Also by Susan Mallery

Published by Pocket Books

SUSAN MALLERY

Sunset Bay

POCKET STAR BOOKS

New York   London   Toronto   Sydney

Pocket Star Books
A Division of Simon & Schuster, Inc.
1230 Avenue of the Americas
New York, NY 10020

This book is a work of fiction. Names, characters, places, and incidents either are products of the author's imagination or are used fictitiously. Any resemblance to actual events or locales or persons, living or dead, is entirely coincidental.

First Pocket Star Books paperback edition March 2009

POCKET STAR BOOKS and colophon are registered trademarks of Simon & Schuster, Inc.

For information about special discounts for bulk purchases, please contact Simon & Schuster Special Sales at 1-800-456-6798 or business@simonandschuster.com.

Designed by Jill Putorti
Cover illustration by Tom Hallman

Manufactured in the United States of America

10   9   8   7   6   5   4   3   2   1

ISBN-13: 978-1-4165-6717-2
ISBN-10:   1-4165-6717-8

acknowledgments

While writing is done alone, sometimes at night and usually accompanied by pacing, eating, and raging at oneself for ever thinking it could all come together and make an actual story, there are more people involved than simply the author.

Yes, we do the word-by-word building of the story. We sweat the big and small stuff. We live with the characters in our heads and try to make sense of it all. But I have always believed true excellence is often achieved through great editing.

So this is for my editor, Abby Zidle, who brainstormed, offered suggestions, and talked me off the ledge more than once. One day I will write your fantasy book about a flesh-eating virus on a submarine. Until then, Travis sweating while using a blowtorch will have to do.

One

"IF ONLY YOU'D BEEN born pretty," Tina Greene said as she glanced at her daughter's reflection. "Or with only one flaw. Like a big nose. That we could fix."

"As it is, we must suffer with my moderate unattractiveness," Megan told her mother, going for sarcasm so no one would know how she really felt. Well, most people could guess, but her mother would take the words at face value. To do otherwise would mean giving thought to another person—something Tina Greene never seemed to do.

"I suppose 'moderate' covers it," Tina murmured as she reached for a brush and eye shadow. "On a good day. If only you were more like your sister. Leanne's only thirteen and she has boys calling here all the time."

Dateless, Megan thought grimly. Eighteen and dateless. "Too bad there's not a recovery center you can send me to. You know, to get over being ugly and not having a boyfriend."

Tina nearly frowned. "Are you being smart with me?"

"No, Mom," Megan said in her most innocent voice.

"There was that one boy. I forget his name. Didn't he end up in prison?"

She refused to answer on the grounds that it was true. Her only boyfriend had been arrested. It wasn't his fault—at least that's what she'd heard. But then she'd also heard Travis had killed someone. She wasn't sure what was the real story.

"You didn't even go to your prom," Tina said. "I could have set you up with someone, but you'd rather sit home by yourself. Do you know how embarrassing that was for me? My daughter not going to the prom?" Tina turned in her chair. "Do you go out of your way to make my life difficult? Does it bring you joy to make me unhappy?"

Megan stared at her mother. She'd read about a study that said babies were more likely to look at attractive faces than unattractive ones. If that was the case, she probably hadn't slept much as an infant. Her attention would have been riveted on her mother's perfect face.

Through some combination of good genes and great luck, Tina had been born beautiful. Stop-traffic, is-she-really-human beautiful. Dark hair that fell in perfect waves, big green eyes and clear, pale skin that practically glowed. It didn't sound all that amazing in words, but in person, Tina was goddess material.

To this day, guys were constantly staring. Men came on to her every time she went out. As her eighteen-year-old daughter, Megan thought it was gross. And depressing. Worse, her baby sister was nearly as pretty. Megan, instead, was the smart sister.

Smart *and* funny, she reminded herself. She had substance. That's what her dad said. They were the regular ones in the family. Tina and Leanne were shallow and narcissistic, but they loved them anyway because she and Dad had *substance.*

"What is that you're holding?" Tina asked, pointing at the blouse on the hanger.

"Nothing."

"It looks like something. Did you make that? The color doesn't work at all on you. Yellow? Megan, how many times do I have to explain the purpose of clothing? To enhance what you barely have. Or in your case, make it look like more than it is."

Megan glanced at the yellow thrift-store blouse she'd bought for three dollars and basically taken apart and put back together so that it looked like a sexy Chanel design. At least that had been the plan. It was pretty enough, and the fit was perfect, but something was missing. Maybe if she changed the buttons . . .

"I worked on this in my design class today."

Tina sighed and returned to face the mirror again. "I swear, I don't understand why your father indulges you the way he does. You can take all the craft classes you want, but don't for a minute think you can make a career out of any of them."

"It's not crafts. It's fashion design."

"Whatever. Be realistic. I don't mean to be cruel, but the truth is you're very unlikely to marry well. You simply don't have that much going for you. You'll have to make your own way. You need skills."

The speech was familiar. A variation on the same theme she'd been hearing for years. Only beautiful women got to marry well. Only beautiful women got to have perfect lives. Lesser mortals simply lived in pain and suffering until they were mercifully put out of their misery by death.

Normally Megan could hear the words and let them wash over her without them touching her at all, but not tonight.

"You're wrong," she said, deliberately inviting trouble. "I have talent, and I mean with more than just eyeliner. My teachers say that—"

Tina rose and tightened the belt on her silk bathrobe. She might have been forty, but she had a body even Megan had to envy. "Your teachers are delighted to cash the checks for the exorbitant tuition they charge at that ridiculous design school. They're going to say whatever they have to so the money keeps coming. Look at yourself, Megan. You're a disaster. Those jeans are cut all wrong, your T-shirt has stains on it. Your hair looks like something cats slept in. When you look in the mirror, do you see 'designer'? You're much more the secretary type. Accept that and move on."

I hate you.

The words boiled up inside, but years of practice kept them from spilling out. Without saying anything, Megan left her mother's room and returned to her own.

Her friend Allegra was sitting on the bed, flipping through a magazine. "And?"

Megan tossed the blouse on the floor. "I'm so stupid. No, what's beyond stupid? I got a great verbal score on my SATs. I should know."

Allegra grabbed the blouse and held it to her chest. The buttery yellow shone against her caramel skin. "I love this. You're doing great work."

Megan joined her on the bed and flopped back on the pillow. "Maybe."

"Hey." Her friend poked her in the arm. "What happened to all the excitement? You love design school. You're going to be a great designer and *I* will be your star model. Let's talk about your collection."

"I'm eighteen and in my first design class. I need to talk about my homework."

"Attack of the Killer Mom?"

"Right to the heart with a quick jab to the creative spirit."

"Want me to call my therapist? I have his home number."

"It's Friday night."

"He's old. Like fifty. What else has he got to do?"

Megan laughed. "I'll be fine."

"Are you sure? Because I can call."

She probably could. Allegra's parents were successful professionals who worried about their only daughter's emotional state. Allegra had been in therapy since she was six. From what Megan could tell, her friend was the most rational, normal, loyal person she knew, but Allegra's parents didn't see it that way.

"I'm beyond fine. I'm in a dimension of goodness

that requires me to get up off the bed. We're going to the party."

Allegra groaned and collapsed in a dramatic swoon. Her long, curly hair fell down, covering her face. "No. Please. Anything but that."

"Or we can spend the evening with my mother."

Her friend straightened. "Party it is."

They looked at each other. "We can do this," Megan said.

Allegra nodded. "Oh, sure. I enjoy going places where people will point and stare."

"They don't do that."

Allegra raised her eyebrows. "I've seen them. It's part of my freakishness."

"You're not a freak."

Her friend stood and put her hands on her hips. "Excuse me? How many other girls do you know who are six feet tall and weigh four pounds?"

"You weigh more than that."

But her friend was right—Allegra was really tall and really thin. And there was something unusual about her face. Huge eyes and wide lips. Cheekbones that seemed on the verge of cutting through skin.

"You have a look," Megan said, meaning it. "One day everyone is going to think you're amazing and want to be just like you."

"Can it be today?"

They'd met in second grade, when Allegra had moved to the neighborhood. She'd been introduced to the class, and a boy had loudly said the new girl was as ugly as

Megan and they should sit together. They did, and a friendship had been born. One bound by time and love and exclusion.

"I'll see what I can do," Megan told her. "But we *are* going to that party."

They'd been invited. At least as much as anyone was ever invited to a big, loud party at the beach. Getting out of the house seemed like the best way to forget how much her mother had hurt her.

Megan felt twisted inside. She knew in her head it was because she'd finished high school and was ready to start college. She was nearly grown up and sometimes, being free and an adult sounded impossibly wonderful. But other times, she wanted to crawl back in bed and hug her teddy bear.

"Come on," she said as much to herself as to Allegra.

She opened her closet and flipped through the clothes Allegra had left behind on her many sleepovers. She paused at a short red skirt, then tossed it over her shoulder.

"That," she announced. "With the tank top you have on."

"I'll be naked."

"You'll be sexy."

"I'll trip and everyone will see my panties."

"Walk slowly and make sure your underwear doesn't have holes."

Megan pulled out the dress she'd finished over the weekend. The sateen cotton had a sheen that made the really dark green look almost black, but when it caught the light, it flashed with color. The dress was simple and fitted, with skinny straps, but the last six inches of the skirt had a really tight pleating that had nearly killed her to get right. It had come out perfect.

"That's so hot," Allegra breathed. "Can you make me one like it?"

Megan flushed with pleasure. "Sure. We'll go buy fabric tomorrow."

They dressed, then tried to decide on makeup. A lot? A little? It was hard to know what to do. Megan made it a point never to listen when her mother tried to teach her.

"Mascara," Allegra said finally. "And lip gloss."

"Right. We'll be fabulous."

Her bedroom door burst open and her baby sister strolled in. "Mom's sick," Leanne announced, plopping on the bed.

"Get out, rodent," Megan told her.

"She has a headache and her heart's beating too fast."

Megan ignored the knot that formed in her own stomach. Her mother not feeling well often meant pain and suffering for everyone in the house.

"Get out of here!" Megan snapped. "This is my room." The room Leanne loved to snoop in.

Leanne glared at her. "I hate you."

"Back at you."

"I'm gonna tell Mom."

An old, tired threat. "About what?"

Leanne flipped her long, blond hair over her shoulder and narrowed her big blue eyes. "There's always something."

The thirteen-year-old left. Allegra stood and smoothed the front of her skirt. "I'm glad I don't have a sister."

"I wish I didn't," Megan said honestly. "She's so annoying. She snoops in here all the time, trying to find out what I'm doing. Then she runs to Mom and rats me out."

"Being an only child is a pain, too, though," Allegra said.

Megan rolled her eyes. "Oh, right. Because your parents buy you everything you want."

Allegra's perfect lips twitched. "They're concerned."

"They're using their credit cards to pay off guilt."

Allegra's parents, both successful doctors, worried they were gone too much. Attempts to heal came in the form of clothes, shoes, and, since Allegra turned sixteen two years ago, cars.

"I'll trade anytime," Megan muttered as she brushed her hair. "You can have my rodent sister, my beautiful mother, and my room with a view of the neighbor's trash can."

"What about your dad and your car?"

"No, you can't have either of them." Megan knew it wasn't totally cool to get along with her dad, but she couldn't help it. They were practically best friends. And the car had been a graduation present.

"Looks like you're stuck with your life," Allegra said.

"I guess."

"But you can share mine."

"Good to know."

Megan applied another coat of mascara, then stood in front of her mirror. Allegra joined her.

They were both tall and thin with long hair. Megan wrestled with pale skin and freckles, red hair that liked to frizz, and breasts that were smaller than her thirteen-year-old sister's. Allegra was similarly built but had been spared the freckles.

"We are perfect," Allegra said. "We are confident. We are going to talk to boys at the party and they will talk back."

"Go us," Megan said. She held up her hand. Her friend did the same and they slapped fingers back and forth three times.

They nearly made it down the hall before her mother called, "Megan? I need to see you."

Megan froze. It was nearly eight. Now that she was out of high school, her curfew had been extended to midnight, which was embarrassingly early for a girl her age. So they didn't have much time at the party. As it was, she was going to drive herself because Allegra didn't have to be home until three in the morning. Dealing with her mother could take a couple of hours.

But she knew she couldn't just walk away, so she sucked in a breath and headed toward the back bedroom.

"Yes?" she said as she stood in the doorway.

The large room was dim, the only light coming from the television. Her mother had moved from the vanity to the bed. Her makeup perfect, her hair tumbling artfully, Tina lay on top of the covers, her silk robe draped over her body. She held one hand to her forehead and winced.

"I have a headache. Could you get me some ice in a

washcloth and make some tea? My stomach's not right. It's stress, of course. You know how the doctor warns me against stress. And maybe you could heat up some soup."

Ten minutes ago her mother had been healthy enough to insult and complain. Megan knew this latest "illness" was a form of punishment.

"I'm going out," she said, doing her best not to whine. Whining only made things worse. "Can't Leanne help?"

Her mother nearly frowned. Not that she would— wrinkles were bad. "Megan, your sister is just a little girl. You have to be the responsible one. We've talked about this."

Meaning Leanne was her favorite and excluded from the caretaking.

"I was going out," she repeated quietly, hoping for a miracle.

"I don't see how that's possible tonight," her mother told her. "Megan, you know I don't do this on purpose. Why are you acting like this? You're being selfish. If you knew my pain and suffering . . . but I pray you never do."

"Because I'll need all my strength to support myself?" Megan asked before she could stop herself.

Behind her Allegra groaned. "You're going to pay for that," her friend murmured.

The lecture was coming. Megan could feel it. Some of it she'd brought on herself and some was just the way things were.

She backed out of the room. "You should go," she told Allegra. "She won't let me out tonight."

"I can wait. I'm not going to the party without you."

"You should."

"Seriously? Alone? I'm going home." Her friend hesitated. "Or we could go together. Megan, you don't have to stay. You could move out. She always does this to you."

Technically, maybe. She was eighteen. But go where? Do what? She wasn't trained to do anything. She wanted to continue her design class and go to college. Her mother or Leanne would simply flounce out, determined to have her own way. Consequences were for other people. As much as Megan wanted to be like that, she couldn't helping thinking about what would happen *after* she flounced.

"I'll be fine," Megan said. "I'll see you tomorrow."

But before Allegra could go, the automatic garage door opener hummed into life. Allegra grabbed her hands.

"You're saved."

Megan grinned and raced toward the kitchen. She kicked off her high heels and flung herself into her father's arms.

"You're back! I didn't think you'd be back until late."

Her father caught her and hugged her hard. "How could I leave my best girl any longer than I had to?" He released her, then looked her up and down. "That's some dress. Did you make it?"

Megan spun in a circle. "Every stitch. Isn't it great?"

Her father kissed her forehead. "You look nice. Hey, Allegra. So you girls are going to a party?"

Megan hesitated. "We were. Mom's not feeling well. She wants me to stay home."

For a second her father looked away. Megan often wondered why he stayed married to a woman as horrible as her mother. A woman who demanded and expected, who never said thank you or talked about anyone but herself. But she knew the answer. She could see the light in his eyes when he looked at his wife, heard the pride in his voice when he walked into a room with her on his arm and introduced her as his.

Her mother was her father's greatest flaw.

He glanced toward the back of the house, then lowered his voice. "Get out of here, kid. I'll take care of things with your mom. Be home by one."

Megan blinked at him. "My curfew is midnight."

He shrugged. "It's summer. Promise you won't get wild."

"Oh, Dad, you know I won't. I have sewing to do this weekend. I'm not going to waste my time getting drunk and then feel sick all day. That's just dumb."

Her dad grinned. "How did I get so lucky with my oldest daughter?"

"How did I get so lucky with my dad?"

The familiar exchange made them both laugh. He pointed to the door. "Get out of here before you have to heat soup and run around with ice."

Megan grabbed her shoes. "Love you, Dad."

"Love you, too, Megan. See you in the morning."

The party was in Santa Monica, in a house less than a block from the beach. Megan and Allegra had to park three streets over. The night was warm and clear. They followed the sound of music to the well-lit house, where the crowd had already spilled onto the lawn.

"The police will be here by eleven," Megan told her friend, knowing the extra hour of curfew wasn't going to matter tonight.

"Maybe the neighbors are cool."

Megan winced at the loud blast of music. "No one over thirty is *that* cool."

They went inside and did a slow sweep of the house, checking out who they knew and who they wanted to get to know. Not that they would actually talk to anyone but each other. Megan had never mastered the art of the party, as her mother called it. Small talk with strangers made her nervous. But they were there and it was fun and that was enough.

Allegra was on cute boy alert, pointing out possible crushworthy prospects. Megan looked but wasn't all that interested. She wanted to work on a pair of tailored pants over the weekend. Once she got them perfect, she could make a pattern, then work with a pinstriped fabric she'd bought weeks ago. The stripes made for a challenge, but if she pulled it off she could—

"Ohmigod! Look!"

Megan turned to glance where Allegra pointed and came to a stop when she saw a tall guy standing by the window.

"I can't believe it," Allegra said. "How long has it been? Two years?"

Nineteen months, Megan thought as her breath caught

in her throat. Give her a minute and she could have actually figured out the number of days. Maybe to the hour. She still remembered everything about the last time she'd seen him. It had been a Tuesday. She'd been standing in front of the school when the police had taken him away.

The moment had been crazy and blurry, like something out of a movie. She remembered thinking that bad stuff never happened on Tuesdays. It was a stupid day. Not like Monday or Friday.

He hadn't said anything when they put the handcuffs on him. He'd stared into her eyes, then looked at her mouth like he wanted to kiss her. He hadn't said he loved her or asked her to wait or anything. He'd been silent and then he'd been gone.

She'd hoped to hear from him. A letter, a phone call. There'd been nothing. And she hadn't known if it was okay to get in touch with him. In the end, she'd done nothing. But she'd always wondered.

Now she stood in the center of the party, not hearing the noise or feeling the crush of the crowd. She was totally alone, like in a bubble, where there were only her memories and the fact that Travis Hunter was back.

"Megan?" Allegra's voice came from a long way away.

Megan couldn't seem to answer as she stared at the only guy who could make her forget her dream of being a designer. It was crazy—they'd only gone out for a few months. They'd barely known each other. She'd been sixteen and he'd been her only boyfriend. He'd been her world, and when he'd disappeared from it, she'd wanted to die.

Without knowing what she was going to say, she walked up to him. He must have sensed her, because he turned just as she reached him. They stared at each other.

His eyes were still dark and looking into them made her want to get lost forever. She didn't think she was breathing, but that was okay, because being close to Travis was enough. His hair was long and shaggy, the way she loved it. The earring was new and made him look like a pirate. He wore a T-shirt over jeans, and stubble covered his chin. Her mother had once described a man as looking like a fallen angel. At the time Megan had thought the description was stupid, but now she got it. Travis was her fallen angel, and if being with him meant going to hell, then she was ready to walk through fire.

Unless he'd forgotten about her.

"Megan," he said, his voice low and thick. The sound of it had always made her tremble.

"Travis. When'd you get back?"

One corner of his mouth lifted in his trademark almost-smile. "Out. When did I get *out*. That's what you mean."

He was angry—she saw that right away. She didn't think it was at her, but maybe it was. Why? Because he thought she was going to pretend nothing had changed? Everything had. They'd both grown up. Him more than her, she would guess.

"When did you get out of jail?" she asked, refusing to let him bait her. "When did you leave prison and come back here?"

He sipped his drink. "A couple of months ago."

Months? And he'd never called or tried to see her?

The flash of pain was as bright as it was intense. She'd missed him, mourned him, wondered if she'd lost the only boyfriend she would ever have. Which made her feel stupid. Like she'd been the only one in their relationship who cared.

"How are you?" she asked, refusing to let him know any of this bothered her. She had plenty of training for that.

"I'm great. A new man. Reformed. I was a model prisoner. They gave me a plaque. Want to see it?"

Was he trying to hurt her or was that just a happy accident? "Did you bring it?" she asked.

He shrugged. "You got me. I left it at home."

"Maybe next time."

She stared into his eyes, hoping to see something—a hint that she mattered, that he'd thought of her at least once, that he was happy to see her. There was nothing. Then a tall, pretty blonde with huge boobs walked up and slid her arm around Travis's waist.

"I'm back," the blonde said, smiling up at him.

"I see." Travis drew her close, possessively. "Heather, this is Megan."

Heather gave her an absent smile. "Hi."

Megan felt beyond insignificant. Her cheeks burned and she wanted to die. Worse, she thought she might throw up. Of course Travis was with someone else. That's what guys like him did. They went out with pretty girls and probably had sex.

She was no one. An awkward, unpopular, ugly person who couldn't possibly be happy because happiness was saved for the perfect.

"Good to see you," Travis said in obvious dismissal.

She nodded, then walked away, her whole body aching. The dress she'd been so happy to wear seemed stupid. Her shoes pinched her toes and she didn't think she was ever going to be able to smile again.

She pushed through the crowd and made her way to the bar, where she asked for a rum and Coke, then took her drink outside. The stars were bright. She could smell the ocean, although she couldn't hear it over the sounds of the party.

Someone joined her on the deck.

"Okay, I asked around and her name is Heather. She's a total ho," Allegra said. "Nobody dates her, they just sleep with her. He's been back two months, working at his mom's business, staying out of trouble. There have been a lot of girls. One night, maybe two, then he moves on."

Megan gulped half her drink, nearly choking as she swallowed. Best friends told you what you needed to know, even when you didn't want to hear it, she reminded herself. Allegra had her back. Now if only someone could protect her heart.

"He's not in love with any of them. Megan, you know that, right? He was in prison. The man is entitled to a little action after that."

"I understand," Megan whispered, hoping she didn't sound as broken as she felt. "It's not like we ever . . ."

She would have, if he'd asked. But there hadn't been time. She'd just been falling for him when he was taken away.

"I hear he has a wicked tattoo on his back," Allegra said. "A tiger."

"It doesn't matter," Megan said fiercely. "He doesn't matter. So we dated and then he was gone. It's fine."

"He didn't leave you. There's no closure. You need closure."

Megan looked at her friend. "What?"

"I know about this stuff. You need the ritual of ending things and then you'll be fine."

"How am I supposed to do that?"

Allegra thought for a second. "I have no idea."

Megan started to laugh. Allegra joined in. They linked arms and went back to the party.

Travis watched Megan make her way to the bar for the second time that night. She wasn't much of a drinker—at least she hadn't been. Maybe she lived to party now. Who the hell was he to worry about her?

Except she didn't look all that different and she'd come with Allegra and not a guy. Was she still into clothes? He would bet that dress she had on was one she'd made.

He remembered a long night when she'd snuck out and met him. His plan had been to get laid, but she'd talked about her dreams and the work she'd done in art class, something about clay and glaze. He hadn't been listening to the words, he'd been lost in the sound of her voice. Then she'd drawn him and the trees in the park and he'd learned that he liked watching her talk and sketch more than he liked screwing anybody else.

"Are you Travis?"

He looked at the kid asking the question. He was maybe fifteen, skinny, and looked like he got beat up on a regular basis.

"Yeah."

The kid looked both excited and terrified. "Is it true? Did you kill someone?"

The truth was Travis had broken up a fight. Some bully had been beating the crap out of a kid as small as the guy in front of him. Travis had stepped in, taken a hit, then decided to teach the bully a lesson. Unfortunately for him, the bully's mother was on the city council and Travis had ended up getting charged and doing time.

At seventeen, he'd been sentenced as an adult— politics-as-usual at work.

Until he'd been taken away in handcuffs, he'd never believed his old man's claim that no good deed goes unpunished. He'd learned it the hard way.

But no one wanted to know that. No one wanted to know about what it was really like to be stuck in jail, to have to watch your back so you didn't become some asshole's bitch. They didn't know it was lonely and boring and that he'd vowed to himself he would never be that stupid again, never end up there, never be like his old man.

He finished his beer and handed the empty bottle to the kid in front of him. "I killed him," he lied. "He deserved it." Then he walked out.

He dug in his pocket for his keys. Coming here had been a mistake. Hanging out with people who used to be his friends only reminded him that he didn't fit in anymore, and seeing Megan again had been the worst of it.

Did she have to be so damn beautiful?

He'd nearly made it to his motorcycle when he saw someone sitting on the curb, next to it. It was dark and she was in shadow, but he recognized everything about her.

"Where's your date?" Megan asked.

"She wasn't my date."

"Just some girl you're sleeping with?"

"She was."

"And now?"

"Why the questions?" he asked, wishing she would go away so he could leave. "What do you want?"

"Allegra says I need closure."

"Allegra needs to stop seeing so many therapists."

She picked up the plastic cup she'd put on the curb, then stood and handed it to him. "Can you toss this? I don't know why I got it. I don't even drink." She sighed.

He poured out the drink and dropped the cup to the grass. She was everything he'd missed while he'd been locked up and exactly what he knew he couldn't have now that he was out. He'd done his best to avoid her. And here she was, looking at him like he was still someone who mattered.

"Go home," he told her.

"Oh, I will. But I wanted to talk to you first."

She meant torture him. Because that's what being

around her was. Torture. It would have been easier if she ripped off his skin and staked him out in the sun.

"I don't want to talk," he said. "I don't talk anymore."

"Because you're big and bad and tough?"

He felt himself start to smile and turned his head so she wouldn't see. "That's me."

"Let's go walk on the beach," she said. "The fog's coming in and my hair will frizz, but I don't care if you don't."

She reached for his hand. He pulled back.

"I'm not interested in talking," he growled. "And I'm not interested in you."

A lie, but the right thing to say. He'd promised himself that, too. That he would do the right thing. Be a man he could be proud of.

Tears immediately filled her eyes. She raised her chin.

"I didn't know what to do. I didn't know if I should write or call your mom. I didn't know what *you* wanted. So I waited to hear from you. I checked the mail every day for a year. I gave up a year of my life for you, Travis. I waited. Then one day I realized you didn't care. You'd probably never cared. But I never forgot you."

She brushed away the tears on her cheeks. "I shouldn't be telling you this. My mother always says never tell a boy what you're thinking. Leave him guessing. But I missed you and I wanted you to know. There it is. All of it. You can laugh at me, or do whatever it is you want to. Say it and then we'll be done."

It was like she was naked before him and he didn't know what to do. She'd waited? For him? Her?

He didn't believe it but knew she wouldn't lie. So now what? Say what he wanted, what was true? Or do the right thing?

He shrugged. "I didn't think about you, babe. Sorry you had to waste your time."

Her expression froze, pain etched in her features. Her eyes widened as fresh tears spilled onto her cheeks.

"Bastard," she whispered.

"You got that right."

Two

MEGAN WATCHED TRAVIS WALK to his bike, unable to believe this was happening. She'd told him how she felt and he'd said he didn't *care*? That she didn't *matter*?

Right. Because that was who she was. The one who got hurt. Would he have said all this to his blond, big-breasted ho?

Without thinking, she bent down, yanked off her high-heeled sandal and threw it at him. It hit him on the side of the head. Before he could react, she went for the other shoe. Then he was there, holding her arms, pulling her against him.

"Megan, don't."

"I hate you."

"Don't hate me." He cupped her chin and raised her head so they were looking into each other's eyes. "Don't hate me." He sucked in a breath. "I'm trying to do the right thing and stay away from you."

"How is that the right thing?"

He swore under his breath, then kissed her, his mouth warm and tender, exactly how she remembered him kissing her. With a gentle sureness that made her want to give him everything.

"I'm sorry," he whispered as he kissed her cheek, her nose, her eyelids. "I'm sorry. I should just walk away. I know that, but I can't."

The pain and humiliation faded, replaced by hope and wonder. "Why would you walk away?"

He straightened and stroked her hair. "Because there's too much crap going on right now. I was in prison."

"It wasn't your fault."

"Don't make a hero out of me. I don't deserve it."

Feelings filled up her chest until it hurt to breathe. Travis was back and here and holding her and nothing else mattered. He made her feel special. He made her feel like there was a chance for her to win.

He kissed her again. She relaxed against him, trusting him to support her. She wrapped her arms around his neck, giving herself up to his kiss.

His mouth claimed hers, touching, teasing, exploring, just as she remembered. When she felt his tongue on her bottom lip, a jolt of heat caught her low in the belly. The familiar aching began, making her squirm.

She parted her lips for him. He slipped his tongue inside, brushing hers, making her skin tingle and her breathing deepen.

It was perfect, everything about this moment. The night, the stars, the whisper of salty air. Outside it was quiet enough for her to hear the pounding of the surf.

"Let's go down to the beach," she whispered.

Travis drew back and stared into her eyes.

She grabbed his hand. He didn't move.

"No," he said quietly, then lifted her hand to his mouth and kissed her palm. "Not like that. Not with you. Not the first time."

Sex? He thought they were going to have sex? The second he was back?

Did he actually think she'd been dating while he was gone? That the guys in her school had lined up to take her out? Didn't he know that she'd been by herself, wishing he'd write and trying to block out her mother's lectures on her lack of social success?

"I don't . . . ," she started, then frowned as she thought about the blonde. "You'll have sex with all those other girls, but not me?"

"Yeah."

She jerked her hand free and walked blindly away. The sidewalk was hard on her bare feet but she wasn't about to go looking for her shoes. At least she had her small purse still hanging off her shoulder. She could get in her car and drive away.

She'd barely made it ten steps when Travis caught up with her, swept her up in his arms, swung her around, then set her back on her feet.

"I will not have our first time together be some fast lay in the sand with a party going on around us. That's not what I want and it's not what you want, either. Dammit, Megan, I'm trying to do the right thing. Don't make me the asshole here."

He was angry. Heat burned in his eyes, almost scaring her. Almost.

"You think this is easy?" he demanded, then took her hand and roughly pressed it against his erection. "You think I don't want to do you fifty ways in the next ten minutes?"

He was hard. She'd never touched a boy "there" before. Had never come close.

Why did he want her? Why did he stand there looking so intense, so male and sexy? Why had he noticed her in the first place? Because he'd been the one who came up to her, to talk to her and ask her out.

Tears returned, but these were a mix of love and gratitude and hope. He was back and he wanted her.

Then his mouth was on hers, their lips parted, tongues thrusting. They kissed until they were breathless. She felt his hardness against her belly and had no idea what to do about it. Still, the sensations were powerful and exciting.

A group of people left the party and walked directly toward them. Travis pulled away. He put an arm around her and led her to her car.

"I wasn't going to see you ever again," he told her. "That's what I told myself when I got out. That you didn't need trouble like me."

"You're not trouble."

"I am, but I'm not sure I can stay away."

She turned toward him and got lost in his eyes. "I don't want you to."

He touched her cheek. "God, I missed you."

Happiness burned inside of her. Her stomach quivered. "I missed you, too."

"Go home," he told her. "I'll be by tomorrow afternoon." He gave her a little push so that she sat in her car. "Stay there," he said, and walked away. A few seconds later, he returned with her shoes. "I'll see you then."

He stood in the road until she drove away. She knew because she kept checking in her rearview mirror.

When she had to turn and lost sight of him, she clung to the fact that he was back. She knew in her heart that they would always be together.

By noon the next day, Megan had changed her clothes eight times. Travis hadn't said what they were going to do, so she had to dress for anything.

He showed up at two, looking tall and sexy in jeans and boots, carrying a black leather jacket. He parked his bike in the driveway and left his helmet on the seat.

She knew she should wait for him to come to the door, but she couldn't help flying down the walkway to meet him halfway. He held a single daisy in his hand.

"You brought me a flower?" she asked, suddenly shy and tucking her hands behind her back.

"Nope." He walked to her VW Bug, opened the driver's door and stuck the flower in the tiny vase that made the new Beetle a true girly car. "I brought your car a flower."

How impossibly romantic, she thought, fighting tears and emotion and feeling as if her driveway had suddenly become the most incredible place on earth. She launched herself at him.

He caught her and held her close, then lowered her to

the ground as he kissed her deeply and thoroughly. Want, delicious and unfamiliar, rose inside of her.

"What are we doing on our date?" she asked, her mouth against his.

"Bowling."

"Seriously?"

"We're going bowling. Then we're meeting a bunch of friends for dinner and we're all going to the movies."

"Okay." Friends. As in his friends and their dates. Like she belonged to a group. She'd never been part of a group before. She grinned. "Sounds like fun."

Leanne sat in her window seat, watching her sister with that boy. The one who had gone to prison. Leanne loved that her sister's only boyfriend had gone to prison. Probably for dating someone as ugly as her.

But Travis was back and now Mom would be happy because Megan was finally out with a guy. Even an ex-con was better than no boyfriend.

Leanne stood and crossed to the mirror. She studied her reflection, making sure she wasn't breaking out, then brushed her long hair.

Except for being blond, she looked a lot like her mother. Big, well-spaced eyes, a mouth boys couldn't stop looking at. She already had bigger breasts than Megan, which wasn't hard but made her happy. She got all the attention.

But if Megan had a boyfriend, Mom would be happy with her and Leanne didn't want that. Which meant making sure Mom wasn't happy that Megan was going out with Travis.

She smiled as she stood and went down the hall to her mother's room.

Her mother looked up from her book and smiled. "Hi there, precious. Finish your homework?"

"Uh-huh."

Leanne climbed onto the bed, where she was always welcome. Her mother pulled her close.

"Are you bored, sweetie? Want to watch a movie with me? We could see what's on HBO."

"Okay." Leanne settled back against the fluffy pillows her mom kept on the bed. "Megan's on a date."

"Impossible. I swear the skies would open and angels sing if someone asked her out."

"She is. It's that boy she went out with before."

Tina put her book aside and sat up. "The one who went to prison?"

"Maybe they have to go out during the day. I think he killed someone. People talk about him."

Tina paled. "Bad enough that she doesn't go out, but to date someone like this? Do you know what my friends will say? What people will think?"

"Nothing good."

"They'll say it's my fault. Why couldn't she be pretty and popular? That's all I've ever asked. But no. And now this?"

Leanne forced herself to look sad. She'd been practicing different expressions in front of the mirror. She blinked hard several times to get tears in her eyes.

"I'm sorry, Mom," she whispered.

Tina hugged her. "You haven't done anything. Now run along. I have to call your father."

"Sure, Mom. I'll go to my room and read."

Her mother sighed. "You're completely perfect. You know that? You're my special blessing."

Leanne smiled. She left the room, but instead of going to her room, she hovered in the hallway and listened at the half-closed door.

Her mother didn't waste any time in calling her father at work.

"Gary, we have to find out about this boy." There was a pause, then, "Do you know what people are going to say about us? Can't she just find a nice boy? But no. She does her best to torture me. She's eighteen. We have to be careful. Megan doesn't have the best judgment. How could she? She has no experience." Another pause. "Oh, I know *you* trust her completely, but I'm not willing to risk our reputation, even if you are."

Leanne slunk away.

When she reached her sister's room, she went inside and pulled out the tray of makeup. There wasn't much there. Megan didn't bother. After putting on some mascara, Leanne picked up several lip glosses before picking the one that tasted like cherries.

Her friends always told her that parents didn't have favorites, but at her house, it was different. Her mother preferred her, and her father, while pretending he didn't love either of his daughters more, had always favored Megan. It was the two of them against her and Mom.

Leanne hated being left out. She wanted to be in the middle of things, to be the favorite and most popular. She was at school, so why not here?

For as long as she could remember, Leanne had been trying to get her dad's attention, to be the daughter he talked with most, laughed with, took out for special lunches. But he never seemed to see her. Maybe now that would change.

Leanne walked to Megan's closet and opened it. She eyed the clothes hanging there, picked up the closest dress and set it on the bed. Then she slipped out of her jeans and T-shirt and reached for the dress to try it on.

"I need you to deliver these to the Santa Monica site, then head up to Malibu and work there today," Karen Hunter said before dropping her pen on the desk and rubbing her temples. "We're struggling to stay on time with the project."

Travis nodded. He grabbed the truck keys from the desk. "Anything else?"

His mother's worried gaze met his. "I need your help," she said. "There's a big bonus for finishing on time. We need the money."

They always needed the money. Landscaping was a competitive business and Hunter's Garden wasn't huge. His father couldn't be counted on to show up when he was supposed to, leaving the family business in the hands of his wife.

"I'll get it done," he said.

She studied him, as if she was trying to figure out what he was thinking. She didn't ask, probably because she was afraid to find out the truth. He caught her watching him all the time, and he knew why.

She'd spent his entire life holding her breath, hoping he wouldn't turn out like his father. That the darkness burning in Burt Hunter hadn't been passed on to his only son. Travis's arrest had terrified her and his conviction had broken her. Now she was waiting for more signs, more trouble, more disaster. There was no point in telling her he wasn't like his old man. She wouldn't believe him and words didn't mean shit anyway. He would have to show her.

"I'll be back late," he said.

"Travis," she called before he could leave. "Are you, ah, still seeing Megan? She seemed like a nice girl."

A nice girl who was driving him crazy, he thought, remembering their last date, when just being close to her was enough to make him want to rip off her clothes. But he was determined to do the right thing. At least this once.

"I'm seeing her."

"You could bring her around if you wanted."

If it was just his mom, he would. But with the old man, he was never sure. Sober, Burt was a hell of a guy, but drunk, he was a bully.

"Sure. I'll let you know."

"See you tonight. I love you."

He smiled at her. "I love you, too, Mom," he said, and meant it. He'd hated hurting her. But with his past, with his father's blood running through his veins, sometimes it felt inevitable.

The pancakes were hot and fluffy. Megan poured syrup over the still-steaming food with one hand while reaching for her fork with the other.

"I'm not sure about the pleats," she said with a shrug. "And you're about done pretending to be interested, huh?"

Her father laughed. "I'm very proud of you."

"But not into fashion."

"Not so much. But it's good that you are. You have a lot of interests."

"You mean beyond the latest wrinkle cream?"

"Megan." His voice warned her not to push.

Right. Because while he could tease Tina about taking forever to get ready and how she was only interested in herself, no one else could.

Her dad's only weakness, Megan told herself. Because they both knew that in the end, she and her dad were the ones who were real people. It had always been that way.

"You did well in your art class last summer," her father said. "I remember when you brought home your first still life for the refrigerator."

She winced. "Let's not talk about those efforts."

"You'll have a real appreciation of the world's beauty when you travel. A lot of kids graduate from college with a single focus. That won't be you. College is only a few weeks away. Are you excited?"

She hesitated. "Um, sure."

Because going to UCLA and majoring in business had always been the plan. How could she tell her dad that things were different now? That she wanted more than accounting and marketing classes? That her design work excited her and being with Travis made her feel that anything was possible?

If there was a time, it was now. Sunday breakfast with her father was a long-standing tradition that she looked forward to every week. She knew a lot of girls who didn't have anything to say to their fathers, but she and her dad had never been like that. Now, her mother was another story—not that she was going to ruin the day by thinking about her.

She put down her fork. "I know we've always talked about my future as being set," she began. "But I'm thinking of maybe doing something different. I'd like to continue with my design classes, which isn't the same as college but still gives me career options."

Gary stared at her. "Give up UCLA? Megan, be serious. You've bounced from one craft to another for years. Yes, you have a creative streak, but it's not a life. It's not a living. You need to be practical." He leaned toward her. "What is this? You're my smart girl. You and I know what the world is like. We don't expect to get by letting other people take care of us."

"What if I want more than to be practical? What if I want to take a chance?"

"You know the world doesn't work that way."

"What way?" She was careful to keep her voice down, which frustrated her. Why couldn't she scream if she wanted to? Leanne would have been screaming. Tina would have walked out, moving like a movie star.

"Mom constantly tells me all the things I can't do because I'm not like her. It's as if I'm expected to have a smaller, less perfect life because I'm not the class beauty. What's up with that? I can be happy. I can be creative. I can have everything I want."

Her father's expression turned sad. "I guess it was too much to hope you'd get through your teens without rebelling."

"I'm not rebelling. I'm talking about my *life*."

He reached across the table and touched her hand. "Megan, you're my daughter and I love you. I see so much of myself in you. I want you to be happy and I know you will be. But you also have to be realistic. You'll probably change your mind about designing in a few months, and then what? You will have missed your chance at college. You need a career you can count on. I have enough to worry about with your mother and Leanne. Don't make me worry about you, too."

Meaning what? Don't dream? Don't hope? Don't expect too much?

"Leanne wants to be an actress!"

"That's different."

"How? Because she's pretty, she gets what she wants and I have to be careful?"

"No." Her father looked both wary and tired.

"Then what?" She knew what he meant; they both did. But she wanted him to say it.

"I want your life to be a sure thing. Why is that so bad?"

"It's not. But I want more than you and everyone else assuming I'm stuck with ordinary. I can do anything I want."

"Yes, you can. Including the right thing. Now, your mother tells me you have a new boyfriend," her father said. "Tell me about him."

She hesitated before accepting the change in topic, then wondered how her mother knew about Travis. She picked up her fork again as she figured out the only answer to the question. Leanne.

"His name is Travis. I dated him junior year. It didn't work out, but it's working out now."

Her father stared at her in a way that made her realize he knew more than she wanted him to. Obviously thanks to her rodent of a baby sister.

She thought about explaining none of it was Travis's fault—that he shouldn't have gone to jail. But would her father care?

"I like him, Daddy," she said instead. "He makes me feel special."

"I guess that's what every father wants to hear. Just be careful."

Oh no. They couldn't have the sex talk. Not over breakfast.

"I am," she said quickly, desperate to head him off. "Super careful. They're putting me on a poster. You know you can trust me," she added.

"You're not the problem."

She met her father's gaze. "Daddy, Travis is a good guy. I swear."

"Then I guess I have to believe you. I'd like to meet him."

Megan thought about her two favorite guys getting together and smiled. "I'd like that."

"What were you thinking?" the instructor asked.

Megan swallowed as she stood next to her model. "I'm into pleating these days. I like the challenge. The assignment called for a dressy cocktail outfit and a dress seemed too obvious. I went with the fitted satin pants. The pleating below the knee adds weight and length while being a little retro. The detail on the halter top connects the outfit without it matching."

There were twelve designers lined up in front of the class. They'd had a week to complete their cocktail party ensemble, fitted to models borrowed from the small agency upstairs. This was their second-to-last project and counted double.

Mr. Bellinger, their instructor, made a few notes, then moved on. Megan had a whole lot more to say about why she'd chosen the satin in that particular color, but he obviously wasn't interested. He discussed choices of fabric and style with the rest of the students, leaving Megan to wonder if she was about to be tossed out on her butt.

She looked at the detailing on the bodice, all the handwork she'd done, and refused to cry. She'd done a great job, and if no one else could see it, they were stupid. This was fresh and stylish and innovative. It had to be better than the tired little black dress half the class had done.

She spent the next ten minutes alternating between wanting to defend her design and deciding she completely lacked talent. There was only one more week of class. Had she spent her whole summer working her butt off only to find out she had zero ability? Finally Mr. Bellinger returned to stand in front of her.

"Ms. Greene, your design is extraordinary. I'm impressed as much by your originality as by your execution. The fit is perfect; the finishing details are exquisite. You show a level of quality far beyond what I have ever seen in a summer class. Bravo."

Megan felt her knees go weak. She grinned. "Thank you."

"I suggest you make a pattern from your outfit. You may find you need it."

A pattern? As in, she could sell the outfit? Maybe sell more than one?

The rest of the class passed in a blur. When she reached her car, she hurried over to Allegra's house, parking in the wide circular drive and running inside without knocking.

"Guess what happened?" she yelled as she took the stairs two at a time. "Guess what?"

She burst into her friend's bedroom. Allegra sat at the antique vanity table, painting her nails. "You're excited about something."

Megan told her what her instructor had said. "If I have a pattern, I can make more outfits. I think he meant I could sell them at boutiques. Wouldn't that be great?"

"You could go offshore and exploit child labor, even."

Megan rolled her eyes. "You're not taking me seriously."

"I am, considering you're now officially twenty-two." Allegra waved her wet nails at a driver's license sitting on the edge of her dresser. "Happy birthday."

"You got it!"

"It was easy. You just have to know who to ask."

Megan picked up the fake ID and rubbed the picture. "It looks good."

"You still going to Vegas with Travis?"

Megan ignored the flutter of nerves in her stomach. "That's our plan. He turns twenty-one on Friday and we're driving up for the weekend." The trip had required lying to her dad about where she was going to be—something she'd never done before. But she wanted to go away with Travis, just the two of them.

Allegra pointed at a small bag on the dresser. "You'll want that."

Megan opened the bag. Inside was a jumbo box of condoms. She blushed. "I'm sure he'll take care of that."

"You take care of it, too. You might think Travis is the greatest guy ever, but you still protect yourself. I don't want anything bad happening to you."

Megan ignored the trickle of fear. "It won't. I trust him."

Allegra only shook her head.

Megan tucked the fake ID in her wallet. "Thanks for this. I appreciate it."

"It was fun. I kind of hope my parents find out. They're

always expecting me to do something bad and I never do. At least this would give them a reason to worry."

Travis could think of about three thousand things he would rather be doing right now, but not one of them was worse than jail—always his benchmark.

He climbed out of his car and walked up to the front door. It opened before he could knock.

"Good evening, sir," he said, hoping Megan appreciated that he'd worn new jeans and a button-down shirt. He'd left his leather jacket draped over his bike and had even removed his earring.

"Travis." Gary Greene stepped back to let him in the house. "Megan will be ready in a few minutes. Thanks for coming a little early so we could get to know each other."

Travis reminded himself that Megan's dad was nothing like his own. Mr. Greene wasn't trying to set him up or find the opening for a good left hook. He was worried about his daughter. That was a good thing.

Travis followed the other man into a comfortable living room. As he walked he pulled a business card out of his shirt pocket.

"Mr. Greene, here's the name and number of my arresting officer. If you call him, he'll explain what happened. I know you're concerned about me dating Megan, but you don't have to be."

Megan's father took the card. "While I appreciate this, I did a little checking on my own. You've gotten into fights before."

"I have a temper. I'm learning to control it."

"You ever hit a woman?"

Travis stiffened. The need to walk out and keep walking grew. "No, sir."

"I don't like the idea of my daughter dating you, but I trust her. I'm willing to be wrong. But if you do anything to her, anything at all, I will hunt you down and kill you myself. Is that clear?"

"Yes, sir."

"Do you have anything you want to say for yourself?"

Travis hesitated, then decided on the truth. "I respect her as much as I care about her. She works hard, doesn't party and wants to be home before curfew so she can get up early for her classes. She's perfect."

Gary Greene didn't look reassured. "I'm glad you recognize that. You're the kind of kid who messes things up. Megan doesn't need that. She doesn't need you screwing with her life."

Travis squared his shoulders. Megan's father wasn't telling him anything he didn't already know. "I'm going to prove you wrong," he said.

"I doubt that, son. I doubt it very much."

Three

"YOU SURE ABOUT THIS?" Travis asked, his hand on Megan's arm. "You need to be sure."

"I am. I can handle it."

"I don't think you're ready."

She pushed him away, then lined up her cue and took the shot. The ball banked off the side perfectly and dropped down. She straightened and blew on the tip of her cue. "Don't mess with me, big guy. I'm good."

He grinned.

Around them, the party was loud and most of the people were already drunk. Megan had passed on the spiked punch, happy to drink a soda from the can. She and Travis were heading out for Vegas tomorrow afternoon. Anticipation was enough to make her feel bubbly and out of control. She didn't need alcohol to help the process along.

Still, it was cool to be there. Travis's friends spoke to her as if she were one of them. As if she were always hanging out at places like this.

Practically popular, Megan thought happily, aware

that she wanted it both ways. She enjoyed feeling superior and real when compared with her mother and sister, but she was desperately happy to have a boyfriend and be included in a group.

A slow song came over the speaker and Travis pulled her to him.

They moved together, staring at each other, their bodies touching.

"You finish the pattern?" Travis asked.

"Last night. I've never made one before. Not for real. It's kinda fun. I'm taking it into class tomorrow. Mr. Bellinger said he wants to talk to me about something." She hesitated. "There's an internship. In New York. I heard some of the teachers talking about it. I think . . . I hope they're going to nominate me."

She watched him as she spoke, half-afraid of his reaction.

He continued to look into her eyes. "Then I guess you'll be moving to New York."

She wrinkled her nose. "That's too scary to think about. I'm not ready to move out on my own."

"Aren't you going to college in a month?"

"Here. I'll be living in a dorm, but I'm twenty minutes from home. Big whoop."

"Maybe New York is a better choice."

Was he being the supportive boyfriend or was there something else going on? "Are you trying to get rid of me?"

He shook his head. "If only you knew how much I don't want that."

She smiled. "Good answer."

"You ready to go to Las Vegas tomorrow?"

Anticipation tightened her belly. "Yes."

"Me too."

"They really have circus acts," Megan said as she stared up at the woman on the trapeze. "I thought it was just a name. But this is Vegas, right? It's all about theme. But it's nice. Don't you think it's nice?"

She'd been talking nonstop since they'd checked in at Circus Circus. While Travis got that everything was new, he hadn't realized how nervous she was until she'd suggested they leave their bags at the bell desk instead of going up to the room. They'd spent the past hour walking around the hotel and exploring the casino. Not that Megan wanted to spend any money.

She kept glancing at the people around them, then looking away. As if she felt guilty about something.

He ached for her. Every part of him wanted her. He'd imagined making love with her so many times, he had a permanent hard-on. But he couldn't ask her. Because Megan was still a virgin and he was determined to make everything about their first time together perfect.

Doing the right thing was a pain the ass, he thought grimly.

He grabbed her hand and pulled her around until she faced him. "Want to go home?" he asked, trying not to grit his teeth. "If you're not ready, I understand."

She stared at him, wide-eyed and pale. "Travis, no.

It's not that. I'm . . ." She leaned close. "I feel like everyone knows I've never been away with a guy before. I feel like they're all staring. I'm half expecting them to throw things and call me names."

He glanced around at the three old ladies passing them. "That one in the middle looks like she has a hell of a right arm. You'd have to duck fast."

Megan's mouth twitched, then she started to laugh. She leaned into him and wrapped her arms around his waist. "Would you really take me home?"

Even if it killed him. "Sure."

"What about our room? Will you take me there?"

Megan watched his face tighten. Something dark and hot flared in his eyes. She waited for the ripple of fear, but there was only anticipation and the knowledge that Travis was the man that she loved.

"Are you sure?" he asked, which made her love him more.

She kissed him. "Very," she whispered.

They returned to the bell desk and claimed their luggage. She still felt like everyone was staring but did her best not to react. It was all in her head. Couples went away all the time. This was Las Vegas—anything could happen here.

They rode the elevator to the twelfth floor and stepped out into a hallway. Travis pointed the way toward their room, then used the card key to open the door.

It was still early in the evening and the summer sun hadn't set yet. The first thing Megan noticed was the view across the Strip and the colors of the sunset. She could see forever. Then she stepped into the room and saw a living area, with double doors leading to a bedroom.

"You got us a suite?" she asked. Didn't that cost a lot?

"It gives us extra space. The sofa folds out in case . . . you know."

In case she couldn't go through with it? In case they couldn't sleep together? Nerves and appreciation battled for dominance. Ignoring her wobbling emotions, she sucked in a breath, then headed for the bedroom.

One door stood open. She stepped in and flipped on the light, then started to laugh.

A round bed sat in the middle of the room. It was huge and covered in an animal print. Travis moved behind her and put his hand on her waist.

"Do you think it's funny or are you getting hysterical?" he asked.

"I love it," she said, still giggling. Because the round bed was funny and something she would remember for the rest of her life. Because Travis cared enough to want her first time to be right. Because without meaning to, she'd waited for him, and now he was here and they were always going to be together.

She turned to him, dropped her purse on the floor and wrapped her arms around his neck. She heard the suitcases fall, then he was holding her and they were kissing.

His mouth was perfect, she thought as she lost herself in the pressure of his lips, the flick of his tongue. She gave herself up to his embrace, to the feel of him against her. He was warm and hard and safe. Always safe.

The kiss was familiar, the way they always did it. She tilted her head so she could take him deeper. His tongue plunged inside. They strained closer, as if they needed to crawl inside of each other, as if being one was really possible. Then he pulled back.

"Give me a second," he said.

He grabbed his suitcase and pulled a box of condoms out of an outside pocket. After setting them on the nightstand, he pulled back the sheets, then returned to her side. He took her hand and led her to the bed, then urged her to sit.

He took off his boots and socks. She kicked off her sandals.

Reality threatened and it was more than a little uncomfortable. They were in a hotel room. On a bed. About to have sex. What if she couldn't do it? What if she was terrible? What if—

"Stop thinking," he told her as he tugged at the hem of her T-shirt and pulled it over her head. "I can hear you thinking. Don't. You're perfect."

She did her best to ignore the fact that he was looking at her in her bra. "I don't want to disappoint you."

"Not possible."

She wished *that* were true. She wished—

He leaned over and kissed her. Once his mouth was on hers, it was easy to stop thinking, to just lose herself in what he was doing. His kiss was sexy and exciting and familiar enough to allow her to breathe.

He put his arms around her and lowered her to the bed. She tried to relax, then forgot to be nervous when she felt his warm hand on her belly. A hand that was moving toward her breast.

Anticipation eased through her as she thought about what it would be like to have him touch her there. She imagined how it would feel, then held in a moan as his palm cupped her curve and his fingers found her nipple.

Heat poured through her, moving from place to place, making her uncomfortable in her skin. Everything felt tight and uneasy, as if something were out of place. She held on to him, because he was safe. Travis would always be safe.

He rolled her onto her side so they were facing each other, then reached behind her and unfastened her bra in one easy motion. Instinctively, she moved her arm to hold it in place, then felt stupid and didn't know what to do. He drew back a little and smiled at her.

"Don't worry," he said quietly. "Don't worry."

Good advice she wouldn't be able to take, she thought frantically, knowing she should be sophisticated enough to toss away her bra and flash her boobs. Except she couldn't. Instead her brain was filled with pictures of the blonde he'd been with at the party. By comparison, Megan's breasts were practically raisins.

He propped himself on one arm and leaned over to touch her face, then he tucked her hair behind her ear.

"You're so beautiful," he murmured. "Nobody has eyes that color of green. It's not natural."

That made her smile.

Then he touched her shoulder and she liked that. His

hand slipped down her arm, then to her side. He used a single finger to lightly stroke the top of her breast.

Electricity shot through her, exploding in her belly, where all her muscles clenched. He moved over her bra and touched her nipple again. Her eyes sank closed and she rolled onto her back.

She didn't notice him pull the fabric away, but he must have because suddenly he was leaning over her. The only warning was a slight brush of warm air followed by his mouth closing around her nipple.

Shock forced her eyes open. She saw Travis at her breast, his dark hair falling against her skin, his eyes closed as he gently licked her. Sexual awareness surged as she felt a gush of wetness in her panties. Hunger burned unlike anything she'd ever experienced before. Wanting grew, fueled by what she was seeing and feeling.

He took more of her in his mouth, then sucked. She felt the tug all the way down to her toes. He moved his hand to her other breast and teased her. They were both breathing hard. Then she closed her eyes and let her head fall back, ready to experience it all.

He moved from breast to breast until she couldn't contain her whimpers of arousal. When he reached for the waistband of her jeans, she actually helped him with the zipper, then pushed them down herself. Her panties went with them and she barely noticed. If he could do all that with her breasts, imagine what he could do between her legs.

Travis slipped off the bed and onto the carpet. He grabbed her hips and pulled her so her legs dangled and her toes just barely touched the floor, then he kissed his way up her thighs.

She knew what he was going to do, at least in theory. She'd seen it in a dirty movie she and Allegra had watched at her friend's house. She was both embarrassed and intrigued. So when he parted her with his fingers and put his mouth to her, she braced herself for the unknown.

His kiss was perfection, open-mouthed and soft. He found her center on the first try and licked it. Megan squirmed in shock and had to bite her lip to keep from shrieking. He licked her again. Pleasure poured through her, making her want to grind herself against him. She had to struggle to keep from screaming.

He circled that one spot, his thumbs moving up and down beside it, working with the movement of his tongue. She was exposed and didn't care. She was confused and scared and excited and would have done anything to make sure he never stopped.

Over and over he touched her with his mouth, moving slower, then faster, harder, then softer. She strained and gasped, her body tensing, her skin heating. She wanted more and didn't know how to ask. She was terrified he would think he was done before she was. There had to be something amazing at the end of this, but what? How would she know?

"Travis," she breathed.

He raised his head and she nearly wept. "It's okay," he told her. "Just go with it."

"But I don't know what I'm doing."

"I do."

"How do I know if I'm . . . you know."

"You'll know."

Easy for him to say, she thought, feeling stupid and inexperienced. What if she—

Something changed. Something deep inside her body tightened and it was as if every cell became focused on something she couldn't explain or touch or even feel, but it was there. Her breathing came in gasps. She grabbed at the sheets and, despite being embarrassed, pushed down. Trevor circled her once, then sucked hard.

Something inside of her ripped apart. She felt it go, then a kind of liquid pleasure poured through her, making her shake and cry out. She couldn't control herself, couldn't stop it, not that she wanted to. The ride went on, a wonderful out-of-time experience that filled every part of her. On and on, slowly, a bit at a time, until she was still and exhausted and energized and amazed.

Megan blinked. "Can we do it again?"

He laughed. "Sure. But first I thought we'd try something different."

Making love. Of course, she thought, suddenly getting it. If this was what sex felt like, no wonder people wanted to do it. It was amazing that they didn't spend all their time in bed.

She shimmied back on the mattress and patted the space beside her. "Hurry."

Travis stood and pulled off his shirt, then quickly stripped off his clothes. She studied his body, dropping her gaze to his erect penis. Thank goodness he wasn't anywhere as big as the guy in the porno. That would have been scary.

He grabbed a condom and got on the bed. She embraced him, wanting to feel his naked body next to hers. There were so many differences. His legs were longer; his chest broad and covered with hair. He leaned in and kissed her breasts, which made her feel all quivery inside again.

While she was enjoying that, he moved his fingers between her legs and gently pushed one inside of her, then two. She wasn't sure she liked the pressure, but then he began to move them in and out and she kind of got into it.

But before she could sink into the tension, he'd shifted between her legs and put on the condom. His face was tight, his expression both determined and worried.

"It may hurt," he told her. "It won't for long."

Fear chased away arousal. "Because I'll get used to it?"

One corner of his mouth twitched. "Because I won't take long. I nearly lost it when I was going down on you."

She was still processing that information to figure out what it meant when he pressed his erection against her and pushed.

He was way bigger than two fingers and it was a little uncomfortable to have him filling her. She did her best to relax, to let it happen, to just go with it. There was more and more until she didn't think she could stand it anymore, then he groaned and withdrew.

Megan lay back, not sure what to do with her arms or

legs, not sure how to move. He pushed in again, filling her, and this time was better than the first. Tentatively, she pushed against him. He stiffened, swore, muttered something she couldn't understand, then pushed in twice more and collapsed on top of her.

Megan stared at the ceiling, not sure what had just happened. Were they done? Travis raised his head.

"I'm sorry."

Okay. "Um, for what?"

"Coming so fast."

Ah, so they were done. "It's okay."

"It's not, but I'll get better. Give me three or four more tries and I'll be able to last more than five minutes." He smiled. "Trust me, if I can last longer, you'll like it."

He rolled onto his back and pulled her close. She snuggled against him.

"This is perfect," she murmured. "Everything I could have wanted."

"I'm glad. We'll get better with practice."

"I don't think it can get better, but I'm up for trying."

He laughed. "Me too."

"Only in Vegas," Travis said as they walked through the art gallery.

Megan nodded in agreement, too caught up in the moment, in being with him, to speak.

Everything was perfect, she thought blissfully. She felt alive and happy and totally in tune with the world.

"Gambling I get," he continued. "But art?"

"It's the new thing. Art galleries." She pointed to a painting on the wall. "These are all reproductions, of course. The setup is interesting. By color rather than artist or time period. I guess these are for decorating, rather than art appreciation."

They paused in front of an early Picasso.

"I don't get it," Travis said as they stared at the nude. "What's wrong with her?"

"This is Cubism. It's from the early 1900s. The theory is that a canvas is two-dimensional and why pretend otherwise? So the paintings are designed to emphasize that aspect. In this work the woman is in pieces, but still recognizable. In later work . . ." She dragged him over a few feet and pointed. "Here we have only hints of the subject."

"It's weird."

"It's art."

He smiled at her, then kissed her nose. "I like you."

Her heart fluttered. "Meaning not so much the gallery visit?"

"I like that one."

He pointed at a metal sculpture that rose to the ceiling. It was black and silver, abstract but with a feeling of violence that made her uncomfortable.

"That's ten thousand dollars," she whispered. "I saw the price when we walked in."

"I don't like it that much."

"I didn't think so."

They walked back into the casino.

Travis looked around at the people. "I bet it's easy to get a job here."

"You want to work in a casino?"

"I want to get away from where I am now."

She was shocked. They'd casually talked about her maybe getting the internship in New York, but what were the odds? Besides, she was going to college ten miles from her house.

"You're leaving?" She tried not to sound hurt but was afraid she failed.

"As soon as I can save enough money."

The slot machine bells seemed to echo in her head. "When were you going to tell me?"

"I'm not going today." He looked at her. "You could come with me."

"To live here?"

"Where do you want to go? New York? We'll go there. You can get a job in a store and go to classes. I'll find something. We'll get an apartment, be together always. Want to do it, Megan? Run away?"

Maybe. Almost. "I'm going to college in a few weeks."

"To study business. That's your dad, that's not you."

"I have to be practical. I need to be able to support myself."

"I'll take care of you."

His dark eyes promised her the world. She'd never thought of anyone taking care of her. All her life she'd been told that couldn't happen. She wasn't special enough. Had her mother been wrong?

She laughed uneasily. "This is crazy. We're not going anywhere but home and back to our lives. Come on. I brought ten dollars to gamble. Maybe we'll win our fortunes."

He didn't say anything for a second, as if he was going to push back. Then he followed her to the slot machines and watched while she put in her money.

Leanne was up early. She waited until her dad had left for his usual Saturday morning at the office, then rode her bike over to Allegra's house. Despite Megan's claims that she was with her friend, Leanne didn't believe her. Megan had been acting weird all week. Something was up and Leanne was going to find out what.

Allegra lived in a big house in Santa Monica with a multicar garage and a full-time housekeeper. Leanne doubted Allegra got up much before noon on Saturday, which meant someone else would be answering the door.

She rode her bike to the stairs leading to the front door and leaned it against the wrought iron railing. Then she took a second to get herself into character.

First she thought about how her dad *always* paid more attention to Megan than to her, how they had their special breakfasts and talks. It was a like a secret club and she wasn't invited. She should be invited. But instead of making her sad, that got her pissed. She tried picturing lost kittens, imagining how she would feel if she had a kitten and it was lost. She got a little sniffly, but there weren't any tears.

Finally she walked over to her bicycle and pushed up

the kickstand. Then she braced herself and pushed it down against her leg. The sharp metal tore into her skin, making her yelp.

Pain ripped up her leg as blood dribbled down. She focused on how much it hurt. When that didn't work, she realized she might have a scar and how bad that would be. Mom hated scars and said they were a sign of bad breeding. Horror filled her and with the fear came the tears. Once they were trickling down her cheeks, she ran to the door and pressed the bell.

A Mexican woman in a maid's uniform came to the door. "Yes?"

"I'm Leanne, Megan's sister. She's spending the night with Allegra. I need to talk to her. Our mom is really, really sick and I'm scared."

The maid looked nervous and concerned. "Miss Megan no here."

Leanne had to bite her lip to keep from smiling, the pain in her leg and the potential scar forgotten. Megan was so going to get nailed. "But she said she was spending the night with Allegra."

"Miss Megan no here." She opened the door. "You can go check. Upstairs. You know the way, yes?"

Leanne nodded and took the stairs two at a time.

Allegra's room was huge, more like a fancy hotel suite than a regular bedroom. Leanne pushed open the door and went into the dim room. Sure enough, Megan's friend was asleep in one bed and the second bed was empty. She checked the bathroom just to be sure, then ran back downstairs.

"Thank you," she yelled as she flew out the front door and started the ride home. She would do what she always did—she would tell her mom, who would call Dad. Megan wasn't getting out of this one. She'd lied about where she was and had been out all night.

Leanne came to a stop as a wonderfully horrible thought occurred to her. What if Megan was with a *boy*? What if she was with Travis? Oh, that was too good for words! Dad would finally see Megan for the bitch she was and Leanne could be the favorite forever.

Four

THE NEXT MORNING TRAVIS watched Megan roll the dice. She looked intense and determined, holding her breath as she threw. The dice bounced against the sides of the craps table before coming to a stop. Everyone cheered.

"I did it!" Megan yelled, jumping into his arms and screaming. "I did it! How much did I win? Is it a lot?"

He eyed the stack of chips. "Four hundred."

"Dollars?" Her eyes widened. "Four hundred dollars? That's amazing. Let's play more!"

"I don't think so." He gathered up their chips and led her away.

"But I'm winning."

"For now. Luck has a way of turning."

She wrinkled her nose. "You're being so sensible. That's not like you."

"Trust me. Keep the money you made and be happy."

"Because you're such a big gambler?"

"I've had some experience." In high school and then later in prison. Not that he wanted to think about that now. They were having a great time and he didn't want anything to spoil it.

She moved in front of him and put her arms around his waist. Heat poured through him, making him hard in seconds. She obviously felt his erection and smiled.

"Again?" she asked.

"No. You'll be sore."

"That's okay. Let's go upstairs."

He pretended to think about it, then kissed her. "Okay, but only because you're asking."

She laughed. "I'll make you like it."

"I don't think so."

Her smile turned knowing. "I so own you in bed."

She spoke with a confidence that was new. It was as if she'd finally found herself, where she belonged, and was comfortable there.

He'd noticed Megan for months before he'd approached her. He'd sensed her shyness but had enjoyed her smile, her comments in class, the way she assumed no one paid attention to her.

She didn't demand. Instead she offered, and that made him want to give her everything he could. But was it enough?

They walked toward the elevators, their arms around each other. She'd just pushed the up button when he felt his pager buzz.

His mom knew he'd gone away with Megan, knew what this weekend meant to him. There was only one reason she would need to get in touch with him.

He waited until they reached the room before telling

Megan he had to call home, then he went into the bedroom and shut the door. Seconds later his mother answered the phone, her voice thick with tears and terror.

"Travis, you have to come back now. I needed the ladder in the garage so I could change a lightbulb. I didn't mean to find anything. I shouldn't have looked. But I did. Oh, God, I did."

He didn't want to know, didn't want to be having this conversation. Didn't want to hear the words. Still he forced himself to ask.

"What did you find?"

"A s-suitcase filled with money and guns. You have to come home, Travis. Now. We have to get rid of this. If it's not here, he didn't do anything. If it's not here, he's safe."

No one was safe, he thought grimly. Not with his father around. The old man had gone too far.

He glanced at his watch. "I'll be there in four hours." It would take that long to drive back.

"Okay. I'll wait. He doesn't know I've found it."

"You're going to have to call the police."

He heard her gasp of air. "I can't. I can't turn him in."

"Then I will."

"No. Travis, he's your father."

"He's a mean bastard who beats the crap out of you, Mom. It's time to walk away."

"No. No!"

A fight they should have in person, he thought, suddenly bone weary of it all. "I'll be there as soon as I can," he said, and hung up.

He stood, walked to the door, then hesitated, not sure

what to tell Megan. The truth? How would that go? "Hey, babe, I forgot to mention that my dad is a criminal. In and out of jail. Apparently he just pulled off something and I have to go home so I can turn him in to the police."

Sure. Why not? She would have already heard plenty of talk. Except knowing would be worse. Then she would look scared and wonder how much of his old man lived in him.

He opened the door. She stood by the window, her arms folded across her chest. She looked worried.

"What's wrong?"

"I have to go home."

"Okay. Why?"

"I don't want to tell you. It's not good. It has nothing to do with me, I swear. I just don't . . ."

She crossed toward him, then touched his mouth with her fingers. "You don't have to say anything, Travis. It's okay. We'll go home."

"Just like that?"

She smiled. "Of course."

"I'll make it up to you."

The smile turned wicked. "I know."

Megan and Travis drove to his friend's house, where Travis had left his bike. He kissed her absently, got on his bike and headed out.

He drove the few miles to the old house where he'd grown up, at the end of a long driveway. The place had always been shabby. It was the kind of building that scared off salespeople and made the post office refuse to deliver packages.

He parked in front of the house. His mother rushed out before he'd turned off his bike.

"He's asleep," she whispered, as if the old man could hear them. "He's been drinking."

"Big surprise."

She cuffed him on the back of his head. "Don't talk about your father like that."

He stood more than a head taller than her. "Don't you get it?" he asked, his voice low with fury. "Don't you understand? It will never get better. Not as long as you let him push you around. He treats you like crap, Mom. He always has." He reached out and touched the new bruise on her cheek and the cut at the corner of her mouth. "I'm done with this."

He walked into the house.

His mother ran after him, pulling at him, trying to stop him. "Travis, no! Don't! You can't. He's your father."

The old man was nothing more than an asshole beating the woman he married. The blood relationship was unfortunate and not enough to slow him down.

He moved deliberately to the back of the house. When he reached his parents' bedroom, he turned to his mother. "Stay out of this."

Tears poured down her face. "Stop. I beg you. Stop."

She always begged the old man, too, and he never listened. Maybe Travis had more of his father in him than he'd realized.

"I have to do this, Mom. Go to the kitchen and call the police. They'll get here before I kill him."

She sobbed and fled. He opened the bedroom door and stepped into the dim room.

His father lay across the mattress, his eyes closed, his mouth open, snores vibrating in the air. He smelled drunk and evil.

Travis looked at him for a long time, letting the anger build. Anger he fought all the time. Except for now. Today he was willing to surrender to the rage that built and built until it was a physical pain that drove him. He grabbed his father's arm and jerked him into a sitting position.

"Wake up," he growled. "Wake up so I can hit you."

The old man's eyes opened slowly. He blinked. "What the hell?"

"Get up. I found the suitcase, old man. I'm turning you in."

His father came to his feet with a roar. He charged Travis, arms swinging, curses flying.

Travis drew his fist back and slammed it against his father's chin.

"Stop hitting her," Travis yelled. "She's your wife. She deserves better."

Burt Hunter wasn't a big man, but he knew how to fight dirty. He lunged low. Travis was prepared, having been beaten many times in the past, when he was younger and smaller and less able to defend himself.

They bounced off the wall and crashed into a nightstand. A lamp went flying.

His father got him around the midsection and started punching him in the kidneys. Travis laid him low with a single crash of his knee against the other man's chest. Burt pulled him down as he fell.

They rolled on the floor, both swearing. There was blood everywhere. Travis didn't know or care whose. He hit and punched, letting the anger give him strength. He finally got his father on his back where he could straddle him and deliberately destroy his face. It was only when he felt his mother dragging at him, screaming for him to stop, that he finally drew in a breath.

His father lay silent and limp, his eyes closed, his face bloodied and swollen.

Travis stood and looked at him. His father's chest still rose and fell rhythmically. "Did you call the police?" he asked.

"Yes," his mother said absently. "I told them your father was being attacked."

Travis wasn't even surprised. She'd always chosen Burt, even when he'd been little and he'd begged her to run away. She hadn't listened.

He walked into his bathroom and washed his hands. He'd taken a couple of hits, but none to the face. He was fine . . . at least physically.

After he changed his shirt, he packed a few things in a small bag that would fit behind him on his motorcycle, then walked to the front of the house. Two LAPD cars pulled into the yard. He kept his arms out as he approached the officers.

"My mom found a suitcase in the garage," he said.

"There's money in it and guns. I don't know from what. My dad's into a lot of shit, most of it illegal."

One officer stayed with him and one went in the house while the other two headed for the garage.

"You help him with his business?" the officer asked.

Travis shook his head. "I've done time. Nearly two years. I'm not going back. I don't know anything about it. I was in Las Vegas with my girlfriend. I just got back about twenty minutes ago."

The man glanced at his knuckles. "Want to talk about it?" he asked.

"Ask me that after you've seen my mom."

The man who went into the house reappeared. "He's in the bedroom. He looks beat up pretty bad."

Both officers stared at him. Travis shrugged. "I guess he fell down the stairs."

They looked at the single-story house and back at him. One reached for his handcuffs. Travis dropped the bag on the ground. They were taking him in.

Megan worried about Travis her whole way home. He'd been distracted on the drive back, pushing her small car well beyond the speed limit. She'd desperately wanted to know what was wrong but had been determined to be the supportive girlfriend. He would tell her later. In the meantime, she would distract herself by working on her design for class.

She arrived home and parked in front, then grabbed her suitcase and walked into the house.

Her father met her before she made it to the living room.

"Megan."

There was something in his voice. Something dark and slightly scary. Her stomach tightened.

"Hi, Dad," she said brightly. "I'm back early."

"Back from spending the night at Allegra's?"

He knew she hadn't been there. She could tell from his tone, or maybe it was just something crackling in the air. She didn't spend a lot of time lying to her parents so she wasn't sure what to say now.

She stared into his familiar face, hoping to see a hint of humor or understanding. Instead he looked furious.

"In the kitchen," he said. "Now."

She dropped her bag on the floor and followed him.

They sat across from each other at the old wooden table. Sunlight streamed through the window and the smell of coffee lingered in the air.

Megan found herself looking at the gleaming surface, then at her hands as she rested them on the wood. The silence stretched between them. The tightness in her stomach increased, spreading to her chest, until she found it difficult to breathe.

"You're my daughter," her father said at last. "My oldest daughter. You and I have always been a team. We're alike. Or so I thought. I've always been proud of you—of what you've done. Of the young woman you've become. You worked hard in school, had goals, followed the rules. Other parents talked about how difficult the teen years were. I listened and felt a little superior because I didn't have those problems. We'd built a trust between us. I knew I could count on you to do the right thing."

Megan swallowed and wished she could run to her room, shut the door, and hide. Her father's words were hard enough to listen to, but everything was made worse by the thick disappointment in his voice.

"Daddy, I . . ."

He continued as if she hadn't spoken. "I was wrong about you. I trusted you, Megan. Doesn't that mean anything? How did this happen? How could you betray me like this?"

"I'm sorry," she whispered.

"I thought I knew you. But you lied, Megan. No, it's worse than that. You made a plan. You did this deliberately. You thought it out for days, maybe weeks. You sat at this table, across from me, night after night, knowing you were going to betray my trust."

She felt tears burn in her eyes, then fall. She ached everywhere. "Daddy, no."

"Where were you?"

"Las Vegas."

She didn't dare look at him. She didn't want to see the disgust in his eyes.

"How is that possible? You're only eighteen. You're not allowed in the casinos."

She didn't say anything.

He grabbed her purse and opened it. She reached for it, then sagged back in her seat. What was the point?

He pulled out her wallet and stared at the fake ID.

"My God, Megan, who are you?"

She began to cry harder. "Don't say it like that. I'm your daughter."

"Are you? I don't think so. My daughter would never do this. I want to tell you that I'm ashamed, but shame doesn't come close to what I'm feeling." He tossed her wallet on the table. "You were with that boy, weren't you? Travis?"

She wiped her face, then nodded.

He stood and walked to the counter. His back was to her. She couldn't see his expression, could only watch as his shoulders slumped.

"Go to your room," he said with a quiet anger that scared her.

"Daddy, don't. Talk to me. Yell at me."

"I can't look at you right now. You're not the person I thought you were."

She cried harder. "Stop saying that. You have to love me, no matter what."

"I know that's true, but it's not something I can think about right now."

She hated this. He was the one person she could always count on. "Daddy, please. I'm sorry. I'm really sorry. You can punish me."

He faced her then, stunning her with the stark pain in his eyes. "Punish you? Don't you think it's too late for that? What I want to know is where I went wrong. When did I fail you so much that you would act like this?" He shook his head. "Just go."

She turned and ran upstairs, hurrying into her room and slamming the door.

Her plan had been to throw herself on the bed and cry out her pain, but she couldn't stop moving. She paced the length of her room, then walked back to the door. Everything inside of her screamed for her to find her father and make it right. She had to make him understand. Only that wasn't possible. How could she justify going off with Travis and lying about everything?

Did her father know they'd had sex? She closed her eyes as her cheeks burned and embarrassment washed through her. Of course he knew. Why else would they have gone away together?

Humiliation joined shame, making her want to crawl into her closet and disappear. How could everything have gone from amazing to horrible so quickly? How had her father found out?

She walked the length of the room again, pausing at her dresser. All the makeup there was out of place. As if someone had been through it.

Leanne.

That little snoop had somehow figured out she wasn't at Allegra's. She'd been the one to tell.

The unfairness of it burned her. Leanne had always resented her closeness with their father. Megan had tried pointing out that Leanne was their mother's favorite. Sure, it was twisted, but that way they each got a parent. But that wasn't enough for Leanne. She wanted it all. Just like Tina, Leanne had to be the center of attention.

Megan distracted herself from her misery by thinking up ways to get even with her sister. None of her ideas came close to being enough. Then she collapsed on her bed, where she must have slept, because when the sound of a motorcycle in the driveway woke her, it was nearly dark.

She looked out the window and saw Travis standing there, looking up at the house.

She stared at him, sensing immediately that something was wrong, but not sure what. Then her father walked out to meet him.

Megan yelped and raced for the door. She flew down the stairs and outside.

"Daddy, don't." She had no idea what her father was going to do, but it couldn't be good.

He didn't even look at her. "Get back inside, Megan."

"No. Daddy, stop. This isn't Travis's fault."

Travis looked at her father. "You don't want to take me on, old man."

"Try me."

Travis looked him up and down. "You really think you have what it takes?"

"She's my daughter, you little thug. I'll do whatever is necessary to protect her from punks like you."

One corner of Travis's mouth turned up. "Punk, huh? I can live with that." He looked at her. "I'm leaving. My dad got arrested for a lot of bad stuff. They're going to lock him up for a long time. That should be a good thing, right? But my mom won't forgive me for turning him in. She'd rather he was running around beating her." He shrugged. "Whatever. They took me in for questioning, then released me. I'm leaving, Megan. Leaving and never coming back. I want you to come with me."

Her father grabbed her arm. "She's not going any-where with you. Megan, get in the house right now."

She pulled free of her father's grip and stared at Tra-vis, unable to take in what he was saying. "I don't under-stand."

"Which part?"

"You're leaving?" she asked, knowing that nothing would be right with Travis gone. "You can't."

"I have to. Come with me. We'll go to New York, like we talked about."

They'd talked about it . . . when? Was it just earlier that day? It felt like years ago. But that was just talk. This was too real.

"You've talked about running away with this guy?" her father asked, his voice low and angry. "Megan, get in the house now."

She ignored him, ignored them both. She couldn't think or breathe.

"You can't go," she told Travis. "You have to stay."

"I've got nothing here."

I'm here. She wanted to scream the words, but she wasn't the type.

"Megan isn't going with you," her father said firmly. "Get out of here before I call the police."

"I've spent most of the day with them," Travis said. "I'm all talked out. Megan, listen to me. We can do this. We belong together." He hesitated. "I love you."

Her heart fluttered. "Travis," she breathed, wishing she could physically hold the words forever. "I—"

"Megan, get in the house," her father ordered again.

She ignored him and stared at the one man who had always had the power to move her. "I love you, too."

He grinned. "Great. Then go grab some clothes and we'll go."

Leave? Just like that? Fill a suitcase or two and go away? From her family and her home and her life? And do what? Live on what? The parade of consequences couldn't be ignored.

"Megan, you can't leave," her father said. "You can't. This is where you belong. You're barely eighteen."

"That's the point," Travis growled. "She's eighteen. She can make her own decisions."

"Stay out of this," her father said loudly, and faced her. "Megan, your life is here. You're not ready to be on your own. New York? And live on what? Dreams cost money. What about college? What about all you've worked for?"

He looked at Travis, then back at her. "You want to go with him? Someone who already has a record? You've been dating for what? Two weeks? Three? Are you really willing to trust him with everything?"

Travis frowned. "I wouldn't let anything happen to her."

"You can't promise that. You don't have a job or a future. Just your motorcycle and the clothes on your back. What happens next? How are you going to pay for anything? What if one of you gets sick or she gets pregnant? Then what?"

Pregnant? Megan felt sick. She didn't want a baby. Not now.

Travis narrowed his gaze. "Either come with me or it's over."

"Wait!" she yelled. "Just wait. Everybody back off."

She needed to think, to figure out what was going on.

"Megan," Travis began.

She held up her hand. "No. You can't just say that. You can't force me to choose."

His expression tightened. "Why not? You're either on my side or his."

"You don't want to be with someone who asks you to walk away from people who love you," her father said quietly, as if the fight had gone out of him. "That's not love. It's wanting what he wants and the hell with the rest of the world."

Her head hurt. "Don't make sense," she told her father. She turned on Travis. "Why are you pushing me?"

"I'm going."

"Why do you get to say? Why can't I choose? Why is it all or nothing?"

"Because that's what life is."

"No. It has to be more than that."

She thought about the last twenty-four hours. Of all the things they'd done and how he'd made her feel. Then she looked at her father and thought about the lifetime he'd been there for her.

Run off? Just like that? She still slept with stupid stuffed animals on her bed. She didn't know anything about being a grown-up. Not really. Love was supposed to be enough and she felt she should be able to trust Travis, but it was too much, too fast.

"I should have known," he muttered, and started for his bike.

Megan raced after him. She grabbed his arm. "Give me a minute."

"No," he told her. "You either love me or you don't."

"That's not fair."

"Welcome to the real world," he sneered. "I should have known you weren't ready to be what I need. Stay home, Megan. Be a little girl. Let Daddy take care of things for you."

She slapped him. The second her palm hit his cheek, she regretted the action. Worse, she knew he could have blocked her, but he hadn't. He'd let her destroy their last chance.

"See ya, babe," he said as he straddled his bike, then started the engine.

"Travis, please," she whispered, not sure what she was asking for.

He put on his helmet and drove away without once looking back. She watched him go, then dropped to her knees in the driveway, hugging herself. The sound of his engine faded slowly and then there was only silence.

Her father came to her and drew her to her feet. He wrapped both arms around her.

"It will be all right," he told her. "Come on inside, Megan. Everything will be fine."

Would it? Or was it now his turn to lie?

"Come in the house," he said.

She went because there was no point in staying outside. Travis wasn't coming back.

Five

Ten Years Later

MEGAN RIPPED OPEN THE silver-wrapped package and lifted the lid off the box. The suddenly expectant silence in the room told her that most of her friends already knew the contents. She stared for several seconds before pulling out the massive, anatomically correct dildo, complete with plastic testicles, and waved it in the air.

"Does it have to be purple?" she asked.

The women sitting around on the overstuffed furniture laughed.

"For those nights when Adam is just too busy," Allegra said, grinning.

Megan rubbed the length of the sex toy. "I don't think it's going to fit."

"Oh, it'll fit," her friend promised. "You just have to want it enough."

That sent everyone into a fit of giggles. Megan put the dildo next to the porn movies, edible panties, and vibrator collection. Only Allegra would think to throw a sex-toys bridal shower.

"And here I thought I'd get flatware and pots," Megan murmured. "What do you suppose happens at the product development meetings at these places? Does someone design a prototype? How would you explain your job description to your grandmother?"

"It could be worse," Allegra said with a hiccup. "How would you explain being the model?"

Megan stared at the dildo. "Not a guy I want to meet."

Payton, her college roommate, picked up a bright pink vibrator in the shape of a tree with a little beaver in front. "While we're on the subject . . . What's up with the little woodland creatures?"

"Sometimes it's a dolphin," Allegra said, then slapped her hand over her mouth.

"Too much information," Megan teased, doing her best not to get a visual of her friend and the dolphin.

"You're going to have some explaining to do," Payton murmured. "Dex would never approve of any of this." She dropped the vibrator and grabbed one of the porn videos. The picture featured three women together. "Okay, he'd probably like this, but that's all."

"Dex has issues," Allegra said. "Adam will be fine with it. He has a great sense of humor, doesn't he?"

Megan nodded. "He'll want to try it all out." Probably on the first night, she thought, imagining her fiancé's suggestive smile when she told him about the presents. He was going to be one tired guy the next morning. But a happy one.

"Just make sure he's not in one of his imperious moods," Sherry said.

Megan glanced at the attractive fortysomething wife of one of Adam's new partners. She didn't know Sherry very well but had invited her because marrying Adam meant getting to know the partners and their wives better.

Sherry drained her mojito and shrugged. "Occupational hazard," she said to the room at large. "Some days cardiologists really do think they're God. Fortunately the mood passes." She looked at Megan. "Or are you two still too much in love for something like that to get in the way?"

"Nobody's that much in love," Allegra said with a grin. "So tell us, Megan. When Adam gets his imperious on, are there whips or does he settle for a spanking?"

"A spanking is usually good enough," Megan joked. "But I'm not worried about him. You're the one who needs a little discipline, girlfriend. It's barely three in the afternoon and you're totally drunk."

"It's my day off. I'm not only drunk, I've had carbs. God, I miss L.A."

"Then give up modeling and come back home, bitch," Payton said. "We miss you."

Allegra blew her a kiss. "I miss you, too. Both of you. But I'm needed in New York. Someone has to fill 'Page Six' and that someone is me."

Megan smiled. She and Payton were the normal ones in the relationship, while Allegra was their shining star. Allegra hadn't lasted through the first quarter of classes at UCLA before she was discovered by a vacationing modeling agency executive while Rollerblading at the beach.

Apparently what their high school classmates, and Allegra herself, had considered freakish was in fact the new "look." Six weeks later, Allegra made a splash in Europe. Two years after that she was on the cover of Vogue. She lived large, played hard, and had sex with entire rock bands.

Talk about a change, Megan thought happily, remembering how socially inept they'd been while growing up. They'd all come a long way. Of course, Allegra had gone on to be a supermodel while she and Payton were simply accountants in a Century City firm.

Not that Megan would trade. It had taken a while, but her life was finally perfect. She was happy and in love and getting married to a wonderful man.

When the guests had left, Megan went into the kitchen of Payton's high-rise mid-Wilshire condo. She grabbed a bottle of water from the stainless steel refrigerator, closed the door, and turned, only to almost run into Leanne.

The sisters stared at each other in awkward silence. "I'm, um, glad you could make it," Megan said.

In truth she hadn't thought to invite Leanne to the shower. Allegra and Payton had sent out the invitation without talking to her. Not that she would have said no. What did she care if her sister came? They weren't enemies. They weren't actually anything.

They might live less than ten miles apart, but they could have been on separate continents for all the contact they had with each other. They were thrown together on major holidays and for the occasional parental birthday dinner, nothing more.

"Your friends are really nice," Leanne said, managing to look both uncomfortable and amazingly beautiful at the same time. She'd grown from a pretty teenager into the kind of woman who could cause a car accident just walking across the street.

With her blond hair and blue eyes, she took after their father, while Megan was a redheaded throwback to a long-forgotten ancestor. Her father teased that she'd been left on the doorstep by gypsies.

"How's the acting coming?" Megan asked. "I saw you on that commercial Mom mentioned."

Leanne wrinkled her nose. "Can I sell shower cleaner or what?" She sighed. "I'm the commercial queen and still struggling to get into movies. I have a couple of auditions I'm excited about." She paused. "How are you?"

The switch in topic was abrupt, as if she'd reminded herself she and Megan didn't get along and that she shouldn't talk about herself too much. Megan wanted to tell her that of course she was interested in her sister's life. Sort of. The truth was she and Leanne had never been close. Friends often told her that was really sad— that sisters should look out for each other. To Megan's mind, it was hard to miss what she'd never had.

Besides, Leanne was still living the dream that she would make it as a famous actress. Sometimes Megan wanted to tell her to grow up, get a real job, and start paying the bills herself. At twenty-five, Leanne continually accepted money from their parents to support her lifestyle.

Not her business, Megan reminded herself. Leanne was not her responsibility.

Allegra strolled into the kitchen and rattled her empty glass. "I'm going to be puffy tomorrow and I'm too drunk to care. I don't have a photo shoot for weeks. Or days." She looked slightly puzzled. "I can't remember."

"Hydrate," Leanne told her. "Eat protein, not carbs, and sleep propped up. Don't forget the lemon juice in water for the next two days. And use tea bags on your eyes."

Allegra smiled at her. "You know I won't remember this for a second."

"You already know all of it. You're the one who taught me how to survive in this business."

Megan leaned against the counter and did her best not to snap that Allegra was her friend, not her sister's. However, she hated looking like a four-year-old, so she resisted the urge to stomp her foot and sulk. Still, it had come as something of a shock a few years ago when she'd realized Allegra and Leanne had gotten close.

Payton always said it was a business thing. They worked in similar industries. They had the same issues. While Allegra was successful and famous, she still had to deal with the reality of making sure she was incredibly beautiful every minute of every day. As an actress, Leanne dealt with the same kind of pressure. Megan couldn't relate—a reality she'd accepted a long time ago.

Leanne set down her drink. "I should go," she said. "Thanks again for inviting me." She looked at Megan. "Maybe we could get together for lunch sometime. I know you're busy with the wedding and all, but after you're back from your honeymoon or something."

The unexpected invitation caused Megan to blink in surprise. Lunch with her sister? "Um, sure. That would be great." She could hear the lack of enthusiasm in her voice, which was as much about being startled as it was about the thought of spending an hour with Leanne.

Leanne smiled tightly, hugged Allegra, then left.

Allegra barely waited until Leanne had walked out before turning on Megan. "What was that? Could you have been more of a bitch?"

Megan stiffened. "Excuse me?"

"She was reaching out. Doesn't that mean anything to you? She wants to be a part of your life."

The attack made her both angry and uncomfortable. "Since when? She was nothing but a pain in the ass when we were growing up. You remember that."

"It was a long time ago. People grow and change, but you've never given her that opportunity. In your mind, she's still fourteen and making your life hell."

"Not all that much is different." She refused to feel guilty about any of this. "We don't have anything in common."

"You might be surprised if you bothered to find out."

"I've bothered."

"When?"

Okay—so maybe Megan hadn't made a serious effort.

"Why are you taking her side? Why does this matter so much?"

"She needs you," her friend said quietly. "She doesn't have a lot of support in her life."

"Not my job. Besides, she and Mom are tight."

Allegra rolled her eyes. "Please. Your mother is the biggest drama queen on the planet. Leanne is stuck with her because her own father ignores her."

"He doesn't," Megan said automatically, although it was sort of true. Their dad didn't have much time for Leanne. "Okay, maybe he does a little."

"It's more than a little."

"Fine. He does. It's not that I dislike Leanne, I simply don't think of her. She's not someone I can respect. It's time for her to grow up and take care of herself."

"What are you talking about?"

"Mom pays her rent, puts gas in her car. All Leanne has to cover is the cost of highlights."

Allegra shook her head. "You couldn't be more wrong. Leanne's been taking care of the bills herself for the past three years. Her commercials pay really well."

"No way," Megan started, then shook her head. How could she argue when her only defense was something her mother had told her? What were the odds of Tina being honest when the story about supporting her daughter played so well to a crowd?

"You know how I hate being wrong," Megan muttered. "I don't want to like her."

"That's clear."

Payton leaned against the counter. "Had I majored in

psychology instead of business I would want to ask why that was."

"You can anyway," Allegra told her.

"Please don't," Megan said, uncomfortable that her sister might be more together than she'd thought. "It's not that I don't want Leanne to do well."

"Sure it is," Allegra said.

"Hey, bride-to-be here," Megan told her. "We are not going to discuss my flaws. There is a very small possibility that I've misjudged Leanne. I'll deal with that after the wedding. Sort of like the calendar. B.C. and A.D. Or in my case, Before Wedding and After Wedding."

"I'm giving in because I'm drunk." Allegra sipped her drink. "This is nice. Us together. We're not together enough."

"You live in New York," Megan pointed out.

"Come live with me. I have a penthouse."

Megan glanced at Payton, who rolled her eyes.

"Honey, you are so going to have a hangover in the morning," Payton said, taking Allegra by the hand and leading her back to the living room.

"My penthouse is nice. Don't you want to come live with me?"

"Not really," Megan told her. "I like my life. I have a great job and a great condo and a great fiancé."

"That's nice," Allegra said as she collapsed on the sofa. "Can I have some more?"

"Silly girl," Megan murmured, wondering if there was enough aspirin in the world to keep her friend from having a hideous morning.

Payton poured the last of the mojitos and pulled the seven-layer bean dip closer to them. Then she raised her glass. "To Megan getting married. May Adam always know that he doesn't deserve her."

Megan grinned. Allegra touched her glass, then Payton's.

"To Megan," she echoed.

They all drank, then collapsed against the sofa.

"When do you fly back in?" Payton asked Allegra.

"I don't know."

Megan grabbed Allegra's glass and put it out of reach. "Two days B.W.," she said.

Payton kicked off her high heels. "Are you about done getting ready for the wedding? Can we help with anything?"

Megan thought of the massive to-do list on her kitchen counter. "I'm actually pretty organized. I've double-checked with all the vendors. I'm still arguing with my mother about the flowers, but fortunately I'm the one talking directly to the florist. I've also warned her that my mother might call and try to change things." She sighed. "Just an FYI—don't let your parents pay for your wedding. It gives them way too much control."

"Why did you agree?" Payton asked.

Megan winced. "A moment of weakness and stupidity. Adam is paying off the last of his student loans. Now that he's in a real practice, he'll be making plenty, but it was tight for a few years. We got carried away with the Laguna Beach location and the menu, not to mention the dress. I could have paid for it all but it would have cleaned out my savings account."

When her father had offered her the wedding of her dreams, she'd accepted. Something she'd had second thoughts about more than once.

"My dad is actually great about it," she continued. "He just wants me to be happy. It's—"

"Your mother," Payton and Allegra said together.

"In some ways I admire Tina," Allegra said, her long, dark hair falling in perfect curls to her waist. "She always gets exactly what she wants. She doesn't care about anyone but herself, which must be very freeing. Imagine the time we'd all save if we didn't have to worry about other people."

"I never want anyone to feel about me the way I feel about her," Megan said, the unexpected rush of honesty fueled by exhaustion and too many mojitos.

Payton touched her arm. "Tell Allegra about the dress."

Megan was grateful for the change in subject. "It's Vera Wang."

Allegra raised her eyebrows. "Aren't you special?"

"It's gorgeous," Payton told her. "Strapless and fitted, then the skirt flares out. It's perfect."

Allegra took another sip. "I thought you were going to design your dress."

Megan thought about all the sketches she'd made over the years. "I considered it and even got a few estimates. It was nearly the same price. I just wasn't sure it would turn out the way I imagined."

Allegra leaned back against the sofa and closed her eyes. "You have to believe in yourself. You have talent."

"You're beyond drunk."

"I know. It's wonderful." Her mouth opened and she began to snore.

"Very pretty," Payton said with a grin. "Okay, are you sober enough to help me pick out an outfit for tomorrow? I'm meeting Dex's mother for the first time and I want to look perfect."

"Sure."

They went into Payton's bedroom.

"I'm thinking conservative, pretty, wouldn't-you-love-me-to-marry-your-son."

Megan laughed. "That's very in these days. *InStyle* did a whole feature on that look."

She opened Payton's walk-in closet door. One side was filled with the dark suits they both wore to the office. She ignored those and flipped through blouses, skirts, and jeans.

"Where are you going?"

"Cheesecake Factory. Apparently it's her favorite."

The Marina del Rey location meant it could be cool and even foggy for brunch. Megan picked out a floral-print A-line skirt and lacy camisole.

"Check the weather in the morning," she said, grabbing both a tailored T-shirt and a cream-colored blazer. "Warm and sunny, wear the T-shirt. Foggy, go with the jacket. Sandals with a heel no higher than an inch." She studied the wall of shoes and grabbed two pairs. "Either of these. For jewelry, keep it simple. You have those dangles with the freshwater pearls. Those, a gold chain and a watch."

"Wow." Payton studied the clothes. "That's great. I would never have thought of layering the T-shirt. But it's perfect. She's going to hate me. She worships Dex. I doubt she'll think I'm good enough."

"Then she's a fool, because Dex isn't going to do better."

Payton blinked rapidly. "I've had too much to drink because I think I'm going to cry. Okay, let's go make sure Allegra's still breathing."

She returned to the living room. Megan lingered in the closet a second, looking at the outfit she'd put together. After a second, she grabbed a handbag from the shelf and put it next to the shoes so Payton would see it when she got dressed.

Her gaze returned to the T-shirt next to the lace camisole. An image came to her of a sundress with a flirty skirt, combining the two fabrics. Of course if the lace was a knit, too, that would be interesting.

Something to play with when she had time.

Megan got home shortly after six that evening. She walked into her Venice town house and pushed the button on the answering machine.

"Hey, darlin', it's me."

Adam's voice made her smile.

"I'm missing you and thinking about you at your shower. Don't forget to tell them all how much I love you and that I'm a total god in bed. Okay? Talk to you later. Bye."

She chuckled, then deleted the message. After putting the piece of cake Payton had sent home with her in the fridge, she headed upstairs.

At the end of the hall was the smaller of the two bedrooms. She went inside and turned on the overhead light. The room was temporarily crowded with wedding presents, but the rest of the space was all shelves filled with folded fabric, several dress forms and covered bins stacked on top of each other.

There were over a dozen clear containers, each jammed with sketches. Some were done on paper, some on thicker board. She opened one of the bins and flipped through the sketches there, then pulled out the picture of the wedding dress.

It was similar to the one she'd bought, but with linked hearts made out of beads and more handmade lace. The intricate pattern continued down the back of the dress and along the train. There were multiple views in her sketch.

Notations on the side showed approximate yardage and a materials list. Underneath that design were fifteen more, of different wedding dresses she would never make, never wear. They wouldn't ever exist in three dimensions.

She put down the drawing and grabbed her sketch pad, then sat on the floor and quickly roughed out the sundress she'd imagined earlier. She studied her fabrics and noted which of them would work. She drew until her legs cramped. Only then did she glance up and realize it was nearly midnight.

No time to sew, she thought. The story of her life. But she would make time. She'd been meaning to work on some of her designs for a while now. A.W., she promised herself, as she put her pad away. A.W. for sure.

Six

MEGAN SIPPED HER MIMOSA. "Trust me, Dad. You don't want to know. Let's just say my friends got creative."

Gary held up both hands. "I'm convinced. You can spare me the details. But did you have fun at the shower?"

"Yes. Allegra flew in, which was great. I don't see her enough."

"Are you all right with the wedding? Everything coming together? You have enough money?"

His voice was filled with concern and love. She reached across the restaurant table, took his hand and squeezed it. "I'm great. Dad, you've been amazing about the wedding. I want you to know I appreciate all you've done."

"You're my best girl. I want you to be happy." He faked a frown. "Adam makes you happy, right?"

She laughed. "Yes. He's still in Hawaii, but he gets home in a few days. I'm finished with fittings, I know who's coming to the wedding and except for a few last-minute details, I'm totally ready."

"Your mother giving you much trouble?"

Megan's good mood faded. "We're fine."

"You need to call her more. You never call."

"I rarely call," Megan murmured. "There's a difference. Besides, she has Leanne."

"Your sister is busy with her career, such as it is." Gary shook his head. "An actress. I begged her to go to college and study something sensible. Anything. But would she listen?" He looked at her. "She could have learned from you, Megan. My sensible girl."

"Just like you, Dad."

"We're a good team."

"We are." Megan looked at the man who had loved her and guided her all her life. "Dad, I want you to know that I'm incredibly happy. My life is perfect and a lot of that is because of you."

He beamed at her. "I'm glad. It's what I always wanted for you."

"I know."

"Your mother wants to talk to you about her dress."

Megan groaned. "I beg you, no."

"Come on. Tina wants to look right on your special day."

More like she wanted to make sure she got even more attention than the bride, Megan thought. Tina was never going to change, and for reasons that Megan couldn't understand, her father was okay with that. But if it made him happy, who was she to judge?

"I'll call Mom," Megan said, mostly to make her father feel better. "How's she doing?"

"About the same. She has her aches and pains."

Tina loved being bedridden. It made for high drama.

The waiter appeared with their brunch order. The Santa Monica restaurant faced the ocean. The large outdoor patio featured big umbrellas and gorgeous views. She and her father met here most Sunday mornings. It was a tradition they'd started while she was in college. UCLA was only a few miles away.

Megan cut into her stuffed French toast.

"Tell me about Adam's conference," he said

"Something about a new surgical technique." She smiled. "I confess, I don't listen too closely. It's the whole blood thing. He can get a little graphic in his descriptions. I wanted to go with him. I mean, hey, it's Hawaii. But it's too close to the wedding and I didn't have the extra vacation time at work." Not with the honeymoon they were planning. A two-week trip to Fiji, where they would do nothing but relax and make love and enjoy being married.

"How is work?" her father asked.

"Great. Busy. I've taken on a couple of new clients, which is good but hectic."

"I thought you were already pushing yourself as hard as you could."

She grinned. "There's always time for more billable hours."

Her father looked worried.

"I'm fine," she told him. "I want to get ahead at the firm and that means bringing in business. Eventually they'll adjust my workload, but for now, I need to focus.

I still want to make partner before thirty. That's only two years away."

He touched her hand. "I'm really proud of you, honey. You know that, right?"

"I know that. The next year will be a push, but then I'm hoping to get promoted and all will be better." She would still have to work the insane hours, but she would be better-paid for her time. "Besides, Adam is going to be working a lot at his practice. They're saying sixty hours is pretty normal. So this way neither of us is home waiting for the other."

"What about kids? What happens then?"

"We'll work it out," she said easily. "I'm a modern woman. I can do it all."

"I just want you to be happy," her father told her.

"I appreciate that. I'm good, Dad."

"Okay. Because if Adam gets out of hand, let me know." He grinned. "I'll hire someone to beat the crap out of him."

She laughed.

Conversation turned to his work and whether the fall Santa Ana winds would bring a big fire season.

"Adam's house is up in the hills," her father pointed out.

"Yes, but we're not in Malibu," Megan said. "We're fine, Dad."

"I don't know why you have to be the one to sell your condo."

"Gee, I don't know," she teased. "Maybe because my place is twelve hundred square feet and two bedrooms, while he just bought a three-thousand-square-foot mansion-in-training?"

"Is your name on the mortgage and the deed? California's a community property state, Megan. But if Adam owns the house by himself before you get married and doesn't put you on the deed, if something happens, you won't get a penny, even if you've paid half the mortgage."

"Dad, you do know I'm an accountant? I understand how money works."

"You're a woman in love, and that trumps accounting training every time."

She supposed she should have been annoyed by his worry, but she wasn't. Knowing she had his love and support had always carried her through the rough times.

"Adam and I are going into his attorney's office the Thursday before the wedding. We're signing a quitclaim deed that puts the house half in my name. I've already spoken to the loan officer at his mortgage company and I'll be added there, too."

"Good. I want you taken care of."

"I want that, too, Dad, but Adam isn't trying to mess with me. We're getting married." She sipped her coffee. "We've actually been discussing me keeping my condo for a while and renting it out. Values are only going to increase over the next few years. It could be a nice investment."

"In your name only, or are you adding him as well?"

She grinned. "Adam isn't worried about my condo. It's staying in my name."

"Good."

She dug into her French toast. "Want to walk on the boardwalk when we're finished here? Burn off a few calories?"

"You have the time?"

Usually she left right after brunch, but with Adam out of town, she had a more relaxed schedule. "Sure."

"Then we'll walk. Or maybe stroll. I'm getting older."

She laughed. "You are many things, Dad, but old isn't one of them."

Megan drove home with the top down. The air was warm, the sun bright. Pacific Coast Highway was slow, but she didn't have to be anywhere specific, so she turned on the radio and enjoyed the drive. Her cell phone rang as she slowed for a red light.

She pushed the speaker button on her steering wheel. "Hello?"

"Hi, gorgeous. Hawaii misses you." Adam's low voice made her smile.

"L.A. is too much into itself to notice you're gone, but it will be happy to see you when you return."

"L.A. needs to think about someone other than itself once in a while. What about you? Do you miss me?"

"Of course. I just had brunch with my dad."

"I know. That's why I waited to call. What are you doing now?"

"Heading home."

"I'm bored."

"You're in Hawaii."

"Yeah, but you're not. Why didn't you come with me?"

"Because I didn't have a conference there and one of us still has to worry about her career."

"I worry."

"Is this before or after you work on your tan?"

"During." He chuckled. "I've been thinking about those shower gifts you were telling me about. I can't wait to try them."

She thought about the massive dildo. "A couple of them scare me."

"I'll hold your hand. And other parts of you. In fact, I'll hold anything you want me to."

"Cheap talk."

"Very cheap, but it's way more than talk. I miss you."

"I miss you, too."

There was a noise in the background. Adam groaned. "Duty calls. I'll talk to you later."

"Okay. Bye."

"Bye."

She pushed the button to end the call. The light turned green and she eased into traffic. Everything was perfect. How did she ever get so lucky?

Megan walked into the break room the next morning. Accountants might have had a reputation for being stuffy and boring, but they knew how to keep their employees wired on caffeine.

A restaurant-grade coffeemaker sat on one counter with two espresso machines parked next to it. There were all kinds of flavored syrups, a clerk whose main responsibility was to make lattes and a refrigerator filled with milk, whipped cream and soy alternatives. High-fructose sugar snacks filled several cupboards.

Megan ignored the cookies and donuts. She brought in whole wheat crackers and fruit from home and kept them in the small refrigerator she'd tucked next to her credenza. But she took advantage of the coffee. Like the rest of her coworkers, she depended on caffeine to make it through the extra-long days.

She'd just finished pouring foamy nonfat milk into her mug when someone else entered the room. She turned to greet them, only to hesitate when she saw Carrie Billings. The petite brunette had recently joined the firm after moving to Los Angeles from Minneapolis. She came highly recommended, was supposed to be a hard worker and had managed to learn everyone's name in less than twenty-four hours.

Megan knew it was irrational, but she'd disliked the other woman on sight and couldn't seem to shake the sense that Carrie had been born half-snake.

"Good morning," Carrie said brightly, carrying her mug to the coffeepot and pouring in regular coffee. "Are you getting frantic about the wedding or is everything on track?"

"I'm fine. It's all coming together."

"No problems with the flowers?"

Megan wondered how the other woman knew about

her flower issues. Had someone been talking about her?

"My mother is a bit of a control freak, too," Carrie said with a smile that made Megan flinch. "It's never easy."

So someone *had* been talking. But who? "It's fine," Megan said coolly, inching toward the door. "Sounds like you're settling in."

"I'm finding my way around, getting to know the staff and a few of the clients. Speaking of which, I was over at Character Creative the other day."

Megan froze. Character Creative was one of her newest clients and landing them had been a coup. They designed characters for advertisers and were difficult, demanding and nearly three million in billing.

"Why would you go there?" she asked, telling herself it was no big deal. Josh had hired her specifically. It had taken her nearly six months to land the account. "I mean, how would you know to go there?"

Carrie clucked her tongue. "Don't get all jealous girl-friend on me, Megan," she chided. "Felicia and I were at lunch across the street. She took me over to meet Josh. I'm not poaching."

If the reassurance was supposed to help, it failed miserably. Why would Felicia, a senior partner, take Carrie there? Megan resisted the need to call Josh that second and make sure everything was all right.

Carrie took a step toward her and patted her arm. "I didn't mean to upset you. I'm sorry. I had no idea you were so . . . possessive about your clients. Felicia said we were all a team, but I guess that's only a theory, right?"

With the insults flying so fast, Megan couldn't both

duck and come up with a well-timed slam of her own. Carrie got the last word and left the break room. Megan watched her go, imagining a sleek tail snapping once before disappearing around the corner.

"I hate that," Megan muttered, taking her coffee and retreating to her office. "I hate not knowing what to say at the right time."

The worst part was she'd allowed Carrie to make her feel stupid and small. Was it just an irrational and unexplained dislike of someone or was her subconscious telling her to beware? She would have felt a lot better if Felicia had hired someone other than snake girl.

Fortunately her morning was busy and she didn't have time to dwell on her encounter with Carrie. A little before noon, she walked into Felicia's office to update her on several clients.

Felicia Graham, a fiftysomething partner who believed in hard work and straight dealings, was the youngest person the firm had ever named partner. She'd been thirty-one. Megan wanted to break her record.

Megan set the pile of folders on her boss's desk. "I always get a workout carrying these around."

"Upper-body strength matters," Felicia told her with a grin. "And we were told that computers would reduce the amount of paper in our offices. Another childhood fantasy crushed. Have a seat."

Megan settled into the comfortable chair across from her boss and picked up the first folder. "The Shoe Factory," she began, and went through all the accounts.

As usual Felicia listened, asked intelligent questions

and offered the occasional insight. When they were finished the other woman said, "Impressive. Even with all you've got going on with the wedding in just a few days. A few of the partners expressed concern when you got engaged, but I told them you would do fine and you have. Bravo."

Megan smiled. "Thanks. Of course the wedding is important, but so is my work. I didn't want any of my clients to suffer. I'm on schedule with everyone and I've assigned all the time-sensitive reports that have to be completed while I'm gone."

"Excellent. If you still have a few things you need wrapped up by someone, use Carrie. She'll have time."

"Sure," Megan murmured, privately vowing that she wouldn't ask Carrie for anything.

Felicia leaned back in her chair. "We're having performance reviews in September. Normally this is where I would tell you that you have another year to do your best to impress the partners. However, we've been talking about changing our structure. There are one or two senior associates who are stand-outs. We don't want to risk those people being stolen away by the competition, so we're starting a junior partner program. Those invited to be junior partners would take a year to transition to regular partner, with all the responsibilities and benefits associated with that title. In the meantime, they would share in the spoils, so to speak, and take on more of the workload."

Felicia leaned toward her. "Megan, you're the person we're considering for that position. You've proved yourself countless times."

Megan felt herself flush with pride and pleasure. To make partner, even junior partner, now? While she was still in her twenties? "Thank you. I'm thrilled and delighted, of course."

"It's not official. It won't be until September. But I wanted to let you know what we were thinking."

There was a kind of warning in the words, which Megan understood. With her getting married, the assumption was she might not be as focused on her career.

"I appreciate the information," Megan told her. "Of course I won't mention it to anyone. This is a great opportunity for me and I will do everything in my power to show you and the other partners that you're making the right decision."

"I had a feeling you'd say that," Felicia told her. "I'm going to enjoy the chance to work more closely with you on the larger accounts. Well done, Megan. Congratulations."

"Thank you."

Megan collected her files and returned to her office. She fought to keep from grinning like an idiot. She'd meant what she said—she wouldn't mention the potential chance to make partner to anyone. She didn't want gossip spreading or word to get back to her boss.

Once she was safely behind her closed door, she allowed herself a victory dance, then spun in her chair until she was dizzy. Finally she looked at her phone and wished she could call Adam. But it was three hours earlier in Hawaii and he might not yet be up. So she would tell him later and call her dad that night.

She thought about telling Allegra but didn't want to

tell her and not Payton, and Payton worked at the office. Not that her friend would spread the news. Still, Megan had given her word.

She returned to the break room, where she celebrated with a mocha latte topped with real whipped cream, then went back to her office and threw herself into her work. The rest of the morning flew by, as did the lunch hour. She hadn't realized how much time had passed until the receptionist buzzed her to tell her a Mr. Johnson, her two o'clock, was waiting.

She walked up front, where a short older man was waiting. After introducing herself, she led him back to her office.

"How can I help you, Mr. Johnson?" she asked.

He settled into the seat across from hers. "I'm an attorney," he began, his tone suggesting that was enough information to explain everything.

"I'm afraid that's not my specialty," she told him. "Were you referred by a client?"

"No. I'm not here to find an accountant. I have one." He looked confused. "You weren't told about me? I spoke with your mother a few days ago and she assured me she would be in contact with you."

Megan frowned. "My mother? What does she have to do with anything?"

Mr. Johnson shifted uncomfortably in his seat. "So she didn't speak to you?"

Oh, she'd spoken at length, about nearly every detail of the wedding, her health, her hair and the search for the perfect nail polish. "Not about you."

"I see. That makes this more . . ." He cleared his throat. "I have been Elliott Scott's attorney for many years now. I handled all his business affairs as well as his personal estate. He recently passed away."

"I'm sorry," Megan murmured, not sure what that or anything had to do with the visit. And why was her mother involved?

"Are you familiar with Mr. Scott? He was a painter who found some measure of success later in life."

"I, ah, haven't heard of him." Should she have? Was he somehow connected with one of her clients?

"Elliott knew your mother many years ago," the lawyer continued. "Nearly thirty. They had an . . . intimate relationship, and you are the result."

Megan heard nothing. She didn't know if he kept talking or not, she just knew she wasn't hearing a sound. Even her heartbeat seemed muted. She had the sensation of falling through space, and it wasn't pleasant. Her stomach clenched, making her regret the whipped cream on her coffee.

"My mother has been married for thirty-one years," Megan murmured. "She was married to my father." This Elliott person didn't have anything to do with her.

"I'm aware of that, as was Elliott. It's the reason he had me get in touch with her directly. We talked about the best way to proceed. Elliott had cancer. His death was not unexpected. He thought if you heard the news from Tina it would smooth things over." Mr. Johnson hesitated. "I'm sorry. When I spoke with her, she assured me she would tell you everything."

"My mother avoids anything unpleasant," Megan said. "Not that it's an issue." She felt cold all over as the last of what he'd said finally sank into her brain. *And you are the result.*

The result of what? An affair? Was he implying . . .

"You're wrong," she said firmly. "I know my father. He raised me."

Mr. Johnson nodded. "Elliott was confident you hadn't been told. He's left a DNA sample at a lab here in Los Angeles. I have the information for you, along with this." He handed her a business-size envelope. When she didn't take it, he put it on her desk.

"Elliott always regretted he never had a relationship with you," the lawyer said gently. "Your mother insisted that was the way it had to be and he respected that. But he never forgot about you, Megan. He didn't expect a check to make up for anything, but he hoped it would somehow allow you to do something special. Something he would, however distantly, be a part of."

She stood. "This is insane. This is not happening. How dare you come in here like this and try to ruin everything?" Someone else her father? Impossible.

He stood. "I'm sorry. I didn't want to upset you. I thought you already knew. That Tina had told you." He reached into his suit pocket and pulled out a business card, which he put on top of the envelope. "Feel free to contact me when you've had a chance to take this in. I would be happy to answer any questions I can."

He paused as if he wanted to say more, then he left, carefully closing the door behind him.

Megan stayed where she was, stiff, cold and sick to her stomach. Her chest ached; her brain felt disconnected from her body. She reached for the envelope, then had trouble opening it because her hands shook so hard. Finally she pulled out a single piece of paper.

Dear Megan,

I realize this is too little too late, but as I near the end of my life, I feel compelled to make contact with you. I have always regretted agreeing to stay out of your life. You are my firstborn and the little I know about you makes me proud.

I realize I will never be your father in the traditional sense of the word. That honor goes to the very good man who raised you. But I hope this bequest can help in some small way. I would urge you to do something special with the money and I will be bold enough to ask you to think of me when you do.

Sincerely,
Elliott Scott

She glanced down at a check made out to her in the sum of two hundred and fifty thousand dollars.

A man she'd never met, a man who believed he was her biological father, had just left her a quarter of a million dollars.

Seven

LEANNE WINCED AT THE twelve-dollar-an-hour parking rate, then reminded herself it was a business expense. That's what she always told herself as she drove around L.A., going to auditions that always seemed to be in expensive high-rises or Santa Monica bungalows. She could deduct parking and gas, even if she didn't get the job. But wouldn't it have been nicer if she didn't have the expense in the first place?

She knew she was fortunate and shouldn't complain. Compared to a lot of struggling actresses, she had it easy. Her commercial work paid the bills and she hadn't needed to get a second job for nearly eight months. That was something. But her expenses were never-ending . . . the gym, the perfect blond highlights, waxing, tanning, manicures, pedicures. Adding to that thrill was the reality of being constantly hungry.

Most of her friends dreamed about finding the perfect guy. Leanne had dreams about an In-N-Out burger with a vanilla milkshake. Instead she survived on less than a thousand calories a day of lean protein and vegetables.

She allowed herself a skinny latte on Sundays and avoided alcohol. All in the name of being an actress.

"Suffering for one's art is a time-honored tradition," she murmured as she pulled into the parking space and turned off her car. Then she checked her makeup in the mirror and made her way to the elevators, her high-heeled sandals clicking on the cement.

Ten minutes later she'd been introduced to Marty, a fortysomething casting director who smiled too much and made her nervous. Mostly because Marty hadn't sent pages ahead of time and doing a cold read didn't produce her best work. She preferred to take her time, memorize her lines and then dig for nuances that would make her stand out.

But her agent had assured her this was an excellent part and Marty was worth meeting.

After the initial hellos and weather chitchat, he took her hand and pulled her to the floor-to-ceiling windows, where the sun fell directly on her face.

"You're a pretty girl," he said. "Surgery?"

"No."

"Good. Scars can be a problem, even the small ones. You've been doing a lot of commercial work?"

She nodded and motioned to her bag. "I've had a few parts on television and a couple of lines in different movies. I brought my DVD with me." It was her hit reel—highlights of her.

Marty didn't even glance at her handbag. "Maybe later."

Two words. Two small, seemingly meaningless words.

But they gave Leanne a knot in her stomach. She swallowed.

"Is anyone else coming to the meeting?"

"No. I thought we could get to know each other first."

My agent sent me, Leanne told herself, fighting the rising tension. This was totally legitimate. A lot of casting directors took meetings. Except she knew she was lying to herself and Marty was lying to her.

He moved close and cupped her cheek. "I've heard great things about you, Leanne. Great things. Take off your panties."

There it was—the boldface command. He hadn't even bothered to buy her a drink. Of course, it was ten in the morning.

Somewhere out in the city, her sister was in a meeting or working on a client's file or whatever it was accountants did. Mothers were taking toddlers to the park or doctors' offices. Truckers were driving and teachers were in class and she was getting screwed by a guy she didn't know for a part in a damn movie.

Anger and shame battled for dominance. She knew why he expected her to put out—because she'd done it before. Because sometimes it was just easier to say, "Fine. Fuck me. Just give me the role." Because she could totally disconnect from her body, send her soul somewhere else for the two or three minutes it took the assholes to get off.

That's all they were interested in. Getting off with a beautiful woman. It brightened their day. It made them feel powerful. It made her feel like a whore.

The internal debate lasted long enough for Marty to

raise his eyebrows. Then she pulled off her thong and set it on the table.

"You'll use a condom," she said.

"Sure." He was already undoing his belt. "Bend over."

Five minutes later, it was finished. She left without saying a word and made it down to the parking garage level before she vomited the little food in her stomach. Then she staggered to her car, where she had to sip water until the shaking stopped.

Megan would never have let that happen, she thought grimly. Her sister would have told the guy off, then walked out. Megan wouldn't have accepted this as the price of what she wanted. Her sister had created a perfect life—one she could be proud of. What did Leanne have to show for her dreams?

The silence is as bad as the violation, Leanne thought as she started the engine. That she couldn't tell anyone. Her agent would say she should have walked out, that of course she wasn't expected to have sex to get a part. Then she would get fewer and fewer callbacks and eventually be dropped by the agency.

Was it worth it? Isn't that what it came down to? Or maybe the real question was: Was *she* worth it? Did her dreams really matter so much? How much longer could she go through this and still look at herself in the mirror?

Leanne didn't have any answers. She just knew she had to get home, get in the shower and pray there was enough hot water to wash away the shame.

*   *   *

Megan didn't remember the drive from her office to her parents' house. One minute she'd been in Century City and the next she was pulling onto the street where she'd grown up.

She couldn't think, could barely breathe. Her skin had that clammy coldness that signals nausea. Thoughts chased each other through her brain, each more confusing than the one before. Nothing made sense.

Had her mother really had an affair? Had she slept with Elliott Scott, gotten pregnant and passed off the baby as her husband's?

"No," Megan said as she hurried up the front walk. "No, no. No!" It couldn't be true. She wouldn't let it. She knew exactly who she was and that person wasn't Elliott Scott's daughter.

She knocked once, then used her key to let herself inside.

"Mom, it's me," she called, walking purposefully through the house to the master bedroom in the back. It was the one place her mother was likely to be.

Sure enough, Tina lay on a chaise, watching television. She glanced up as Megan entered and half raised her arm.

"I'm so glad you came," her mother said. "I'm feeling weak today. So tired. I'm not sure I can make it to the kitchen myself. Would you fix my lunch, Megan?"

Megan couldn't believe it. She waved the envelope the attorney had left with her. "Mr. Johnson stopped by my office today, Mother. Do you remember him? He said he was here last week. He said he talked to you and that you told him you were going to get in touch with me. He said you were going to tell me—" She couldn't say the words. As if saying them might make them real. "What the hell is going on?"

Her mother blinked at her. "What are you talking about? You are not allowed to speak to me that way, Megan," she said, but her expression was wary and her eyes darted around the room.

Megan sank onto the bed and the possibility of the impossible became real. "No," she whispered. "No. It can't be true. You slept with another man while you were married to Daddy?"

"Of course not," her mother told her. "I would never do that. I love your father. I'm not sure who this Elliott person is."

Megan desperately wanted to believe her. "So you did see the attorney. He came by."

"Yes, but so what? He's wrong. I told him he was wrong."

"He didn't believe you. And if you denied everything, why did you tell him you'd talk to me? Saying you'd tell me what happened makes me believe you have something I need to know."

Her mother rubbed her chest. "I'm having pains, Megan. Serious pains. You may have to call 911."

Megan stood. If anyone was going to pass out, it was her. She couldn't take this. Nothing was right. Nothing made sense. "I'm not calling anyone. There's nothing wrong with your heart or any other part of you. You can't use being sick to get out of this." Her voice began to rise.

"What the hell is going on?" she demanded again. "What did you do?"

"Nothing." Her mother began to cry, then gasp for breath. "Nothing."

Megan desperately wanted to believe her, but she couldn't. "You did," she whispered, the awfulness of it filling her. "You slept with him. You cheated on Daddy and got pregnant with me."

"No. Never. I didn't tell you because it was ridiculous. That man coming here after all this time. It's all lies."

But Megan wasn't sure anymore. She was terrified that it was true, and that if it was true, it would change everything. "Is it? Elliott Scott says he's my father. He says he left a DNA sample at a lab, so I can confirm the connection."

Color drained from her mother's face. She seemed to age in a heartbeat. "DNA? Like on TV?"

It was true, Megan thought. Her mother's face was as much an admission of guilt as a written confession. She wanted to shriek or hit or throw something.

It was true. She sank back onto the bed as her legs gave out. She could hear the blood pounding in her ears.

"You slept with Elliott while you were married to my father." No. Not her father. "While you were married to your husband." And if Gary Greene wasn't her dad, who was she?

"I didn't mean for it to happen," her mother whined. "It's not my fault. Your father traveled so much. He was gone and I was lonely and no one paid any attention to me. I met Elliott and he was kind. I needed that."

"Needed the attention," Megan said bitterly. "My God, Mother. How could you do that? Are you saying this is Dad's fault because you couldn't go fifteen minutes without being told you're beautiful? Not even you are that shallow."

"How dare you?" Tina said reproachfully. "I'm your mother."

"You're the woman who not only cheated on her husband but lied to her entire family." Anger filled her. She welcomed it because maybe if she was furious enough, she wouldn't be so scared.

Tears filled her mother's eyes. "Megan, don't. You can't understand what it's like to suffer all the time."

"The only people who suffer are those who have to listen to your constant complaints. You never think of anyone but yourself. That's why you didn't tell me. You didn't want to deal with the truth, so you ignored it. You let me take a meeting with an attorney at my office because you're a selfish coward. You cheated on my—on your husband, because you're a selfish bitch."

Megan had a whole lot more to scream, but a noise caught her attention. She turned, then froze when she saw her father—the man she would always think of as her father—standing in the doorway. He stared at his wife.

"Tina?"

There was stark pain in his voice, a thousand years of hurt. Megan walked to him, arms open. He pushed her aside and crossed to the bed.

"Is it true?" he asked harshly.

"Oh, Gary." Tina cried, tears pouring down her cheeks. "It's not true."

"Don't lie to me."

She covered her face. "It's not my fault. You have to understand that."

Megan felt nothing but disgust for this woman who always needed to be at the center of the universe. She waited for her father to look at her, for them to connect over Tina's deceit, but it was as if she wasn't in the room.

"I didn't mean for anyone to find out," Tina whispered. "No one has to know. We can pretend it never happened. Please say it will be all right." She gave a little gasp and widened her green eyes. Despite everything, Tina looked stunning.

"My heart," Tina gasped. "It's beating so fast."

He turned and walked toward the door.

Megan grabbed his arm. "Dad—"

He cut her off with a cold, distant expression she'd never seen before. It was as if they were strangers, as if he'd never known her at all. Without saying anything, he stalked out of the room. Seconds later, she heard the front door close.

Tina brushed her face. "I hope you're happy. You've ruined everything."

Megan touched her cheek. It felt as if her father had slapped her. "Me? I'm not the one who cheated and lied for twenty-eight years." It hurt to speak, to breathe, to *know*.

Her mother didn't bother to look upset or embarrassed. "If he doesn't come back, this is your fault, Megan. You couldn't keep your mouth shut. It's always about you, isn't it?"

"No," she said quietly, strangely unmoved by the attack. "But this time, it should be."

With that, she left. But she didn't slam the door. She was already too broken inside and was afraid the sharp noise would cause her to shatter.

Once in her car, she scrolled through her cell phone until she found the number for Adam's hotel and dialed. With the time difference, he might still be in his room.

"Hello?"

Megan frowned at the sound of a woman's voice. "I'm looking for Adam Nolan. Do I have the wrong room?"

"Uh, no. Let me get him."

Seconds later she heard a familiar voice. "Megan?"

"Hi. I . . . what's going on?"

"I'm having a few people in to talk about the morning lecture. Hold on. I'll go to the bedroom where it's quiet."

She had the brief thought that there hadn't been any background noise on the connection, then forgot when she heard him say, "Okay, now it's just us. What's up?"

"There was this man. An attorney. He came to my office." Her voice began to shake as tears filled her eyes. "Oh, Adam, you won't believe what he said. I can't believe it."

"Tell me. Whatever it is, we'll handle it."

His words made her feel better. She wasn't alone in this—she had Adam. "It's about my father."

"Is he sick? Did he have a heart attack?"

"He's fine. Actually, no. He's not. He's dead."

Adam swore. "Your dad died?"

"I'm not explaining this right. Gary Greene isn't my father. At least not my biological one." She told him about the attorney's visit, the inheritance, the DNA sample and her mother's reaction. She started to tell him about Gary walking out on her, but it hurt too much for her to say the words.

When she'd finished there was only silence. Finally Adam drew in a breath. "That's a hell of a day."

"Tell me about it."

"I'll be on the next flight out."

Relief eased the tightness in her chest. "Really?"

"Sure. Megan, I love you. You matter more than any conference. Let me call the airlines and find a seat, then I'll call you back. Give me fifteen minutes."

"Okay. Thanks."

"You're my best girl. What else would I do?"

Eight

TRAVIS HUNTER CHECKED THE printout on his clipboard, then motioned to the front three trucks. "I want them fully loaded. Get it all on now so there's no return trip. I mean it, Billy."

Billy inhaled on his cigarette, then saluted. "Yes, Mr. Boss-man. Whatever you say."

Travis shook his head. "Yeah, I'm the man." He walked toward the back of the yard, where the smaller vehicles were parked.

"Trees to the association," he muttered, then looked up to see them being loaded. "Mrs. Crandall wants new roses." Those were being stacked by a pickup.

He went down the rest of the line to confirm the crew was doing what they were supposed to, then he glanced up at the sky. It was barely after seven in the morning, but the sun was out and it was going to be damn hot. Of course, it was Houston. The air conditioners clicked on sometime in late April and didn't take a rest until October.

He returned to the front, where topsoil and bark

poured into the three largest trucks. Billy stood by the back of them.

"No, all the way. We're not coming back later to top up." Billy glanced at him. "Ain't that right?"

"You give me a pain in the ass, Billy," Travis told the other man.

Billy grinned. "Then it's gonna be a good day."

Travis chuckled. Billy was one of his best guys, but he wasn't easy or cooperative. Still, he led a good team and the other men respected him. Some days that counted as a win.

He headed for the office but before he got there, the door opened and Jenny yelled for him. "You got a call. Long distance. Says she's your mama."

Travis paused in mid-stride. His mother? He spoke to her three times a year. Christmas, her birthday and Mother's Day. The calls were short, uncomfortable and lacking in detail. They discussed their health; he didn't ask about his father, though she always told him anyway; then they hung up. So why was she calling now?

His first thought was the old man was out of prison. It didn't seem possible. He shouldn't even come up for parole for another fifteen years. But if not his father, then what?

He entered the office.

"Line two," Jenny told him.

He thanked her, then went into his office and picked up the phone.

"Hello?"

"Travis. It's your mother. I'm sorry to bother you at

work. I've tried calling you at home for the past week, but I can't seem to catch you."

"I've been out a lot."

"Oh. Is everything . . . Are you all right?"

What did she think? That he was hanging out in bars? Getting in trouble? He'd learned his lesson. He did his thing, didn't get involved. He wasn't his father. Not that they would have that conversation.

"I'm fine."

"Good. Good. I've been . . ." Another pause. "It's hard, Travis. The business. I'm having a hard time with everything. I guess I'm getting older and the world is changing. The business is all I have. There was never any money to put away for retirement. I just don't know how long I can keep doing it. I want to sell. Take what I can, you know. But right now, it's not what it should be."

He'd thought she would be calling about his father, so he didn't get what she was saying at first. "Why would you sell?"

"I'm sixty-two years old. I can't do this forever."

She'd been in her early thirties when he'd been born. Funny how in the ten years he'd been gone, he'd never thought about her getting older. He always imagined her the same. Desperately in love with a dangerous man who regularly beat her.

"I want you to come home," she said quietly. "Just for a few months. You can help me get the business in order so I can sell it. That's all I'm asking. Six or eight months. Please, Travis. I don't know what else to do. This is all I have."

He sank into his chair. Six months probably didn't seem like much to her, but moving back to L.A. would change everything for him. He had a feeling if he left Houston, he would never come back.

He glanced out the window and saw rows of trees and shrubs ready for planting, piles of topsoil and wood chips. Then he wondered if leaving was such a bad thing. He'd traveled fifteen hundred miles only to end up in exactly the same place where he'd started, working in the same business.

He hadn't thought about L.A. in years, mostly because the place reminded him of the person and he sure as hell didn't need that.

"Travis? Do you want to think about it?"

She was his mother, which meant he had to care, even if he didn't want to. Even if he'd vowed he would walk away and never look back.

He rubbed the scar on his cheek, the physical reminder that time had passed.

"Give me a few days to pull things together," he said at last. "Then I'll drive back. I'll be there in less than two weeks."

She was silent at first, then he heard a faint sob. "Thank you," she whispered. "Oh, Travis. Thank you. I'll see you soon." She was still crying when she hung up.

Megan paced the length of her living room, then flew into Adam's arms when he walked in. He set down his luggage and pulled her close.

"I'm here," he whispered into her hair, then kissed her. "I'm here."

She'd been holding herself together by a thread. Now, safe and supported, she gave in to the tears that had been threatening her all day. She shook all over and still felt sick to her stomach.

"I can't believe it," she said, hanging on to him. "None of this feels real."

He was warm and strong and familiar. She breathed in the scent of him and finally allowed herself to believe that it might all work out.

"We'll figure it out," he told her. "We're both smart. Me a little more than you."

The familiar joke made her laugh, then a sob caught in her throat and she felt tears on her cheeks again.

"It's okay," he said, rubbing her back, then touching her chin and kissing her. "We'll get through this. Tell me what you know."

"Just what I told you on the phone. This lawyer showed up in my office, told me that Elliott Scott was my biological father, then handed me a check. It's my inheritance, I guess."

"Your mom didn't deny anything?"

Megan hated thinking about that conversation with her mother. "She tried, but it was obviously true. She finally admitted everything. But my dad was there and he heard her and then he left . . ." She started to cry again.

Adam led her over to the sofa and eased her down. "I know this sucks, but you're going to be okay. I'm here for you."

Magic words, she thought, relieved and comforted. He *would* be there for her. He loved her. He was her rock.

She raised her face so she could stare into his blue eyes. Adam had the blond good looks of a surfer. He was more tanned than usual, what with spending nearly a week in Hawaii. They had so much in common. Payton joked that they made the perfect couple because they looked good on paper.

Now, hurt, confused and lost, Megan let him comfort her and told herself that moments like these were the ones that would make or break a relationship. Adam had come through for her. He was all in. They would be together forever. Whatever happened with her parents, she had him.

"It's so horrible," she murmured. "It's less than two weeks before the wedding. I've tried calling my dad, but he won't pick up his phone."

"He's got a lot to deal with."

She sucked in a breath and voiced her greatest fear. "Do you think this changes anything? You know, with him and me? We've always been close. I can't believe he's not talking to me."

Adam's hesitation made her stomach knot. "I'm sure he still loves you," Adam hedged.

"Why do you say it like that? Is there any doubt? He's my *father*. He raised me. I'm his daughter in every sense of the word. Are you saying now, after twenty-eight years, he's going to turn his back on me? He's just going to walk away because of this?"

Adam squeezed her hand. "I believe my exact words were *I'm sure he still loves you.* That's a long leap to him turning his back on you."

She sniffed. "I know. I'm just scared. My head says everything will be fine, but my heart says nothing will ever be the same again." She wiped her face with her free hand. "He's my dad. He's the one I count on. The one I depend on. What if that changes?"

"You'll have me. You know that, right?"

She nodded. "I can't get my mind around this. It's too surreal. How can I be someone else's child? I feel like I should go look in the mirror to see if I look different, or grew a tail or something. But nothing's different."

He leaned toward her. "It's a little different. I know it sounds crazy, but there's biology at work here. For guys, there's a primal connection. Our DNA wants us to reproduce, to pass on our genes. Finding out your child isn't your child screws with a man's head. His genes want to know why he's been wasting his time with another man's kid. It all goes back to us being cavemen."

Not exactly what she wanted to hear. She pushed to her feet. "So you're saying my father is going to turn his back on me because of this? You're saying it will never be the same?"

Adam rose and tried to hug her. She jerked back. "Tell me!"

He sighed. "I'm saying he'll need some time."

"But I need him now."

"He can't be there for you right now, but that doesn't mean he won't still love you. Give him a couple of days.

It's not just about you, Megan. His wife cheated on him and passed off another kid as his own."

She covered her face with her hands. "I can't believe you said it's not all about me. My dad isn't my dad and now I'm turning into my mother. I can't figure out if I should start laughing or just rock back and forth in the corner."

He winced. "Do I get a vote?"

She dropped her hands to her lap. "Let me guess. You want the hysterical laughter."

"You never said it was hysterical." He smoothed her hair behind her ears. "Give him a second to catch his breath. Your dad loves you. In a day or two, everything will be back to normal."

"Promise?"

"Yeah."

She wanted to believe him because the alternative took her into an emotional pit. "Everything was so good," she said. "Why did this have to happen? Why did my mom lie about her affair? It all comes back to her. Once again she's at the center of the drama. She must be delighted."

Adam was smart enough to just listen. He pulled her close and hugged her. "Want me to go get you some chocolate?"

She managed a very shaky smile. "No, but thanks. I just need to . . . I don't know. Something. Maybe go for a walk. Or scream."

"I wouldn't do them together. You'll frighten the neighbors." He hugged her. "Dammit, Megan, I'm sorry. This sucks."

"I know."

"You're still my girl. I love you."

She stared into his blue eyes and told herself she was very lucky. She had a great man and a job she loved. Yes, she'd just gotten a body blow from life, but she would deal. She was good at dealing. The rest of her world was exactly where it needed to be.

He held out his hand. "Come on. We'll walk until we're so tired we can't think anymore."

She let him lead her outside. "Not thinking sounds really good right about now."

Megan had never been one to medicate her emotions with anything but work. She barely bothered to take ibuprofen for a headache. But Friday morning, she sat at her desk and wished she had a medical way to escape from the emotions crushing her.

She'd never felt so unsure of herself. She'd always known who she was and where she belonged. But now . . . nothing was right.

She stared at her computer, trying to make sense of a quarterly report. Analyzing it was part of her job and she was confident that eventually her brain would kick in. She just didn't know when. She'd been in a mental fog ever since she'd found out about Elliott Scott. What she didn't know was what to do with the information.

She'd avoided her mother's phone calls, hadn't talked to her sister, and had waited to hear from her father—although she still hadn't. Adam had been completely supportive and when this was over, she was going to order him a plaque telling him so.

"Daydreaming about the dress or the honeymoon?"

Megan glanced up and saw Carrie Billings standing in the doorway. She forced herself to smile. "A little of both," she lied. "What's up?"

Carrie strolled in and set a file on her desk. "That's actually my question to you. I e-mailed you and asked you for an update on Wayward Productions, but you sent me information on Film Rats. Just for a laugh, I went over the statement. There are a couple of errors on the P&L. Did you know?"

Megan couldn't remember e-mailing either to Carrie, although she obviously had. She really had to get a grip on her mental fog. Work was constant. Work didn't care about her personal problems.

Carrie's smile turned predatory. "Maybe you should take a few days off so you can deal with the wedding. An associate in the office where I worked before got so caught up in preparations that she missed three tax filings. The fines were huge and she ended up getting fired."

A warning or a promise? Megan forced herself to lean back in her chair and look as relaxed and confident as possible.

"Thanks for the advice," Megan said, her voice friendly, but firm. "I'm doing fine. I'm sorry I sent the wrong file. I'll get you the right one within the hour. As for the P&L for Film Rats, it's not wrong. I haven't finished it yet. Not that you're on their account."

"Oh, I know. But I like to know what's going on."

Megan stood. "As you were kind enough to give me a warning, I'll return the favor. While we all work together in this firm, we're also careful not to get too involved with other people's clients. One of the associates who used to work here tried to steal someone's account. She got fired." Megan smiled. "I'm sure that's not anything you would do, but I know how hard it is to learn a new company culture."

"Aren't you the sweetest?" Carrie looked annoyed.

"I consider myself more fair than sweet. Integrity is important to me."

"It's important to all of us."

"Good to know." Megan glanced at her watch. "I need to get you the file you want. So if you'll excuse me?"

Carrie started to say something, then turned and left. Megan found the correct file, checked it quickly, then sent it on. Then she turned off her computer and grabbed her purse.

She needed to get a few things settled one way or the other. And the only way to do that was to face them head-on.

Thirty minutes later she stood in front of her father's secretary. Janey had to be in her sixties. Megan had known her all her life. She remembered playing by her desk when she was little and Janey bringing in homemade cookies.

"Janey, you can let me into his office, or I can push my way in," Megan said, meaning every word of it. "But one way or the other, I *will* see my father today."

Janey sighed. "Megan, you know I'd do anything for you, but he's insisted he doesn't want to see you. I don't know what's going on between the two of you. He hasn't been himself for a few days now. What's wrong?"

"I can't talk about it. Janey, please. He's my dad. I have to see him."

Janey glanced at the closed door behind her. "I'm going to take my break now, which means I'm leaving my desk. What you do with that is up to you."

Megan smiled. "Thanks."

She waited until the other woman had left, then walked to the closed door, knocked once and entered.

Her father sat behind his desk, staring at his computer. He wore glasses to read these days, and they sat on the end of his nose, as always in danger of falling off.

He looked tired. His shirt was wrinkled, as if he'd slept in it. His shoulders slumped forward and his skin had a gray cast to it.

"Daddy?"

He stiffened but didn't look away from the computer.

"Daddy, please. We have to talk."

"I have nothing to say to you, Megan."

Her stomach knotted. "I didn't do anything wrong. You have no reason to be angry at me. I'm as horrified and shocked as you are. I had no idea. This lawyer showed up and just told me. Apparently he'd been to visit Mom the previous week but she never said anything. I guess she thought if she ignored it, it would just go away."

But Gary Greene didn't respond to anything Megan

said. He sat there, staring at his computer, barely breathing.

Megan fought tears. "I know you're devastated and confused and angry, but nothing is different between us. You're still my dad. You'll always be my dad. I love you."

He leaned back in his chair and tossed his glasses on the desk. "Megan, this isn't a good time for me."

She brushed away tears. "Not a good time for you? I'm getting married in a week. I don't know what to think about anything. We're both dealing with something terrible and it would be better if we dealt with it together. We're a team, remember? You and I. The sensible ones. There's a way out of this. Let's find it."

He finally looked at her. His eyes were as cold and distant as they'd been the last time she'd seen him. When he'd found out about his wife's affair.

"Everything is different," he told her.

"I agree. Mom lied to both of us."

He looked past her. "She was supposed to be mine. That was what she said. It's what we both wanted. She betrayed that."

Annoyance pushed a little of the hurt out of the way. "I understand that, but there's more going on than just you and Mom. There's you and me."

"You're not my daughter."

The words crashed into her, hitting so hard all the air left her lungs.

"That's not true," she told him, determined to keep control and not cry. One of them had to think straight. "You raised me. We're alike."

"That's what I thought, but we're not. You're not . . ." He leaned back in his chair and closed his eyes. "You're not mine."

But Tina was supposed to be his. That's what he'd said. Megan didn't want to hear any of this, but she couldn't stop her brain from pushing everything into place. Like a puzzle being completed.

She thought about what Adam had said—the primal need to pass on DNA.

"Let me see if I understand this," she said, trying to hang on to anger because there was more power in that than in tears. "You're turning your back on me because we don't have a biological connection. Twenty-eight years of loving each other suddenly doesn't matter. We can't be a team, we can't be alike. We're now nothing?"

He looked at her. "I'm sorry if this hurts you."

"Sorry?" she shrieked. "You're *sorry*? I didn't do anything wrong. I'm the kid here. Some lawyer shows up and says a few words, and that rips everything apart? I'm getting married, Dad. Do you remember that? Do you remember how we talked and planned and you wanted to make sure Adam took good care of me? Doesn't that mean anything to you?"

He glanced down at his desk.

"No!" she yelled. "Look at me, Dad. Talk to me."

"I'm not your father, Megan. Stop calling me that."

The anger faded into mist, leaving a hole for the pain to fill. It was all she could do to keep standing. It hurt to breathe. "I . . ." He couldn't mean it. "But you love me."

"I loved who I thought you were. Now . . ." He shrugged.

She couldn't have been more stunned it the earth had suddenly stopped rotating and aliens had burst from the seas.

"What do you mean, I'm not your daughter? We never had a relationship? All the times you told me you loved me were conditional? 'I love you, Megan, but only because you're my biological child. If you're not, screw it.' "

He didn't answer.

She began to cry. "So this is it. The last twenty-eight years are meaningless. Are you even coming to the wedding? Are you walking me down the aisle?"

"I don't know. Maybe it would be better if—"

She didn't wait to hear the rest of it. She couldn't. She'd accepted he was upset, but she'd never really considered the possibility that anything would be different in the long run. She'd been so sure he would know that no matter what, he was still her father.

Barely able to see through the tears, she ran out of the building and back to her car. Her chest ached with the effort of gasping for breath.

She crawled into the front seat and gave in to the hurt that flowed through her. She sobbed and choked on the worst pain of her life. There was nothing beyond this. There couldn't be. She simply couldn't survive one more blow.

Minutes later, or maybe hours, she managed to stop the tears and wipe her face. She glanced at herself in her rearview mirror, then wished she hadn't. She looked horrible, pale and blotchy. Her eyes were swollen. She couldn't go back to work looking like this, which was just as well. There was no way she could function right now.

She decided it was late enough in the day that she could just go home without an explanation. Once there, she changed into a T-shirt and sweatpants, then crawled into bed.

Every cell in her body throbbed. She felt like something that had been tossed in the garbage and left to rot.

Her father had been the one constant in her life. He'd been there for her, protecting her from her mother's craziness and her sister's spying. He'd loved her, adored her, encouraged her. He'd wanted what was best for her. She'd known she was her dad's favorite and had reveled in the safety and comfort of that position.

In return, she'd taken care of him. She'd fussed and made his life better. They were close—they'd always been close. How could he turn his back on that? How could he pretend that didn't matter?

Unless it didn't matter to him. Unless Adam was right and DNA changed everything.

She didn't want to think about that, didn't want to think about anything. So she lay in her bed, watching the room darken, wondering if it was possible to cry enough to use up all the water in her body.

She ignored the phone and the shivers that made her tremble and hated her mother for making this all happen.

Sometime later Adam appeared, turning on lights, then crawling into bed and holding her.

"He's not walking me down the aisle," she whispered into

his chest, feeling the heat of him and realizing how bone cold she was. "I don't think he's coming to the wedding."

"I'm sorry."

"It's all her. She did this. She destroyed everything and she doesn't even care. I know she doesn't. She's making this my fault, or his. Maybe both. But not hers. I hate her. I know it's wrong to say that, but I hate her."

"Megan." He kissed her head. "This is hard, but eventually you'll figure it out."

She pushed away. "Figure out what? Who I am? What it means that after all this time, my dad turns his back on me?"

"Yeah. All of that. You're strong. You'll make this work."

How was that possible? She had a hole inside that would never be filled. "I don't even know who I am anymore. I thought everything was perfect. I worked so hard to make my life exactly what I wanted."

"Nothing about you has changed. You're exactly who you were a week ago."

"I can't believe that."

"That doesn't change the truth. We're starting a new life together. I love you. I want to marry you. Does that matter at all?"

She forced herself to let go of some of her anger. "It does. You're being really good to me. I'm sorry this is happening now, days before the wedding. I don't mean to be difficult."

He smiled. "You're doing great. I admire how you're handling this. I just want you to remember that you're not different. And none of this is your fault."

"I know. I just wish I could feel better." She flopped back on the pillow. "I should have gone with you to Hawaii. Then none of this would have happened. Instead I let you go by yourself where you probably had wild monkey sex with a dozen other women."

She managed a smile at the image, but something flashed through Adam's eyes. Her face froze.

Megan didn't realize she was moving, but suddenly she was up and out of the bed, standing next to it, staring at him.

"Adam?"

"What?"

"Is there someone else?"

He threw up his hands. "Megan, no. Why would you even think that? There's no one but you." He dropped one hand and left the other in the air. "I swear, Megan, there is no one in my life but you." He drew in a breath. "If you're looking for a distraction, this isn't a good one. Don't go there. I love you. We're getting married."

She believed him, so why didn't she feel better?

"What?" he asked, leaning toward her. "Why are you doing this? I'm not in a relationship. I'm not seeing anyone. I'm not interested in anyone but you."

He answered all her questions before she even asked them, so why wasn't she happy?

She moved back a few steps, stopping only when she felt the wall. As if she needed the support. He'd answered her questions. That was good. That was better than good—except he'd been so specific.

Her stomach tightened; her legs felt weak. The coldness returned and with it a disbelief that spread like a chilling mist.

"You're not seeing anyone," she repeated. "Now. Were you before?"

He looked at her for a long time, then stood. He was on the other side of the bed. They faced each other across what felt like miles. She'd never felt so alone before.

"You cheated." She hadn't meant to say the words. They came out of nowhere, but she knew in her gut they were true.

"It's not what you think."

Oh, God.

She was beyond pain. That was the good news. She'd gone into some weird numb state, because while she was in the room and having the conversation, she couldn't feel anything. Maybe she'd died and this was hell. An eternity of betrayals.

He shoved his hands into his front pockets. "Megan, I've wanted to tell you for a while. I was going to after I got home from Hawaii, but how could I? Look at what you're dealing with."

"So you did cheat." It wasn't even a question. It didn't have to be. A question implied there was uncertainty.

"Not with a dozen women in Hawaii. I've been having a . . . relationship with someone I met a while ago."

She'd been prepared for an "it didn't mean anything" conversation. Not the revelation that he'd been emotionally involved.

"You've been having an affair?" Her voice was amazingly calm, as if from a great distance. As if someone else was speaking.

"I met this girl getting coffee a couple of months ago. I was stressed, deciding on which practice to join, the wedding was getting closer. I saw her, but it was just sex. A distraction. It didn't mean anything. She was, you know, young."

Too little, too late, she thought. Information clicked into place. "I'm only twenty-eight. How young could she be?"

"Nineteen."

Megan swore. "Let me guess. Big boobs? Gorgeous?"

Adam looked away.

"So those late dinners with the partners. A lot of them were lies?"

He nodded.

She remembered the woman on the phone in Hawaii. "You took her with you, to the conference." She frowned. "Was there a conference?"

"Of course. I went with two of the partners."

Humiliation burned hot. "They *knew* about her?"

He hung his head.

"You felt comfortable enough to take your piece of ass with you on a business trip? How?" Then she got it. "Oh my God. They're all cheating, too. What? It's a club? This is the practice you joined? Cheating Bastards R Us?"

He glared at her. "We're doctors. Cardiologists."

"Oh, and that makes it all right. Silly me." She pressed

her hands against the wall. "Okay, let me see if I understand this. You've been cheating on me for a couple of months and you took her to Hawaii, which your new partners know about. But hey, it's okay."

"I ended it. That's why I wanted to take her away. To say good-bye."

"One last screw in the tropics? You wouldn't want to miss that. So how many others were there? I can't believe this is the first time. You're too good at it."

His expression tightened. "We're getting married. I wanted to come clean about what had happened because once we're married, everything will be different. I plan to be faithful to you, Megan. That's important to me."

"Sure. If you plan to, then it's gonna happen. Why wouldn't I believe you? You have a plan."

"Don't make this worse than it has to be."

"Make it worse? Is that possible? Did you have to do this now? Wasn't losing my dad enough shit for one week? But no. The other man in my life, the man I'd planned to marry, tells me he's been cheating on me for months. Do you really think I believe she's the only one? How many others, Adam? Cough up a number. Any number. I'll probably accept it."

"This isn't helping."

Anger replaced the numbness. "Don't you dare try to make me the bad guy, you bastard! You've been lying to me, probably from the beginning. I can't believe anything you've ever said. My God, who are you? What kind of man does this? Worse, you wanted to tell me so you could feel better about yourself."

There were a thousand things she wanted to say. She wanted to hurt him, crush him, destroy him until he was nothing but an emotional bug she could squash under her shoe.

But as quickly as it had flared, the anger faded, leaving only pain and emptiness.

"Get out," she told him.

"Megan, we have to talk."

"We don't have to do anything. Get out."

She turned her back and waited. After a few seconds, she heard him walk away. When the front door closed, she sank to the floor, curled up in a ball and sobbed.

Nine

"IF YOU'RE LEAVING, THE least you can do is sell me the bike," Will said as he eyed the motorcycle parked by the garage door.

Travis looked from his friend to the nearly finished motorcycle. He'd done all the custom work himself, night after night, in a rented bay in a garage in Tomball. The 120-cubic-inch Patrick racing engine and six-speed transmission had been the easy part. He'd spent weeks on the sheet metal, customizing everything from the fenders and bars to the gas tank and seat. The bike still needed paint and he hadn't figured out the color scheme he wanted. He had several options pinned to the wall.

"It's not ready," he said, knowing he was going to have to let at least a couple of the bikes go. He didn't have room to take them all back with him and he wasn't leaving anything behind. He had a feeling he wasn't coming back.

"Seven thousand," Will said.

"It's worth twelve as it is. It'll be worth twenty when I'm done."

"Cash," his friend added.

Travis grinned. "I wouldn't take your check. I know you."

Will laughed. "Come on, Travis. You gotta sell me one of 'em and where am I gonna get twelve grand?"

"You can have that one for seven," he said, pointing to a bike that was more parts than structure. "I finished the last of the bodywork Saturday. You can put it together yourself."

Will studied the pieces. "What's the engine?"

"124 S&S."

"Sweet." Will considered for a second, then nodded. "Okay. I'll bring by the cash tomorrow. When are you leaving?"

"Noon."

"I'll be here at ten. I can help you load up." Will poked his head in the trailer. "You're taking everything. You gonna stay in L.A.?"

"I don't know. Maybe." He had no idea what he would do next. Helping his mother for six months would give him time to think, time to figure out what he wanted to do for the rest of his life.

"You could take out an ad in the paper or online," Will told him. "Sell these for real. You do good work. You could start a business."

It was something Travis had thought about for a long time. For years, the bikes had been a hobby of his. He'd been taking them apart and putting them back together since he was twelve. It was the one good thing his old man had taught him.

After leaving L.A. ten years ago, he'd started customizing the bikes. At first it had been a way to fill the nights and chase away the past, but after a while he'd realized he enjoyed the work. The sixteen months he'd spent in jail had given him plenty of time to work on designs.

"I didn't know your mama was still alive," Will said. "You never talk about her."

"She owns a landscaping business back in L.A."

Will frowned. "So why are you working here in Houston and not back there?"

"Long story."

"Your old man dead?"

"Close enough."

"What does that mean?" Will asked.

Travis ignored the question and loaded the second bike, but he couldn't shake Will's question.

Ten years ago, Houston was where the money had run out, so he'd stopped and gotten a job doing the only thing he knew how to do. After he got out of jail, he'd needed to stick around as part of his parole. Now he was free to go wherever he wanted, which should have felt good but instead left him with too many choices.

"I've never been outside of Texas," Will said. "What's it like?"

"Big."

"You taking I-10 the whole way?"

California was a straight shot. Three days due west and a man would run right into the Pacific Ocean.

"I'm going to head up to Vegas for a couple of days."

Will grinned. "Oh, man, that's one place I want to see. Lots of pretty ladies there. You're gonna have a good time."

"That's the plan."

"You've always had a way with the ladies, Travis. I've seen you. You walk into a bar and they don't see nobody else."

"Women love a tortured soul."

"I don't think it's your soul they're looking at."

Travis secured the bike. "Probably not, but they see it all the same."

They thought the darkness was romantic, that they could be the one to heal him. No matter how much he tried to convince them he was long past healing, they wanted to try. Most nights he let them, because it was easy and he was a man who enjoyed getting laid. But in the morning he always walked away. He'd learned a long time ago there was no point in trying to stay.

Leanne carried the mug of tea into her mother's bedroom. Tina lay on the chaise, the blinds closed against the bright sun, the swishing sound of a scented humidifier providing white noise. The scene should have been peaceful, yet Leanne's stomach clenched as she moved closer to her mother.

Most of the time she could deal with her mother's imagined chronic illnesses and demands, but every now and then, she wanted a real parent she could talk to. Someone who actually cared about her as more than a prize in a competition. Gary had gotten Megan, so Tina had claimed Leanne.

She wanted to be able to talk about her life, her problems, the situation she'd gotten herself into—her tattered, hey-I'm-a-slut-so-just-fuck-me reputation. But Tina wouldn't want to hear any of that. Her idea of a deep conversation was comparing eye creams. If Leanne tried to talk about anything significant, her mother would simply pretend to faint or have some kind of mock seizure. At least Leanne didn't have to wonder where she'd gotten her acting ability.

"Here you go, Mom," she said.

Her mother opened her eyes, took the mug and sighed. "Thank you. It's such a relief to have you stop by. I've been in constant pain for weeks now. Nothing gives me relief. I'm not sleeping at all. Every sound is excruciating."

She kept on talking, but Leanne wasn't listening. She found herself thinking about how her mother was like Mrs. Bennet in *Pride and Prejudice*, but without the charm. Then her mother brushed away tears.

"It's been so lonely," she whispered.

Leanne frowned. "Is Daddy out of town? I don't remember him mentioning a trip." Not that her father called her all that much . . . or ever. But she usually ran into him when she stopped by.

Her mother looked at her. "You don't know? Megan didn't tell you?"

"Tell me what?"

Tina hesitated, which Leanne knew meant she was trying to decide the right way to spin events. She wouldn't have cared, except if Megan was involved she wanted to know. Not that her sister would call her.

Another broken relationship, Leanne thought grimly.

"Mom," she said, her voice stern. "Tell me exactly what happened."

Tina's eyes filled with tears. "Megan upset your father so he moved out. He's left me because of your sister." She covered her face with her hands. "She's always resented me because I'm beautiful and she's not. I tried with her. I tried to help, but did she appreciate my effort? No makeup, handmade clothes . . . she went around looking that way deliberately, just to hurt me. If she'd had her way, he would have left me years ago. She hates that your father loves me. He worships me, you know. I'm his prize."

Leanne ignored the crap and got to what she hoped was the real information. "Excuse me? Why would Megan want you and Dad to break up? That's sick and borderline incestuous. Besides, what could Megan do to make Dad move out?"

As she spoke, she glanced at the closet and debated getting up to check if his clothes were gone. There was no way to know if her mother was telling the truth or not. Gary could simply be working extra hours at work, or on an unexpected trip.

Leanne was very clear on the dynamics of her parents' relationship. Gary was an ordinary guy who had won a princess. He wanted to adore and Tina lived to be worshipped. She'd never known them to fight for very long.

"Megan told him . . ." Tina paused for a well-timed sob. "She told him I'd had an affair and he believed her."

"What?" Leanne couldn't imagine her mother sleeping with her father, let alone someone else. "That's crazy. Why would she say that? How would she get the idea? Mom, it's a week before her wedding. She's too busy to worry about stuff like that."

Tina's eyes shifted suddenly. Leanne tensed.

"What did you do?" she asked, aware that she'd yet to hear the truth. "What did you do to Megan?" She rose and crossed to the closet. Most of her father's clothes were gone. She spun back to face her mother. "What did you do to Daddy?"

"It's not me," Tina sobbed. "You know that, darling. It's not me. They just don't understand. It's not my fault. You have to understand. It was so long ago and then that horrible attorney came here. He said things. Lies. They were lies, but he told them to Megan and she came here and yelled at me. Her own mother."

Leanne walked back to the chaise and stared down. "Tell me *exactly* what happened."

Tina's cheeks glistened with tears. "There was another man some years ago. It wasn't my fault. Your father was gone all the time, ignoring me. He was awful, really. He deserved it."

"You cheated on him?" She couldn't begin to imagine it, not that she wanted to.

No wonder Gary was pissed. She'd broken their most significant rule. She was supposed to belong only to him.

"Briefly. But Megan . . . Well, she's his daughter. He

died and left her some money, which is how this all started. If only he'd left well enough alone, but no. Elliott was always selfish that way. It's not as if he left *me* any money, and he should have."

Once again Leanne tuned out her mother's words, but this time for a different reason. Megan, another man's daughter? Tina cheating on her husband? It was more shocking than a sweeps week cliffhanger.

She sank onto the ottoman by the chaise. Thoughts chased each other, tumbling and diving, splitting and joining.

"How did Dad find out?" she asked.

"He came home to check on me and heard everything. Megan was happy, too," Tina said angrily. "She wanted him to know. She wanted him to leave me."

"There's no way Megan was happy to find out she'd been lied to her entire life," Leanne said. Megan would have been devastated. Not her father's daughter? They were so close.

Leanne felt horrible and hurt at the same time. Because no one had called to tell her. Certainly not Megan. They'd never been close and no matter how many times Leanne tried to connect with her sister, she was always pushed away.

"She's always hated how intimate your father and I are," Tina said. "This is just so like her."

Leanne stood. "Will you stop?" she yelled. "This isn't about you. Megan's getting married in a week, Mom, and everything is screwed up. She's dealing with a ton. For once think about someone else."

Tina stared at her. Color drained from her face. "You will *never* speak to me like that again," her mother told her. "Remember who I am, young lady."

For once Leanne wasn't intimidated by the words or the implied threat. "Remember who I am," she snapped back. "It seems to me you've run off everyone else in this family. I'm all you have left."

Tina pressed her lips together but didn't speak. Leanne crossed to the far side of the room and tried to think.

"How's Dad taking it?" she asked.

"Your father isn't speaking with m-me." Tina's voice broke. "He *left* me. He wouldn't listen. He's so angry. I've never seen him so angry."

Leanne looked at her and thought maybe this time the tears were genuine. "You lied to him for nearly thirty years, Mom. Did you think that would be okay?"

"But I'm his wife. We have a life together. What if he never comes back? What if I'm alone forever?"

Not something Leanne wanted to think about. If her mother was alone, then her own life would sink to a new level of hell.

"I've called him," Tina whispered. "He won't talk to me."

Leanne didn't ask if she'd called Megan. At this point her mother didn't care about anyone but herself. Leanne couldn't stop thinking about her sister. How bad she must feel. How this would change everything. Megan was probably questioning who she was. The complication of a wedding in a few days would only make it worse.

"He'll have to talk to you at the wedding," Leanne said,

knowing the guests could be getting more of a show than they expected.

"If he goes."

Leanne sucked in a breath. "He has to go. He's walking her down the aisle." Their father not go to Megan's wedding? Was that possible?

She wanted to leave and go see her sister. She wanted to talk to her and offer comfort. Only Megan wouldn't see it that way. Megan would think there was something else going on and Leanne didn't know how to convince her otherwise.

Pints of Ben & Jerry's, spoons, glasses and an empty pitcher that had once held margaritas crowded together on Megan's coffee table. Megan sat curled up in a corner of the sofa, Payton next to her, Allegra beside her on the carpet.

"All men are jerks," Allegra said, stroking her arm. "Total and complete jerks. I have a friend who's a personal trainer. He'll beat up someone for eight hundred dollars. The guy is right here in L.A. Do you want me to call him? He could get Adam in the parking garage where he works. No one would have to know it was you."

Megan hugged her knees to her chest and wondered when she would run out of tears. "Thanks. That's really nice of you, but I don't want him beat up." Actually she did, but she couldn't bring herself to say that. Not yet. "Check back with me in a couple of days."

"You know I will."

Allegra would, too, because she was a good friend. The kind of friend who flew across the country to be with her.

Payton held her other hand. "I don't know what to say. I have a really good sense about men who cheat. Why didn't I know he was doing this?"

"Because we trusted him," Allegra said. "Because he played us all. He acted like one of the good guys. That's worse than the ones who are bastards all the time. At least we can see them coming."

They continued to debate the worst kind of man, but Megan didn't bother joining in—she didn't have an opinion. Was it worse to cheat on someone you claimed to love and want to marry? What about turning your back on your daughter after twenty-eight years? That ranked right up there.

"I can't believe they're both gone," she murmured. "Adam and my dad. Just gone. And they're not even dead. If they were dead, it wouldn't be a decision, you know? But they chose to act this way. They decided to abandon me. They chose to say I didn't matter."

Both women hugged her. "I'm floored about your dad, too," Allegra told her. "I don't get it. You guys were always so close. When we were growing up, I always envied your relationship with your dad. You guys had the best connection." She looked at Payton. "I used to offer her my life in exchange for her dad."

Megan nodded. "I remember." She remembered so much. How he'd supported her, loved her. They'd had so much fun together. Their Sunday brunches and phone calls. Now it was all over.

"I know it's a shock," she said. She'd felt sick to her stomach for days. "I know it's horrible and he has to take it all in. I'm dealing with it, too. But even if I'm not biologically his kid, I'm still his daughter, right? He raised me. I am who I am because of him. Doesn't that matter?"

"It will," Payton said. "He'll get it."

Megan wanted to believe that, but she wasn't so sure. It had been days and he still hadn't called. He had to know how devastated she felt, but where was he?

"I miss him," she said. "I miss my dad."

"I know, honey." Allegra stayed close. "I wish I could fix this."

"Thanks. It's just too much. I start to figure out how to deal with the stuff with my dad, then I remember Adam and it's like the wound opens all over again. He cheated. For months. It wasn't just sex, it was a relationship. He had a relationship with someone else, while we were engaged. That's not okay. That will never be okay. How am I supposed to trust him now?"

"You can't," Payton told her. Allegra nodded.

She stared into their eyes as the truth hit her. She couldn't trust him. She could never trust him. He'd broken something inside of her and it couldn't be fixed.

She sat up. Her friends moved back to give her room. She looked down at the engagement ring still on her finger.

"I can't marry him."

The words were more test than fact. She wanted to hear them, feel their weight. But once they were spoken, she realized they were the truth.

"I can't marry him," she repeated.

Payton and Allegra shared a look that told her they'd been talking about this very thing.

"You really can't," Allegra said. "Not now. He can't just dump this on you a week before the wedding and expect it to be okay. It's not okay."

"You can't know if she's the only one," Payton added hesitantly. "Maybe she is, or maybe he's a chronic cheater. You need to know. You need to be sure and right now you're not sure."

Megan nodded slowly. Tears made everything blurry. She felt like she was trapped in a room of knives. Everywhere she turned, she got cut. Two weeks ago, she'd had everything she ever wanted. She'd built her life, piece by piece, and now it was hanging in tatters.

"I'm not marrying Adam." She took off the ring and set it next to the spoons. It glittered in the afternoon light. "I'm not getting married on Saturday."

Her friends watched her. "You okay?" Payton asked. "Are you going to start screaming or foaming at the mouth?"

Megan managed a smile. "No foaming, I promise." She kept watching the ring, as if expecting it to come to life and attack. "I might scream." Would screaming make it better? "How do I get over this?"

Allegra stood and ran upstairs. She returned with a couple of pictures in frames, then disappeared into the kitchen. Seconds later she was back with a cutting board, a knife, matches and a big glass bowl. She handed one of the frames to Payton.

"Get this one out."

Megan had no idea what she was doing. When both the pictures were free, Allegra set them on the cutting board and gave her a knife.

"Have at it, girlfriend."

Megan took the knife. "I'm supposed to stab him?"

"Well, just the picture. You don't want to go to jail over the jerk."

Megan picked up the first picture. It showed Adam leaning against a railing by the beach. The wind blew his hair and he was smiling into the camera. She jabbed the point of the knife squarely into his chest.

"I feel stupid," she said.

"Just keep doing it," her friend told her. "He cheated on you, Megan. He slept with someone else. He said and did all the intimate things with someone else. They were supposed to be just for you. His heart and his dick."

She stared at the photos. The second one was of the two of them. She looked so happy in the picture. Stupidly happy.

She dropped the knife, ripped the picture so that she was left with only his image, then dropped it back on the cutting board.

"He cheated," she said, and stabbed the picture.

"He had an affair," Payton told her. "He took the bitch to Hawaii."

Megan stabbed again. "He didn't take me to Hawaii. He took her to Hawaii to end it. Can you believe it?" She poked the picture harder.

"You bastard!" she yelled, and stabbed the pictures

again and again, faster and faster. "I hate you. I hate you! Fuck you. I hate you."

She stabbed the pictures until they were sliced into pieces, then she dropped the knife and ripped up the shreds. When the pictures were confetti, she scooped them into the bowl and set them on fire.

The flames quickly burned out. When there was only smoldering ash, Megan leaned back on the sofa and started to cry.

"Why did he do this? Why wasn't I enough?"

Payton hugged her. Allegra squeezed her hand.

"He wasn't the right guy," Payton said. "I know it hurts, but you'll heal from this and go find someone else."

"I don't want anyone else."

"Do you want Adam back?" Allegra asked.

"No. Of course not."

"If you could make him never cheat again, would that be enough?"

Megan wanted it to be, but it wasn't. "He betrayed what we had," she whispered. "Who we were together. I want someone who's a good guy. Good guys don't do that."

The engagement ring sparkled on the coffee table, next to the bowl of ash. She wasn't getting married. Piece by piece, her very perfect life had crumbled into nothing.

Ten

THE INSTANT SHE SAW her sister's car in the driveway Megan regretted coming to see her mother without calling. Not that Leanne wouldn't find out about it eventually, but she didn't feel strong enough to deal with her right now. Unfortunately, the choices were to put off the inevitable or get it all over at once.

"I can do this," she told herself as she sat in her car.

She'd managed to survive the night and a morning at work without anything really horrible happening. She tried telling herself change was good, that she would rise out of these ashes a much stronger person. The problem was, she knew it was all a crock.

After locking her car, she made her way to her parents' front door, knocked once, then entered.

"It's me," she called.

"We're back here."

Megan recognized her sister's voice. Before she could change her mind, Leanne walked into the living room, her expression concerned.

"Are you okay?" she asked. "Mom told me what happened a couple of days ago. I wanted to call, but . . ." She cleared her throat. "I'm sorry. I know that's a stupid thing to say, I just can't think of anything better."

The words were all correct and the tone matched. Looking into her sister's beautiful blue eyes, Megan wanted to believe her. But she'd been lied to by enough people that she was wary.

"I'm dealing," she admitted. "Not especially well, but I'm dealing."

"She's not." Leanne pointed over her shoulder, toward the bedroom. "She's in full diva mode. Apparently Dad came by last night and collected more of his stuff. He really moved out."

"Finding out his wife cheated on him and had a child by another man is kind of a big thing to get over," Megan said, not sure why she jumped to defend her father.

"I know. I totally get why he's doing it. The last thirty years have been all about her, and now this? It's probably the last thing he can handle."

Megan frowned. "You're not siding with Mom?"

"Why would I? I'm very clear on all her issues." Now Leanne looked confused. "Do you think I like being her favorite? It's a nightmare. She just happens to be the only parent I have left."

"Not anymore. Dad's available." Megan shook her head. "I'm sorry. This isn't about anything you've done. The good thing about being this far down is I can only start heading up."

Leanne nodded. "I'm sorry. You must be so mixed up by everything."

"More than you know." Megan started down the hall.

"Leanne, darling, would you make me some tea? This cup you brought me is a little cold. It doesn't taste right. I'm just so exhausted."

Megan walked into the bedroom. Today her mother was receiving from a pile of pillows on the bed. Her silk gown was the same color as her green eyes and her hair looked magazine perfect.

"What are you doing here?" Tina asked. "I'm not speaking to you, Megan. This is all your fault. Did you know your father left me? Just like that, with no warning." Her mother's eyes filled with tears. "How could you do this? How could you hurt me like this? Why do you hate me?"

"I don't hate you," Megan said, determined to stay rational and in the moment. It was what she'd promised herself on the drive over. "I probably should, but I don't. What amazes me is your total failure to take responsibility for any of this. Your husband left you because you lied to him for years and passed off another man's kid as his own. *You* cheated on him and *you* lied to me my entire life. There's no way you're the victim, Mom. Sorry. Someone else gets to wear the crown this time."

Her mother waved one hand in the air, then slumped onto the pillow, eyes closed, apparently unconscious.

Leanne came and stood next to Megan.

"Did she faint?" Leanne asked.

"I guess."

"She'll recover," Leanne said. "Want some coffee? I just made a pot."

"Thanks, but I'm already wired."

"Are you sleeping at all?"

"No."

"You're just going to ignore me?" Tina snapped, raising her head.

"You seem fine," Megan told her. "Which is great for you. Me, I'm not fine. Do you know Daddy isn't talking to me? He won't return my calls or see me. He doesn't consider me his daughter anymore."

"I don't have time to deal with this right now," her mother said. "I've been abandoned by my husband. Do you know what that means?"

"It means you're a selfish bitch!" Megan yelled. "You've always been selfish and now you're getting what you deserve."

Tina shrank back in the pillows. "Megan! I'm your mother."

"So what? That doesn't make you a good person. You've been horrible for years and no one has ever called you on it. You've done everything you've wanted to do and never once cared about the people around you. You've manipulated all of them, constantly. Well, that's over. At least for me. And I'm guessing your husband, too, although I can't speak to that. You see, the man I have loved as my father for twenty-eight years has turned his back on me. Because of you."

"You don't know what it's been like for me—"

"You're right, and I don't care. Your marriage is broken and you earned that. *You* made it happen with your lies and your self-absorption. You've lost him and you've lost me. Not that I expect you to care except for how it may inconvenience you. You might actually have to get out of bed and get your own tea once in a while."

Tina sat up straight. "You will not talk to me that way, young lady."

"Watch me."

Tina turned to Leanne. "See how spoiled your sister is? I always said your father spoiled her and now she's ruined. Adam won't like you acting like this, Megan."

"I don't actually care what Adam thinks, Mom. I'm not going to marry him. That's why I came by. To tell you the wedding's off."

Megan had never seen her mother move so fast. One second the older woman was in bed, doing her best to look frail, and the next she was on her feet, hands on her hips.

"What are you talking about?" Tina demanded. "You're marrying Adam on Saturday."

Talking about all this made Megan tired. "No, I'm not. The wedding is off."

"Now? Less than a week before the date? Do you know what this will cost? We won't get any of our money back."

Of course, Megan thought, noting that for an invalid, her mother actually looked pretty good. Her makeup was perfect, her pedicure fresh.

"I'll pay you back," she said, knowing the money mattered a whole lot less than the reason, but of course her mother wouldn't bother to ask why the wedding was canceled. That would mean showing interest in someone else.

"It's not about the money!" her mother shrieked. "You can't cancel. What will people say?"

"Now we're at the heart of it," Leanne murmured. "What will the neighbors think?"

The comment surprised Megan and nearly made her smile. She glanced at her sister. "Yeah. Who cares if we're bleeding inside, as long as it all *looks* good?"

"Stop it, you two," Tina said. "I insist you stop this right now. There will be a wedding, do you hear me? Whatever it is you did to upset Adam, you'll apologize for it. You'll promise to change. He's a good man, Megan. You don't want him getting away."

"I have to get back to work," Megan told her. "I came by to let you know, Mom."

Megan turned and left. Leanne came with her.

"I want to ask why," Leanne admitted when they reached the living room. "But I won't. If you're serious about canceling, there's going to be a ton of phone calls. The whole guest list. Want some help?"

Megan stared at her. "Why are you being so nice to me? I would have thought you'd be having a party, celebrating the various disasters in my life."

Leanne took a step back. "That's a nasty thing to say. Why would you think that?"

Because you are as selfish and narcissistic as my mother, Megan thought, not sure how to politely phrase that.

"What have I ever done to you?" Leanne asked, her eyes bright with annoyance. "And don't you dare talk about all the stuff that happened when we were kids.

What have I done in the past five years to make you say something like that? Or think it? I'm your sister. I care about you." She folded her arms across her chest. "Oh, wait. I get it. I'm incapable of feelings, right? I'm just some dumb blond actress who thinks with her tits."

Megan opened her mouth and then closed it. She felt as shocked as if a garden gnome had suddenly turned on her. What did Leanne have to get all pissy about?

"I know you don't think with your breasts," Megan said, feeling both annoyed and foolish.

"Because that would imply I have a brain? And I can't, right? I'm just a blond version of Mom. Well, you don't know anything about me and I think it's pretty crappy of you to assume I'm a horrible person when you haven't taken the time to get to know me at all."

Megan's mild annoyance blossomed into anger.

"You want to have it out?" she demanded, glaring at Leanne. "Fine. Let's have it out. Is your life painful? Is being the most beautiful girl in the county a serious burden? You're right—I don't know anything about you, and amazingly enough, this isn't a good time for me to learn. I'm dealing with, in no particular order, some bitch at work trying to steal my clients and a possible promotion that could rock my world, but I don't get to enjoy that because I just found out I'm not my father's daughter. The one person on the entire planet who has been there for me since I was born suddenly won't take my calls. But that's okay, because I have a loving fiancé to lean on. Except I *don't,* because Adam cheated on me with some nineteen-year-old twit. So I'm very sorry if your feelings are hurt, but I don't have the time or energy to deal with that right now."

She expected Leanne to back off, but her sister leaned into her face. "Because it's always about you."

"What?" Megan yelped. "You can't be serious. *You're* the little princess."

"I'm Mom's lapdog. You got to have Dad. You got a parent, not a life-size annoying doll to take care of. He's always talking about how proud he is of you. He can barely remember my name. And let's not forget where this all started. I offered to help. You're going to have a lot of stuff to do to cancel your wedding. I'm willing to be there. But you can forget it! I hope you drown in the details. I hope the damn presents fall on your head."

Megan couldn't believe it. "Bitch."

"Super bitch."

"Slut."

"Bean counter." Leanne glared at her. "I swear, I just want to pull your hair until you scream."

"Back at you."

"I hate you."

"I hate you more."

Megan had never felt such rage. Maybe it was about her dad and Adam, but it was directed at Leanne. Somehow, in her mind, her sister was suddenly responsible for everything bad that had happened in the past few weeks.

Instinctively, she picked up a vase from a nearby end table and raised it above her head. Leanne shrieked and jumped back.

"For God's sake, don't bruise my face. I have an audition." Leanne grabbed the vase from her and thrust a pillow in her hands. "Hit me with this," she said, sounding perfectly serious.

Megan stared at the vase, then the pillow and finally her sister. One corner of Leanne's mouth twitched. Megan felt herself start to smile. The anger disappeared as if it had never been and she began to laugh.

It started as a chuckle, then moved lower until she was laughing so hard she couldn't breathe. She sank to the floor and kept laughing. Leanne joined in and then they were sprawled on the carpet, unable to stand.

"You called me a bean counter," Megan said with a gasp. "Is that the best you can do?"

"I'm an actress, not a writer. Give me a break. You called me a slut."

"I take it back."

"Don't bother. Some days it's true." Leanne sighed, then straightened, crossing her legs in front of her. "I meant what I said. I'll help with canceling everything."

"Why would you want to help me?" Megan asked. "I'm not being mean or angry. Just, why?"

"Because you're my sister."

"That's not an answer."

"It is to me." Leanne stared at her. "I'm not the enemy. I've always wanted us to be friends. But I've offered twice, I'm not going to beg." She scrambled to her feet.

Megan stood as well. They looked at each other.

Her instinct was to say no. Of course these were the same instincts that had told her it was safe to fall in love with Adam and that her father would always be there for her.

"There's a lot to do," Megan said slowly. "I'd appreciate some help."

Leanne smiled. "Great. Tell me when and where."

Leanne checked herself one more time in the mirror. She'd dressed in tight jeans, boots and an off-the-shoulder T-shirt. Not exactly avant-garde fashion, but the look suited her character and she wanted this part more than she'd wanted anything in a long, long time.

She'd practiced the pages that had been sent over for three days and had even arranged a private session with her acting coach. She knew the lines, knew the motivation, understood the movie. This was more than about proving herself, it was about taking her career to the next level.

After the disaster the previous week, she'd seriously thought about giving up acting. But this was her dream, and she was determined to make it happen. So she would go into this audition and dazzle them.

She picked up her handbag and walked out of the restroom. The offices were across the hall. She went in and smiled at the receptionist.

"Hi. I'm Leanne Greene."

"They're expecting you, Ms. Greene. Go right in."

Leanne nodded and walked through the open door into a large office where several men sat behind a large conference table.

They were all successful—the producer, the director, a couple of assistants—but one more so than the others combined. Connor McKay. He was in his midforties, a writer-director with three Academy Awards to his name and a string of hit movies. He was known for his eclectic style, his attention to detail and his ability to cast exactly the right person, however unexpected. The other guys might have been wearing suits, but in this meeting, Connor was the one with the power.

"Gentlemen," she said with a smile. "Thanks for seeing me."

Nerves danced in her stomach, made her weak. Her heels seemed impossibly high and she desperately wanted to collapse somewhere in a corner. Not that she would. She would get through this. No, she would do more than that. She would be great.

"Leanne. Hi. Good to see you." The producer did all the talking, explaining the process, asking her if she had her pages.

She answered him but couldn't seem to tear her eyes away from Connor. He'd gone gray in his twenties and now his hair was almost white. He had piercing blue eyes that seemed able to read every flicker of fear, sense every whisper of trepidation.

It was as if he looked into her inner being and knew she wasn't good enough. That she was just some pretty face who slept around to get better parts than she deserved.

She took a step back and forced herself to pay attention to the man who was talking.

"She's an unlikely rebel leader," the producer continued. "We want a combination of vulnerability and passion."

His voice seemed to linger over the last word. Was he
checking out her breasts? Was she expected to sleep with
them all to get the part?

A week ago she would have done it. A week ago she
would have sold herself. But that last encounter had been
her rock bottom and there was no way she was going
back. She forced herself to stand tall.

"You want to read from the pages?" he asked.

She shook her head. "Just give me a second."

She turned her back on them and focused on the
character, on what she'd been through. Her entire family had been killed and she'd seen it all. There was pain
inside of her, but also a fire that burned. She wanted the
past made right—an impossible task. She wanted justice,
at any price. Later she would learn the price was too high,
but in this scene, she still believed.

She turned back to the men, careful not to get trapped
in Connor's gaze again. "I'm ready."

The producer picked up a script. "Val, you can't keep
doing this."

Leanne dug deep for the feelings, ignoring the sense
that this would all go easier if someone just wanted to
have sex with her. "I can do this forever. I'm not stopping.
This is all I have left and I will see it to the end. I don't
care what it costs me."

Despite all her emotions, or maybe because of them,

the words fell completely flat. Leanne shook her head. "Sorry. Let me try that again."

She repeated the lines, desperately trying to make her voice and her body a conduit for her heart, but she couldn't seem to force it out. One of the suits started to smirk. She heard someone whisper she was a better piece of ass than an actress.

She ignored him. She was good. Better than good. This was her chance. She'd been born to play this part.

"I'd like to try it again," she said, aware that the men had already disengaged.

"Sure." The producer read the intro line again.

She knew what they were thinking. That it was true—that she was nothing but a piece of ass. She didn't belong here.

"I'm sorry," she said, grabbing her handbag. "Thank you for the chance."

Without saying anything else, she walked out.

Her steps sounded loud on the tiled floor. Her heels clicked with the rhythm of failure.

She'd lost it. Somewhere along the way, she'd lost the passion. Or maybe it was just her integrity. Did it matter? She was through and everyone knew it.

Megan arrived at Adam's office shortly after four thirty. She knew his last appointment was at four, so she had plenty of time to catch him.

The receptionist recognized her and showed her back to Adam's large office. The space was impressive, with a big desk and plenty of diplomas and awards on the walls, along with a painting they'd bought together the last time they'd been in Santa Barbara.

She walked around the room, then paused by the window, not sure what she was supposed to be feeling. Anger? Confusion? Hurt? There were all those emotions and others she couldn't name. But there was also a sense of certainty. She'd made her decision and she knew it was right.

It hurt. Knowing her relationship was over kept her up at night as she alternated between tears and rage. For a while she'd wondered if the problem was her—had she forced Adam into acting this way? Then she'd come to her senses, mentally slapped herself hard and accepted that Adam had cheated because that's the kind of guy he was.

With certainty came a kind of relief. It hurt, it was relief with claws, but it promised that in time she would heal. It promised that she would one day accept that Adam wasn't the love of her life. He was just a jerk with an expensive education and unlimited earning potential.

"Megan!"

She turned and watched him hurry toward her. He was as handsome as she remembered, but that information no longer mattered.

"Megan, you're here. I'm so glad." He pulled her close and kissed her. "I've been calling and calling. I understand you've needed time to think everything through. I want you to know that I'm very sorry for what I did. I know it came at a bad time and I'm sorry about that as well. You mean the world to me, Megan. I would never want to hurt you."

"Wouldn't you?" she asked, stepping back and putting the desk between them. "But you had to know that finding out about your affair would be devastating."

"Yes, but it's over. I told you that."

He said the words as if he meant them. She would have put money on him passing a lie detector test. At least today. But in a month? A year? He would cheat again.

"I'm too tired to argue," she told him, knowing the long nights of angst had left her with all the emotional strength of cooked pasta. "This wasn't a onetime thing, Adam. You were too good at it. You must chronically cheat. Is that part of what goes on here? You repair your patients' hearts while ripping out your wives'?"

He looked confused. "Megan, I know you're upset, but—"

"I'm not upset," she said, interrupting him. "I'm actually very calm. I'm more hurt by what my dad is doing than this. Which tells me we have a bigger problem than you cheating."

"The wedding is in less than a week. You're going to *have* to forgive me."

"This isn't about forgiveness." She pulled off her engagement ring and set it on the desk. "I'm not going to marry you. I'm canceling the wedding."

He stiffened. "You can't. It's Saturday. Everyone is coming. What will we tell them?"

"You can tell your friends anything you like. I'm telling mine the truth. That you were screwing around. It's not pretty but it gives a clear picture. Good-bye, Adam."

She walked toward the door. He grabbed her arm and pulled her around until she faced him.

"Just like that?" he demanded. "You're ending things without an explanation?"

He looked good, with his intense blue eyes. She stared at him, expecting to feel some sense of loss or longing. Adam would be out of her life forever. She should have wanted to cry.

What she felt instead was . . . relief.

It shocked her, like a jolt of electricity.

"I don't want to marry you."

The words came from somewhere deep inside. They stunned her, as if she'd started speaking Mandarin or Dutch.

"We can fix this," he told her. He put his hands on her shoulders. "I love you."

She tested the words again. "I don't want to marry you."

Her anger drained away, the pain faded to something bearable and she was left with a lightness she hadn't felt in weeks.

"I don't want to marry you."

"Would you stop saying that?" he yelled. "I get it."

"Good."

She left his office and walked toward her car. She was practically buoyant. She felt like a cartoon character floating inches above the ground.

She didn't want to marry Adam. Why hadn't she figured that out before?

The crash would come. She knew that in a few hours she would be curled up somewhere, desperate for him to be back, but for now there was only relief that she'd gotten off so easy.

Eleven

MEGAN OPENED THE FRONT door and found Leanne standing there with a plastic bag.

"KFC," her sister said. "I don't know how your afternoon went, but mine sucked."

Megan held up the pitcher of mojitos she'd made. "Mine was actually okay." She stepped back to let in her sister. "I'm planning a hideous night later when I come to my senses, but for now, I'm self-actualized and shopping on QVC."

"Lucky you. What happened?"

"I broke up with Adam. It was incredibly freeing. Either I did the right thing or I'm having some kind of psychotic break. For now I'm just going with it until I plummet back to reality. What happened to you?"

"I blew the most important audition of my career. It was my big break and I totally lost it."

"I'm sorry to hear that."

Leanne rolled her eyes. "Right."

"I am." Megan took the fast food bag and set it on the table. "Can't I be sympathetic? Are you the only one who gets emotional depth?"

"You don't think I have emotional depth. You think I'm useless and that I'm mooching off Mom. Seriously, did you actually believe she would continue to pay my rent? It might take away from her skin care treatments and Botox."

A point Megan hadn't considered. "You're right. She wouldn't be that supportive."

"She's not supportive at all. The only thing she likes about what I do is that she gets to brag to people. I'd say friends, but she doesn't have many. Just to be clear, I have friends, okay? I'm a regular person. I'm not like Tina."

"Defensive much?" Megan asked, wondering where the attack was coming from.

"Do not push me."

"Or what? You'll hit me with a pillow?"

"You were going to throw a vase at me."

"You deserved it."

"Not as much as you. You've been a real shit to me, Megan. If I didn't already love you, I would walk out of here and never want to see you again."

Megan took a step back. "What have I done?"

"Nothing. Exactly nothing. You dismissed me years ago and never felt any reason to change that. I'm your sister. You should have tried, but no. Every second we're together, you make it clear I don't matter. Well, fuck you." She grabbed the KFC and turned to leave.

"No!" Megan yelled and stomped her foot. "I'm tired of fighting with everyone in my family. If you want to go, then go. But you are leaving the damn chicken."

Leanne clutched the plastic bag to her chest. "This is my chicken. I bought it."

"You'll just throw it up later."

"I am *not* bulimic. Why do you do this? Why do you assume the worst about me?" Tears filled her eyes. "I admire you and you don't even care that I'm alive. When I was sixteen and Billy Wade asked me to go to his college homecoming dance, I begged you to come home and help me buy a dress. I was scared I would look like a kid. You always knew how to dress and what to wear. But you wouldn't even return my calls."

She sniffed and still managed to look beautiful. "When I had my very first ever movie audition, I called you and asked you to come with me. I wanted someone who mattered to share the moment. You didn't show. When I got home, you'd left a message saying you were too busy and good luck. You never even send me a birthday card."

Leanne shoved the plastic KFC bag at her. "Here. You eat it. I'm not hungry."

She started for the door.

Megan stared after her. Everything Leanne said made sense. Worse, it was true. She'd been a horrible sister. She felt like crap.

"I didn't think you cared," she said, setting down the food. "I thought you assumed I was ridiculous with my normal life and my average happiness."

Leanne spun back to face her. "I swear to God, if this is about me being the pretty sister—"

"Of course it is. Do you know what it was like to have

Mom going on and on about the boys calling when I couldn't even get a date to the prom? You were the perfect one. I was just—"

"Dad's favorite. You're not the only one who didn't send me a birthday card last year. Neither of my parents did. They both forgot. Feel the love."

Megan felt small and mean. "I'm sorry."

"Yeah, yeah."

"I mean it."

"Well, excuse me if I don't believe you right now."

Megan didn't know what to do. She found herself wanting to reach out to Leanne, which was odd and uncomfortable.

"You want a mojito? They're really strong."

Leanne hesitated.

"I really am sorry about the audition. Was it for a movie?"

Leanne crossed to the table, opened the bag, popped the top on the plastic tray covering the first dinner and grabbed a leg. "I don't want to talk about it. I want to get drunk and eat and pretend I have a life."

"Can you do that here?"

"Are you going to throw anything at me?"

"No."

"Okay."

Megan went and got the drinks. They sat at the table and ate, not saying much until dinner was finished.

Megan hadn't thought of things from her sister's perspective before. Had Leanne been reaching out to her and had she really not noticed? She'd always thought of herself as a kind and sensitive person. Apparently she'd been wrong.

"How many people do we have to call to tell them the wedding's canceled?" Leanne asked.

"I didn't think you'd still . . ." Megan pressed her lips together. "I'm going to stop assuming where you're concerned."

"That won't make you any less of an ass."

"Nice. Do you kiss your mother with that mouth?"

"Yuck. We don't kiss. I might mess up her makeup. Besides, I learned all my swearing from you."

"That is not possible. I'm the perfect sister. Except for the pretty thing."

"You're certainly annoying."

Megan smiled. "There are two hundred guests. Most of the numbers will be in my address book. I've marked which ones are Adam's family or just his friends. I'll e-mail him a list and he can contact them himself." She bit into the chicken and chewed, then swallowed. "That's only about twenty names, leaving us with the other hundred and eighty."

"Just so you know, I plan to be totally drunk before I make the calls. They'll go faster that way. What about the gifts? They have to be returned."

Megan thought about all the boxes piled in her second bedroom. "It's a nightmare. At least I kept a list of who sent what. But I'm going to have to pack them all up and send them back."

"I can help with that, too."

Megan looked at her. She swallowed the first three

things that came to mind. "Thank you. That would be very nice."

Leanne smirked. "Kinda hurts when you talk like that, doesn't it?"

"A little."

"I plan to be smug. Just so you know. You've been smug for years and now it's my turn."

"What?" Megan yelped. "I'm not smug."

"Oh, please. Miss I-Have-the-Perfect-Life? With your UCLA degree and your great job and your blond, pretty doctor boyfriend. You own your condo, your car is paid for. Your best friend is a supermodel. You're smug. You have it all and you're delighted to rub it in my face. Mom's too. Mostly Mom's, to be honest." Leanne drained the rest of her mojito.

"Are you drunk? You can't be drunk already."

"Right. Because I couldn't be telling the truth sober."

"That's not what I meant. I'm not smug."

"Take a poll. Ask anyone."

Megan felt insulted. "I've worked hard for everything I have. I earned it."

"That doesn't make you flaunt it less."

"You couldn't be more wrong."

"Maybe."

"I'm not sure you should be making calls."

Leanne smiled. "Afraid of what I'll say about Adam?"

"Good point. Let me get my address book."

Megan went upstairs to collect the information.

Two hours later, they'd made a serious dent in the

guest list. Megan leaned back on the sofa and rubbed her temples. The room had a bit of a spin to it.

"If I hear one more 'that's just so awful' I'm going to throw myself in front of the UPS truck."

"People don't know what to say," Leanne told her. "Plus they really want details but they're mostly too polite to ask."

"I guess. It would have been easier to just marry Adam."

"But a mistake."

"Oh yeah. Big time. It's going to get worse, too. Mom insists I come by tomorrow to talk about all of this. I'm sure she's going to try to convince me to change my mind."

"Ignore her," Leanne said from the overstuffed chair next to the sofa. "I'll take care of it."

Megan looked at her. "There's that nice thing again."

"I know. You might want to take advantage of it now in case I get over it later."

"You won't." She blinked. "Did I mention I had a pitcher of mojitos before you got here?"

"No."

"I did. I'm fuzzy. But thank you. For the Mom thing."

"You're welcome. Allegra said she and Payton were taking you to Las Vegas this weekend. That will be fun."

"I don't know. I'm supposed to be on my honeymoon."

"You didn't want to marry Adam, remember? Are you having second thoughts?"

Megan shook her head, then wished she hadn't. "Right now I'm not having any thoughts. I just don't want to be pathetic. Wouldn't that be pathetic? My friends taking me to Vegas because my fiancé cheated on me and I had to cancel the wedding?"

"It's not like they'll make you wear a sign. No one has to know. It would be better for you to be somewhere else on Saturday. Do you really want to spend what would have been your wedding day around here, by yourself? You won't be able to think about anything else. That would be awful."

Leanne had a point.

"I haven't been to Las Vegas in a long time," Megan said. "I went with Adam a couple of years ago." But that wasn't the trip she remembered. The one she remembered had been a lifetime ago, with the first boy to love her and leave her. "I lost my virginity at Circus Circus."

Leanne nearly spit. "Are you kidding? Oh, yeah. You went with that guy. Travis. I had a thing for him."

"Me too," Megan murmured. "He was gorgeous. Those eyes and how he talked to me. He treated me like I mattered."

"Why'd you let him go?"

A question Megan had asked herself a thousand times. "Because he needed me to be an adult and I was still a kid. I wouldn't stand up to Dad. Travis asked me to choose and I picked my father." She looked at Leanne. "What an idiot, right?"

Her sister looked sympathetic. "You're still not talking to Dad?"

"Nope. He won't return my calls. I had to leave a message that the wedding was canceled. I thought he might phone to find out why, but he didn't."

She felt the familiar burning of tears and blinked them away. "I'm done crying," she said, more to herself than Leanne. "I've cried more than a river and I'm done. Adam isn't worth it and Dad . . ." She swallowed more of her drink. "I still haven't figured that one out yet."

Leanne got up, came around the table, crouched down and hugged her. Megan hugged her back. She couldn't remember the last time they'd touched, but it felt good to be comforted.

"Go to Las Vegas," Leanne told her. "Try to forget about all this. I'll keep Mom busy so she doesn't bug you."

Megan sniffed. "When did you get so nice?"

"A couple of weeks ago. It was a Tuesday."

Megan's hangover was a living, breathing creature inside of her. One determined to crack her skull and reduce her brain to dust. She downed two more aspirin, made a latte with four shots of espresso, then steeled herself for a conversation she didn't want to have.

I'm not getting married. I'm not getting married.

The words pounded in her head as she walked, keeping time with the click of her heels.

Felicia's door stood open, but Megan knocked anyway. When she heard the familiar "Come in," she entered.

"Morning," she said, hoping she looked a whole lot better than she felt.

Her boss smiled at her. "Getting excited? You're only a couple of days away. Your last day is Thursday, right? Then you're gone next week. Mike and I are really excited about the wedding. I've heard so much. I can't wait to see how the details play out in person. The flowers are going to be . . ." She paused. "Are you all right? You look a little pale. Are you coming down with something? Megan, you can't get sick now."

"I'm fine," she said, sitting and ignoring the dozen or so tiny hammers pounding the back of her eyes. "I wanted to talk to you because, well . . ."

Felicia leaned toward her. "What's wrong?"

"The wedding has been canceled. My sister and I have called most of the guests, but I wanted to tell you in person. I'm going to e-mail everyone in the office who was invited. I'm sorry there's going to be gossip for a few days. It's not professional, but I don't know how to stop it."

Felicia stood and came around the desk. "I don't care about the gossip. Are you all right? Can I ask what happened? Is that too personal? Oh, Megan, you were so excited."

"I'm okay. I'm not happy, but I'm not destroyed. I found out something about Adam that made marrying him impossible."

Felicia's eyes widened. "He's gay?"

Megan managed to smile. "No. He cheated."

"Ouch. I can't decide if that's better or worse. What a bastard. I always liked him, too."

"Everyone did." Megan clutched her latte and wished

the aspirin would kick in. "I'll be fine. I'm going to take off Friday and probably Monday, but then I'll be back."

"Are you sure? Maybe you should take the week."

"No. It's better for me to work. My clients' problems seem easier to fix."

"Okay. But if you need more time, just let me know. Can I help with anything?"

"I have it handled, but thanks."

"Okay. Let me know if you need anything."

Megan nodded, then left. She had the e-mail ready to send out. Then the talk would start. People would come by her office to check on her. Some would be genuinely concerned, but many would just want the scoop.

"It'll be over in a couple of days," she told herself. By next week there would be a new scandal to keep everyone talking. But first she had to get through this one.

Leanne walked quickly past the young woman parked outside the closed door. "He's expecting me," she said.

The assistant went to stop her, but Leanne had already opened the door and moved inside. Connor McKay looked up from his desk.

"I'm sorry," his assistant said, coming up behind Leanne. "She just pushed her way in."

"It's all right, Heather. I'll see Ms. Greene for a few minutes."

Leanne waited until Heather left, then faced Connor, her anger giving her courage. "You know why I'm here?" she asked.

"Not a clue."

"I got the call this morning. The rejection. You probably don't get those anymore."

One corner of his mouth turned up. "I get rewrites."

"You get millions, but that's not the point." She crossed to his desk and stared at him, determined not to be mesmerized by his dark blue eyes. "I hate this. It's a rigged game and I don't know the rules. You get to screw around all you want. Girls half your age line up to sleep with you and no one cares. You get a pat on the back and a new deal."

He rested his elbows on the arms of his chair and touched his steepled fingers to his chin. "I get the deal because I wrote a damn good screenplay or because I'm going to get the movie. The screwing is incidental."

"Of course it is. Because hey, what does a piece of ass matter?"

She was beyond furious. She wanted to scream and hit and throw.

"I have done things I'm not proud of," he said. "But what does that have to do with you, Leanne? You didn't sleep with anyone."

"No, and I didn't get a callback either. You want it both ways. I heard them talking at the audition. That I was just a piece of ass. You punish actresses who use what they can to get ahead and don't hire the ones who don't. I know it was a bad audition. I was nervous and scared and all I could think about was if I slept with one of you, I'd get it. But I don't want to be that piece of ass anymore. It's disgusting. I'm worth more. You don't get to treat me like that."

"Why are you telling me this? I'm just the writer."

"That's the credit you're taking on this project, but it's your production company calling the shots." She crossed to the tall windows, then turned back to him. "Explain it to me. How am I supposed to get ahead? People look at me and assume I'm an idiot. I read well and they assume it's a fluke. But if I show them this"—she pulled up her shirt, exposing her bare breasts—"that makes sense. That they can understand. So they do me and give me the role. If it goes well, they take credit. If it goes badly, they tell the world they gave it to me for a piece of ass and everyone understands."

She dropped her shirt. "Tell the truth," she said, her voice rising. "Just tell me the truth. Who would I have to screw to get the part? Is it you? Does it make you feel like a man to force a woman to do it with you? Does that make you hard? Because it mostly makes me sick to my stomach."

She covered her face with her hands, then dropped her arms to her sides. "I'm done. I won't do this anymore. I thought it was my dream, but nothing is worth turning myself into a whore. Fuck you, Connor McKay. Fuck you and the whole damn business."

She started toward the door.

"Stop!"

His command made her freeze in her tracks. She looked at him. "What?"

He rose and walked around the desk. He moved in front of her, standing inches from her. His dark eyes seemed to be able to swallow her whole.

"If you'd brought that to the audition, the part would have been yours."

The unfairness of it all surged through her. Without thinking, she raised her hand to slap him. He grabbed her wrist.

"I don't think so." His voice was low and silky.

She felt it then—a jolt of awareness that went through her body and settled in her groin. Heat and need burned. An answering flare tightened his face. He released her and stepped back.

"Go with Heather," he said. "She'll take you upstairs."

"I'm not sleeping with you," Leanne told him.

"No, you're not. Several people from the studio are having a meeting. We still haven't cast the part. You're getting a second chance to read, Ms. Greene. See that you use it wisely."

"I could still get the part?"

"If you do well on the read, you'll be called back. That's the best I can do."

She couldn't believe it. "Why?"

"Because you're right. There is a double standard. And because I think you might have what it takes. Don't disappoint me."

By four o'clock on Friday, Allegra, Payton and Megan had checked into their rooms at the Venetian, lost money in the casino and shared a round of margaritas.

"How are you feeling?" Allegra asked as they rode the escalator up to the shopping level. "Good? Bad? Resolved?"

Megan considered the question. The noise and crowds were oddly comforting, as if being around people made her feel less alone.

"I'm okay," Megan admitted, a little surprised it was true. "Breaking up with Adam was the right thing to do. The worst of it was having to cancel everything."

"So you're okay?" Payton asked, sounding skeptical. "Seriously."

Megan smiled. "I promise not to throw myself out the window. I'm going to hang with my friends, gamble, eat too much and sleep as late as I want. It's a perfect, healing weekend."

"You forgot taking a bath," Allegra told her. "Did you see the size of the tubs in our rooms?"

"I did and it's on my to-do list."

They stepped off the escalator and headed toward the shops.

"Women with credit cards," Payton said. "Move aside."

They all laughed and went into the first store.

A half hour later, Megan was restless. She couldn't seem to get into the shopping zone. Maybe it gave her too much time to think.

"I'm going back downstairs," she told her friends. "I'm going to grab a drink and play blackjack."

Payton and Allegra looked at each other. "We'll come with you," Payton said.

Megan shook her head. "Come on, you two. I can survive on my own for a couple of hours while you shop. Maybe some cute guy will want to buy me a drink. I'll be fine," she added. "Seriously. I'm feeling almost normal, which is pretty spectacular when you consider what I've been through in the past few weeks." She pulled her cell phone out of her purse and waved it. "You can reach me in a heartbeat."

"All right," Allegra said slowly. "But call us if you start to get sad or anything."

"I promise. Have fun."

Megan waved and walked toward the glass doors that led outside. She walked down to the front of the hotel, then paused, not sure what to do. She should go inside, of course. That made sense. She wanted to gamble a little more, absorb the craziness around her. So why was she suddenly thinking about being somewhere else?

"What the hell," she muttered, and walked toward the cab stand.

"Where to?" the bellman asked.

"Circus Circus."

Twenty minutes later she stood inside the hotel she'd visited all those years ago with Travis. Memories vied for her attention, crowding her brain with images.

She'd been so incredibly nervous. It had been her first time going away with a man and she'd been convinced that everyone knew they were going to be having sex later. She'd felt scared and excited and a thousand other emotions.

She walked around the casino, then to a railing where she could look down on the lower level. She'd been so young then. Too young. Travis had lived a different kind of life and he'd wanted things from her she wasn't ready to give. Did he know that? Did he understand that she hadn't wanted to reject him? Everything had happened so fast—he'd insisted on her leaving with him that second. There was no way she could have gone.

But what if she had? How would her life have been different? Maybe she would have found work in a New York design studio. Maybe she and Travis could have made it. She would never know, which was probably for the better. Fantasy was often so much more interesting than reality.

She'd been forced to grow up that summer. Her parents had grounded her and she'd had to quit design school. At the time that decision had seemed like the end of the world. Then she'd started college, majoring in business, and gradually the idea of designing clothes had slipped away. Sometimes she looked back and wondered if she'd ever really been that creative, or if she'd been playing a childish game of dress-up.

She'd made a life—a good life—for herself. Despite Leanne's comments, she was happy, not smug. She had everything she wanted . . . at least, she'd had it until a few weeks ago.

She walked over to where they'd had drinks before going up to their room. Travis had been so good to her, she thought, remembering their night together. Her first time had been perfect, thanks to him. He'd been gentle and sexy and caring, with the right amount of intensity. He wasn't the kind of man who would cheat weeks before his wedding and then expect it to be okay.

Megan took a deep breath. Apparently she might not

have been as emotionally disconnected from Adam as she'd thought. Which was fine. Healing took time. She'd lost Travis twice and both times she'd taken months to heal. Of course, he had the advantage—he was forever young in her memories. The perfect boyfriend. The kind of guy who—

"Hello, Megan."

She stood motionless, unable to move or breathe or think or speak as she stared at the man standing in front of her. It was as if she'd summoned him from her mind. Only not him, exactly. An older version of what he'd been.

His eyes were the same; that was the first thing she noticed. The scar on his cheek was new. His hair was just as shaggy, but he'd filled out more. He'd become a man. And he was here . . . in the hotel where they'd made love so many years ago.

She swallowed and forced herself to meet his powerful gaze. "Hello, Travis. It's been a long time."

Twelve

WELL, HELL, TRAVIS THOUGHT as he stared at the beautiful redhead in front of him. He hadn't meant to come to the hotel. He was staying down the Strip, but after checking in, he'd found himself taking a cab to the place to look around. He wasn't sure what he'd expected to find, but it certainly hadn't been Megan.

She looked as surprised as he felt and more stunning than he remembered. She'd been appealing before, with big green eyes and a mouth designed to make a man think about things that were illegal in seven states. But she'd been a kid and now she was a woman, and there was something to be said for grown-up beauty.

She smiled and it was like someone hit him in the gut. "Is that really you? Oh, my God. I can't believe it. I was just walking around and . . ." She flushed slightly. "How embarrassing. I was just walking around and thinking about you. What are you doing here?"

"Passing through."

"I'm here with some friends." She stared into his eyes.

"I don't even know what to say. How are you?" Her smile widened. "You look good. The scar is new."

He rubbed his cheek. "Don't ask."

"Okay." Her gaze slipped to his earring. "Still the bad boy?"

"In some ways." In others, he'd learned his lesson. One of those lessons said he should just walk away. Instead he found himself saying, "Come on. I'll buy you a drink."

They made their way to the bar. She ordered a soda and he did the same. For once he wasn't interested in getting drunk and forgetting. This time, he wanted to remember everything.

"Passing through from where?" she asked, leaning toward him.

Her hair was long and curly, a tumbling, sexy mess that made his fingers twitch. Her skin was pale and the curves were pretty much as he remembered. She might have filled out a little, but in the best ways possible.

"Houston," he said, wishing he'd thought to get laid before leaving town. "It's where I ended up when I left L.A. My mom's looking to sell her business, so I'm heading back to help her for a few months. What about you? Living in New York?"

She frowned. "Why would I be . . . Oh. I'm in L.A., too. Never left, actually."

"I thought you were going to get that internship and move to New York."

"Let's just say that it was several weeks before I saw daylight after our weekend together. My father was not happy with what happened. I had to quit my design class and spend a lot of time in my room."

She spoke lightly, as if she were hiding something, but what?

"And now?" he asked. "What do you do?"

She shrugged. "I'm an accountant in west L.A. I mostly work with the entertainment business, which is interesting but demanding. Those Hollywood types want to be creative with their money. It's my job to make sure they don't get too wild."

"An accountant? Seriously?"

She stiffened a little. "I like it. I'm good with numbers. I play with designing as a hobby. I help my friends when they need a special outfit."

Defensive, he thought. He held up both hands. "I'm not judging. Hell, I'm still working in the landscape business."

"Which will make helping out your mom easier." Her gaze settled on his scar. "So, is there a Mrs. Hunter waiting for you at the hotel?"

"No. Never married. You?"

"No. I was engaged, but things didn't work out." She picked up her soda, then put it down. "He cheated. Why do men do that?"

Her fiancé cheated on her? "Because they're assholes."

"I was hoping for something more definitive." She sighed. "It doesn't matter. I found out in time. Better before the wedding than after, right?" She tilted her head.

So Megan had been engaged. Travis had never found a woman he felt that sure about. Women were forgettable and interchangeable. He looked at Megan. Except, maybe, for her.

"Still riding your motorcycle?" she asked.

"Sometimes. I build them now. Custom bikes. I'm starting a business, but it's slow going." He shrugged. "I like it. I like the work and how I can make each bike unique. I do one at a time."

"I can see you working with your hands. I'm glad you're doing that." She smiled. "If the ladies are seeing you on your motorcycle, I'm surprised they let you get away."

"Maybe I'm not interested in getting caught."

There was something in the way he said the words, Megan thought, doing her best not to shiver. She told herself she was emotionally on edge. The last few weeks had been stressful, she was running on almost no sleep and despite the soda in front of her, she'd had several drinks with her friends and was definitely feeling the liquor.

Still, part of her reaction was about seeing Travis again. He was so much the same and yet so different. Darker, stronger, bigger. The air of danger was more subtle but no less potent. How was it possible they were sitting here now, talking, like the last ten years hadn't happened?

Silence stretched between them. She sensed he might excuse himself and leave, and she didn't want that.

"You said you're going back to L.A. to help your mom. Is she all right?"

"I guess. She wants to sell the business, so I'll work there for a few months, get it ready, then leave."

"And go where?"

He shrugged. "Somewhere. It doesn't matter."

She'd had so many plans, she thought, remembering her dreams for the first time in years. They'd been as powerful as her love for Travis, yet she'd walked away from both in the course of a weekend. Until this second, she'd believed she'd made the right decision. The smart decision. Had she?

Rather than answer the question, she asked, "What about your dad?"

Seconds later she remembered Travis's troubled past with his father and wished she'd thought of a different topic.

"Still in jail. Going to be there a long time."

"I'm sorry."

"Don't be. It doesn't matter to me. The longer he's away, the better it is for my mom. Not that she'd see it that way. For reasons not clear to me, she's always loved the old bastard."

She leaned toward him. "It's like my parents. My mother has been awful. Selfish, a professional victim."

"I remember you talking about her."

"Probably to the point where you were desperately bored, right?" She managed a slight smile. "My dad stayed. All this time and he stayed. You know why? Because she's beautiful. Because he wants to walk into the room with the prize on his arm. It's a shallow reason to stay married."

Not that they were together now, she thought, remembering what had happened.

"Megan?"

She drew in a breath. "Sorry. Brain freeze. I just . . . Let's talk about something else. The Dodgers are having a winning season. That's exciting. Or do you follow a Texas team?"

Travis studied her as if debating which topic to pursue. She really hoped it would be baseball, because the exhaustion had caught up with her and she felt seconds from a breakdown. Better to get up and walk away than risk sharing that with him. Not that she wanted to leave.

"What's going on?" he asked at last.

"Nothing. Nothing. I'm fine."

"You're still not a great liar."

Her smile was real this time. "Isn't that a good quality?" She rested her hands on her lap and squeezed her fingers together. "It's my dad. We're not getting along. No, that's not right. I'm . . ." She drew in a breath. "A few weeks ago I found out he's not my biological father. My mother had an affair and I'm the result. But she wasn't the one to tell me. She left that up to some attorney I'd never met. My father—my real father, Gary—found out. He left her, which I guess is bad enough, but he won't have anything to do with me. He's turned his back on me, like I don't matter. Like I'm not his daughter anymore. He won't even speak to me or see me and I don't think he loves me anymore. Maybe he never did."

Tears burned hot, but she fought them, fought to stay in control. She forced a laugh. "This is so not the conversation you want to be having. I need to go and let you enjoy yourself." She stood. "I'll get a cab back to the hotel and meet up with my friends. It was really good to see you again and good luck with everything."

She looked around to find the exit. Why had she told him any of that? He would think she was some psycho emotional train wreck.

The sound of his chair scraping as he pushed back was loud enough to make her wince. She looked around, prepared to try to smile and at least leave him with a last memory that wasn't scary. But he didn't turn from her. Instead he drew her against him and wrapped both arms around her.

"He's an idiot," he murmured, his voice soft and low. "And he still loves you. You were his world, Megan. You have to believe that."

Soft words. Tender words. And a familiar, safe, wonderful embrace that made her want to melt.

"I want to," she whispered. "You don't know how much I want to. But he won't even talk to me."

"He's dealing. He'll get over it."

"I want to believe you."

"Hey," he said, straightening and staring into her eyes. "It's me. I know stuff."

She laughed. "You are so full of crap."

"Maybe, but it sounds good." He brushed her cheek with his thumb. "He'll come around."

"I hope so. He's my dad."

Which, given his family situation, was probably the wrong thing to say.

"I'm sorry," she told him. "For being a mess. Aren't you afraid some of the crazy will rub off?"

"No." He wiped her other cheek.

His gaze was exactly as she remembered, as was the feel of his arms and his body against hers. It was as if the past ten years had never happened. This was Travis, her first love, and no matter what, she was unable to resist him.

Being with him made her see possibilities, made her believe.

"I've missed you so much," she admitted. "I didn't realize how much until right now."

"I've missed you, too."

Did he mean that? She wanted to believe him. Because having him miss her made her feel a little stronger.

She became aware of their bodies touching, of the heat brewing between them. It aroused and embarrassed her in equal measures. What happened to the girl she'd been? Ten years ago, Travis had wanted to give her the world. Instead she'd settled for becoming an accountant.

No, not settled, she told herself, finding it hard to think about anything but the man who held her. She loved her job. She loved . . .

Looking into his eyes reminded her of all she'd planned to be. It was like looking at the sun. It burned her and threatened to make her go blind.

"You must be so disappointed," she said, not meaning to speak the words out loud.

"You couldn't be more wrong."

Still holding her in his arms, he dropped his head and kissed her.

His mouth was everything she remembered. Warm,

soft, firm, teasing, provocative. The light touch was probably meant to be comforting; still, she felt every millimeter of the contact and desperately wanted more. Being with him had always been right.

He breathed her name against her mouth, spoke it like a sigh. Then he pulled back and took her hand in his.

"Where are you staying?" he asked.

"The Venetian."

Without saying anything else, he led her through the casino to the front, where he flagged a cab. They rode back in silence, not touching. She was aware of him, of his breathing, the warmth of his body, how her own trembled slightly in anticipation.

The cab ride took about fifteen minutes. When they arrived, he took her hand again. This time she led the way to the elevators, showed her room key to the security guard, then pushed the up button.

They went up to the seventeenth floor, down the carpeted hallway, and stopped in front of her door.

He took the key from her and unlocked the door. Then they were inside, facing each other, the faint light of sunset spilling into the quiet room.

"Megan," he whispered again before reaching for her.

She dropped her purse onto the floor and went willingly into his arms. As they reached for each other, she heard the door slam shut.

He kissed her again, but this time with an intensity that stole away her breath. He claimed her with lips and tongue—took, offered, tasted her, teased her until she was helpless to resist. Not that she wanted to.

He kissed her deeply, plunging inside of her mouth, making her strain for more. Each stroke aroused, each flick made her tremble. Wanting grew and with it the promise that making love with Travis would ease some of the pain inside.

She touched him everywhere. His arms, his shoulders, his chest. He touched her in return, skating over her body with quick, sure movements. Rediscovering? Exploring? She didn't care as long as he promised not to stop.

Sexual hunger made her bold. She closed her lips around his tongue and sucked. He stiffened slightly, broke the kiss, then trailed his mouth along her jaw. He nipped at her earlobe, licked her neck, then bent down to draw her tight nipple into his mouth.

Even through the layers of her cotton dress and bra, she felt the deep pull. A clench answered between her legs. She managed to kick off her sandals, but it wasn't enough. She wanted to be naked in every way possible, to have him inside of her, filling her, making her respond until she had no choice but to surrender.

He reached behind her for the zipper of her sundress, then pulled down the fabric. Seconds later her bra went flying.

He explored her curves, brushing against her nipples over and over again. She was already wet, could feel the thickness of his erection and didn't see any reason to wait.

She unfastened his belt buckle, then popped the button on his jeans. He was so hard, so big, she had to tug on the zipper to get it down over the thick ridge.

He drew back just enough to shove down his jeans and briefs. She flung off her panties. Then he pushed the lamp and the silk flowers off the entry table, lifted her into their place, spread her legs and found his way home.

Later she would remember the crash as the lamp shattered. Later she would come up with a story to tell housekeeping and figure out what the replacements would cost. Later she would wonder what had gotten into her.

He filled her completely, thrusting deeply, banging her against the wall. She opened her legs more and grabbed his hips, digging her fingers into his muscled flesh.

It was hot and fast and lacking in elegance. It was exactly what she needed.

He took her without saying anything, their bodies straining, both of them gasping as they stared into each other's eyes. It wasn't gentle or seductive, which made it perfect in every way.

She lost herself in an orgasm as loud as the crash of the lamp on the floor. Her eyes sank closed, her body shuddered, she forgot to breathe. Then he groaned and pushed in one more time and was still.

When the pleasure faded she became aware of the cold table against her bare butt and the way her skirt was pushed up to her waist. She opened her eyes and found him watching her.

"Impressive," she murmured. "I don't believe I've been responsible for breaking furniture before."

He glanced at the lamp and grinned. "Sorry. I'll pay for it."

"No, no. It's fine."

He stroked his knuckles against her cheek. "Don't move. There's glass everywhere and you're not wearing shoes."

He collected her sandals, then carefully slid them onto her feet. When they were secure, he eased her into a standing position.

Her insides felt squishy and her legs were a little shaky. She pulled up her dress and managed to stagger into the bedroom. He fastened up his pants and followed her.

She glanced from the broken lamp to him, not sure which to deal with first. But Travis didn't seem to have that same problem. He moved past her into the bathroom.

"Did you see the tub?" he asked. "It's big enough for two."

She trailed him into the bathroom. "You want to take a bath?"

He stepped behind her and cupped her breasts. Even through the dress, his touch was enough to make her nipples hard.

"I want to do a lot of things."

Her cell phone rang. The loud music reminded her that she hadn't come to Las Vegas alone.

"I have friends who are probably wondering where I am," she said, and dashed back to grab her purse. After flipping open the phone, she said, "Hello?"

"Where are you?" Payton demanded. "We've looked everywhere. Are you okay? Are you alone in your room feeling sorry for yourself?"

Megan glanced over at Travis. He'd fastened his jeans but left his shirt out. He leaned against the door frame, looking two parts satisfied male and one part ready to do it again.

"I'm totally fine," she said, smiling when he met her gaze. "Seriously. I'm great. I'm just going to, um, stay in for a bit."

"Megan, no! You can't sulk."

Her smiled widened. "Trust me, I'm not sulking. I'm having a great time."

"What are you talking about?" Payton asked. "Allegra, talk some sense into her."

"What do you think you're doing up in your room?" Allegra asked.

"The question isn't what," Megan told her. "It's who."

"I have no idea . . . Megan? Do you mean what I think you mean?"

Megan hung up and put the phone back in her purse. "Sorry," she said. "They're checking on me."

"I can tell. I don't want to get in the way of any plans you might have for tonight."

"No plans," she told him. "Unless you have to be somewhere."

"Just here."

"Good."

He nodded toward the bathroom. "Want to start filling the tub? I'll call housekeeping and room service. Any requests?"

Just that this night never end. "I'm good."

"Yes, you are."

*   *   *

Forty-five minutes later, they were stretched out together in the tub. Champagne sat in an ice bucket, candles flickered in the bathroom and something soft and soothing played on the stereo.

Travis had taken care of all of it, including paying for the lamp and tipping the housekeeper who had efficiently cleaned up the glass. Now Megan leaned back into his arms, the warm water lapping at her shoulders.

"Tell me about the scar," she said.

He tightened his arms around her. "It's not a fun story."

"Were you drunk?"

"No. Some guy was beating up his kid. I got between them. The dad had a knife."

She broke free and turned to face him. "Are you serious? A man attacked you with a knife?"

"I'm fine."

She touched the scar on his face. "No, you're not. Look what happened. Is the kid okay?"

"He's not with his dad anymore. Is that better? I don't know."

"You rode to the rescue."

"I was a damn fool. Don't romanticize it. I'm not a hero."

She stared at him for a few more seconds, looking for more changes. Except for his ability to hide what he was thinking, she couldn't find any. She slid back into the tub and settled against him.

"Tell me about Houston," she said.

"It's hot and humid. The people are nice. I like Texas.

Great food. I missed the mountains. It was cloudy the first winter I was there and I kept thinking that when it cleared, I would see the mountains. But they're not there. Tell me about being an accountant."

He ran his hands down her arms, then laced their fingers together. Her skin was already wrinkled from being in the water, but she didn't want to get out. She liked being close to Travis, sensing his strength, feeling she was perfectly safe. At least that was the illusion.

"You really want to know why I gave up on design." She reached for her glass of champagne with her free hand.

"That, too."

"I got scared," she admitted. "That weekend we went away, my dad got so mad when he found out. I'd never done anything like that before in my life. Lying, going away with a man. When we got back and he was so disappointed, I couldn't stand it. I would have done anything to make him . . ."

What? Love her again? She'd never thought of it in those terms, but that had been her darkest fear. That he wouldn't love her anymore.

A month ago she would have chided herself that a father's love wasn't so conditional. Now she knew better.

"He grounded me and told me I had to quit the class," she continued. "I guess I could have fought him, but I never considered that a possibility. I stayed in my room for the rest of the summer, then went to UCLA. I told myself I was fine with it."

"Were you?"

"Yes. I have a great life. Okay, make that had. There are challenges. I always thought that if I could walk away from something that it didn't mean enough. Now I'm not so sure."

She put the glass back on the edge of the tub. "You were a part of that," she admitted, staring at his hand and grateful she couldn't see into his eyes. "The dangerous part of who I could become. At first I knew I couldn't go with you because I was too scared, but later I knew you would test me in ways that were terrifying. You would have expectations I could never fulfill."

She touched her fingers to her forehead. "Okay, I'm obviously more drunk than I realized. Where did that come from?"

"You thought I would want you to have all the answers. I just wanted a chance. Or maybe an escape."

She glanced at him over her shoulder. "So we both ran, only I did it standing still."

"Aren't you happy? Not about your dad, but about other stuff?"

She thought about Adam and what had happened with him. Carrie possibly making trouble at work. Her confusing relationship with Leanne.

"I don't know. What about you?"

"I'm not in jail and I haven't killed anybody."

She faced him. "Is either a possibility?"

He shrugged. "Some days it seems like it."

"I don't believe that."

"You don't know me, Megan. It's been ten years. A lot has changed."

"Trying to scare me?"

"It seems like a good idea."

"Why?" Why would he want her nervous around him? As a warning? To keep her from wanting to get close?

Instead of answering, he stood, then pulled her to her feet. They were both naked and dripping, but she didn't care when he drew her close and started kissing her.

She kissed him back, hanging on when he stepped out of the tub. He lifted her onto the tile next to him, wrapped her in a towel, grabbed one for himself, then drew her into the bedroom.

"You're going to silence me with sex?" she asked as he began to rub her body with the soft towel, paying particular attention to her breasts and that heated area between her legs.

"Whatever works."

By eight the next morning, Megan was boneless. She would have to spend the rest of her life in bed, unable to walk or even lift her head, but it had been worth it.

She and Travis had spent the night making love. He'd made her climax a dozen times, sometimes by being inside of her, sometimes with his mouth or his fingers. She'd done the same to him. It was as if they had a lifetime to experience in only a few hours.

Now they lay together, waiting for breakfast to be delivered. She ached in the best way possible.

"I'll probably be dead by noon," she told him, running

her fingers across his chest. "I'll leave a note saying it's not your fault."

"Thanks."

He put his hand over hers. She noticed the burn scar there. "Should I ask?"

"Blowtorch," he told her. "Working with metal. Sometimes I have to learn the hard way."

"The bikes, right?" She sat up and grabbed a robe from the foot of the bed. "You make custom bikes."

"That's the theory."

"Are they like those ones on TV?"

"Sometimes. Mostly I make changes for guys I know. I've built a few and sold them. I can modify a standard bike or build from the ground up."

"Tell me you wear a helmet when you ride."

He tucked her hair behind her ear. "Still a worrier?"

"Still? Was I before?"

Someone knocked at the door.

"Food," she said as she scrambled off the bed. "At last. I'm starving." She waved him back into the bed. "Stay there. I can handle this."

She tightened the robe, then crossed to the door. Before she reached for the handle, she heard a familiar voice say, "Megan? It's Adam."

Thirteen

MEGAN STUMBLED. TRAVIS GOT up to help her, but she wasn't falling. She was just standing. The knock came again.

"Megan? Are you going to let me in?"

A man's voice. Megan turned to face him and the guilt in her eyes told him enough. That while she might not be married, there was a guy. Sure. Because why would someone like her be alone?

He wasn't surprised. Last night had been great. Better than great. But so what? He'd had good sex before and he would again. Not with Megan, but what did that matter?

"You'd better answer that," he said as he collected clothes. "I'll be in the bathroom."

"Travis, I—"

He closed the door behind him.

The mind is a funny thing, he thought as he stared at himself in the mirror. Ten years ago there had been another man in Megan's life. Her father. Two days ago he would have said those memories were long gone and meaningless, but somehow they all came back to him.

The sense of not being enough, the knowing that she would choose someone else over him.

"Bullshit," he told his reflection. He wasn't that kid anymore and Megan was just someone he used to know.

He shrugged out of the robe and reached for his clothes. Voices drifted in to him.

"Adam, what are you doing here?"

"What do you think? Checking on you. Your mother told me where you were, and gave me your room number. I know you need time, but this is ridiculous. You're not answering your phone or returning my calls. Now you're running away."

Note to self, she thought grimly. Don't ever call Tina again. "I'm not running. I'm here with my friends. Besides, you and I aren't together anymore. I don't have to answer to you."

"Megan, we were supposed to get married today."

Travis pulled on his shirt. Married? Was that the engagement that didn't work out? It was a little more recent than she'd let on.

"No, we weren't. The wedding was a mistake and I stopped it."

"What's gotten into you? Why are you acting like this?"

Probably because she has a man in her bathroom, Travis thought. He stepped into his boots and jerked them into place.

Last night had been about forgetting. At least for her. He wasn't sure what it had been for him. A great fuck, maybe. He didn't need it to be more. He felt nothing, except maybe anger. Anger was always safe.

He pulled on his leather jacket and opened the bathroom door. Megan stood in the narrow hallway, by the table where they'd first had sex, looking trapped. He looked past her to the guy standing by the door.

He was blond, older, successful looking. Professional type. Someone an accountant would marry.

Adam looked from Travis to Megan, then said, "I'm not happy, but at least we're even."

Travis ignored him, nodded at Megan, then left. He didn't expect her to come after him and the door stayed shut behind him. The good news was this was Las Vegas, where the bars never closed and no one cared if a guy got drunk at ten in the morning.

"A biker?" Adam asked. "Is that the best you could do?"

"Shut up," Megan snapped, unable to think clearly.

Travis was gone. She told herself that was for the best, that under the circumstances, she needed him to leave, but nothing about this felt right. She was exhausted from being up all night, confused about everything going on in her life and surprised that Adam had bothered to come after her.

"Why are you here?" she asked.

"Why do you think? I want to make things right with you. I was going to apologize again, but now that we're on an even playing field—"

"Oh, right. You don't have to, or so you think. Forget

it, Adam. We will never have an even playing field. You cheated on me for months. You had another relationship while we were engaged. I slept with someone *after* I'd called off the wedding, returned the ring and told you it was over. That is hardly the same."

She tightened the belt of her robe and returned to the bedroom, where the rumpled covers reminded her of all that had happened in the past twelve hours. Adam followed her.

"You're not being reasonable," he said.

"I don't have to be. You cheated. I'm still angry." Angry, but also worried about Travis. Had he already left the hotel? What was he thinking about her? Was he upset?

Stupid question, she thought. He sure wasn't happy. Unless none of this had meant anything to him.

Adam crossed to her and grabbed her arms. "I can smell him on you. Take a shower and we'll go to breakfast. We can talk and figure things out. I don't want to lose you."

A month ago, she would have said she didn't want to be lost. A month ago, she'd thought she would love Adam forever. But now, everything was different. She couldn't imagine being with him again, touching him, marrying him. It was as if he'd become a stranger overnight.

"You've already lost me," she said, wondering why she wasn't more sad. "It's been over for a long time, I just didn't know. I guess I'm not sorry you told me about your affair. It forced me to look at things and see them as they really were. We wouldn't have made it, Adam. You have to see that."

"I don't." He shook her. "What's gotten into you?"

She jerked free. "Stop it. You don't own me. I don't want to be with you. I don't want to marry you or date you. I don't love you, Adam. Not anymore."

He looked stunned. "Just like that? You can't fall out of love that fast. You're just saying this to justify sleeping with that other guy."

"Travis has nothing to do with you and me." She walked past him to the door. "You should go."

He stalked behind her. "I don't accept this. What am I supposed to tell everyone? Do you know how this looks?"

He sounded so much like her mother that she didn't know if she should bolt in terror or start laughing.

"I don't care how it looks," she said, opening the door. "I only care how it is."

As she watched him go, she had the thought that the only other person who could possibly appreciate the irony of the moment was Leanne. For perhaps the first time ever, she wished her sister was with her.

Megan knew she was on borrowed time. So far her friends hadn't said a word. Not through the massages or the pedicures. But when they were finally alone in the relaxation room with plates of organic raw vegetables and mugs of soothing tea, Allegra turned to her.

"Who was he?"

"A complication," Megan said, not sure if she was proud, shocked or a little of both. Talk about stepping out of her comfort zone. "Travis."

Allegra choked on her tea.

"Who?" Payton asked. "I don't know anyone named Travis."

"Are you kidding?" Allegra stared at her, then turned to Payton. "He's an old boyfriend from high school. *The* old boyfriend."

"Interesting," Payton said. "How was it?"

Megan studied her newly painted toes, then sighed. "I don't know. Technically—fabulous. Emotionally—confusing. I'm not the kind of girl who sleeps around."

"It's time you tried something new," Allegra said. "That's what they say in all the magazines."

Payton shook her head. "They're talking about nail polish or shoes. Not a guy." She turned to Megan. "Are you okay?"

"I don't know. I can't stop thinking about Travis. It was magic and amazing and in a lot of ways like we'd never been apart. But I'm not that eighteen-year-old girl anymore and he's different, too."

"Megan's own private bad boy," Allegra said, sounding a little bitter. "He was so hot and totally into her. He was beyond gone. Everyone could see it. She was his princess. I've always said I'll marry the first guy who looks at me the way he looked at Megan."

Megan frowned. "You never told me that."

"I didn't? I've told everyone else. I was so jealous of you back then. Travis was a man in a sea of boys." She grinned at Payton. "He was her first time and apparently the sex was excellent."

"I didn't think that was possible. Not the first time."

"I'm telling you, Travis was special. Isn't he still?"

Megan thought about the Travis she'd known ten years ago. Had he really looked at her the way Allegra said? She'd been wildly in love with him but hadn't been as confident about his feelings for her.

She sipped her tea and did her best to ignore the sense of loss that filled her. It was ten years ago. What did it matter now?

"Megan?" Payton spoke her name. "Was he still special?"

She thought about how he'd held her and the hours they'd talked. "Yes," she murmured.

"I knew it," Allegra moaned. "But did he ever even look at me? Of course not. So how did you end things? Are you going to see him again? Where is he living now?"

Megan looked at her friends. "Things ended badly. Adam showed up."

"What?" the other women said together.

"That bastard," Payton muttered. "Typical that he appears and ruins your good time. What did Travis say?"

"Good-bye. He left. Adam and I had it out. He seems to think we're even now that I've slept with Travis. I told him that didn't matter. That I just wanted him gone. We're done. I can see that. I don't love him and I'm not sure what I ever saw in him." She shook her head. "How did this all happen? How did I get so messed up?"

Allegra grabbed her hand. "You're dealing. There's a ton of crap going on with your dad and Adam and everything else and you're dealing. Don't beat yourself up over this. It'll work out."

Would it? She wasn't sure how. Even if her dad came around, how could she ever trust him again? And what about Travis? He was back in L.A. but would he want to see her again? What had last night been to him and what did she want it to be to her?

Travis pulled into the familiar long driveway. The old house looked more run-down than he remembered. The fence had fallen, leaving only a few weathered posts to mark where it had once stood. The window by the front door was cracked and the cement stairs had crumbled at the corners.

He parked and climbed out, refusing to feel guilty for leaving his mother with all this. The last time he'd seen her, she'd been furious that he'd insisted she call the cops on his old man. She'd chosen and it hadn't been him.

A curtain moved, as if someone had been watching for him, then the front door opened and his mother stepped out onto the small porch.

"You came," she said, folding her arms over her chest. "I wasn't sure you would."

She looked the same, but a little older, a little smaller. There was gray in her dark hair and more wrinkles around her eyes. When he'd been little, he'd loved her more than anything in the world. But as he'd gotten older, he'd learned that given the choice, she would always run back to the man who beat her. The man who made her life a living hell. It didn't matter how much Burt hurt her, how often he left her broken and bleeding. She would love him forever and no one else really mattered.

"I'm here," he said.

"How was the drive?"

"Good."

"I missed you," she said, surprising the hell out of him. "I'm sorry you went away."

He wanted to believe her but wasn't sure he could. Still, when she walked down the stairs and moved toward him, he hugged her. She felt tiny and frail.

"Oh, Travis, it's been so hard, with you and your father both gone."

Meaning what? That either of them would have done? Or any man to help with things?

This was his mother—he shouldn't be cynical. But he wasn't willing to trust her. Not right away. Still, he went with her into the house, which was just as battered on the inside.

"I've washed your sheets," she said as she hurried into the kitchen to pour him a cup of coffee. "I didn't touch anything else. I left your room like it was before."

"That wasn't necessary, Mom," he told her, accepting the mug.

"I want you to feel welcome."

"Tell me about the business."

She fussed with a plate of cookies, rearranging them over and over. "There's not much to tell. Money's tight. There always seems to be enough work, but the bills are harder to pay. I can't keep track of it anymore. I've all the orders there." She pointed to a stack of folders on the table. "You can go to the office whenever you want and check the books. I don't know what's wrong."

She sighed and put down the cookies. "I want to sell, Travis. I need to. I've been . . . sick for a while. I'm fine," she added before he could ask. "But I'm too old to be running this business. I need your help. This is all I have."

Sick? How sick? Did he want to know? "I'll take care of things," he told her. "We'll get the business fixed and then you can find a buyer."

She smiled. "Thank you. I didn't know what I was going to do."

The room seemed too small. He set down his coffee. "I'll go grab my stuff and unpack," he told her. "Then I'll go to the office and see what's going on there."

She nodded. "Do you want . . ." She hesitated. "Do you want to go see your father later this week?"

"No." If he got his way, he'd never see the old man again.

"Travis." His mother sounded reproachful.

"No," he repeated. "This isn't about him. This is about me helping you. That has to be enough."

She nodded and seemed to shrink a little, which made him feel like crap.

He ignored the guilt and left the kitchen. After picking up his duffel and a second bag with the rest of his stuff, he returned to the house and made his way to the back bedroom, where he'd grown up.

She wasn't kidding, he thought as he stared at the room. She hadn't touched anything.

There were still posters of girls on motorcycles taped to the wall, a few books, an old board game and an ancient-looking computer. Most of his old clothes still hung in the closet.

He dumped the contents of a couple of drawers onto the closet floor and shoved his stuff into them before slamming them shut.

What the hell had he been thinking, coming back here? It was like reentering a nightmare. He didn't belong here—this wasn't his life. So what if his mother needed him? He could turn his back on her.

Except he couldn't. No matter what he said or how he complained, he couldn't. So he was stuck.

He walked over to the desk and stared at the bulletin board. A piece of pink paper caught his eye. He pulled it off the board and stared at the handwriting.

It was a note from Megan. Nothing significant, just something she wrote. But he'd saved it because it was from her and back then he couldn't believe he'd gotten lucky enough to find someone like her. That wasn't supposed to happen to guys like him.

And last night? Had she used him to make a point, to heal a broken heart or just to get laid? Her motivation didn't matter. It was over now and he wasn't going back. If he couldn't stop thinking about her, he had only himself to blame.

Megan walked into her mother's house. "It's me," she called.

An unintelligible response came from the back of the house.

Bracing herself for what was likely to be an award-winning scene, Megan walked down the long, dark hallway and pushed open her mother's bedroom door.

Tina lay in bed, a washcloth across her eyes. There were dozens of over-the-counter medicines on the nightstand, the TV was playing with the sound off and the scent of VapoRub filled the room.

Her mother held up her hand. "Can you get me some tea?" she whispered, her fingers with their perfect manicure fluttering. "I haven't had anything to eat or drink in nearly two days. I'm just so weak."

Megan walked into the bathroom, where she saw a Taco Bell bag crunched up in the small trash can, then returned to the bedroom.

"I'm here to talk about Elliott," Megan told her.

"I can't," Tina said with a moan. "It's been so horrible. Do you know what I've been through? All those calls. All those people wanting to know why you broke off the wedding. I didn't know what to tell them." She removed the washcloth and dabbed at her eyes. "They're saying I'm a bad mother. That this is my fault."

Megan crossed her arms over her chest. "I doubt that. I'm sure you've explained that this is all my fault. That I wasn't willing to overlook Adam's cheating." After all, her mother had also been unfaithful. She was unlikely to believe fooling around was a serious problem.

Her mother sat up and glared at her. "I don't appreciate your attitude. You took off with your friends and left me with a mess."

"How did I do that? Everyone on the guest list had been personally notified the wedding was canceled." At least her half of the list had been. She didn't take responsibility for Adam's friends and family.

"That doesn't mean people didn't call, wanting to know what happened."

"The only people who would have called you were your friends, Mom, and you would have talked to them anyway."

"There were questions. I can't imagine what they're thinking about us now. About how we raised you."

"Maybe that I made a smart choice, breaking things off before the marriage rather than after."

"So you're only going to think about yourself," her mother said. "That is just so typical. You have no idea what I suffer. What about the other calls?"

"Which ones? Everything else was canceled. The florist, the caterer, the DJ. All of it."

"Which sounds just so perfect, but did it ever occur to you that it all has to be paid for? You canceled too late for us not to have to pay for it all, let alone get our deposits back. Those are the calls I'm talking about. The ones telling us how much they're putting on our various credit cards. It's over forty thousand dollars, Megan. Did you think about that when you had your little temper tantrum with Adam?"

She hadn't, Megan admitted to herself. But the point

of no return on the deposits and payment had been crossed weeks ago.

Forty thousand dollars. Ironically, the wedding had been as much the one her mother had wanted as her own. Not that it made any difference. The decision to cancel had been hers.

"I'll pay you back," she said.

Her mother collapsed back onto her pillows and covered her eyes with her washcloths. "Oh, please. As if that will ever happen."

"I mean it. I'll pay you back." Or at least her father, as he would be the one paying the bills. "How much is it exactly?"

"There's a paper on the dresser with all the totals." Her mother pulled off the cloth. "You'll be using your inheritance, I suppose. The money Elliott left to you. I'm not sure why he didn't leave me anything. I'm the one who raised you while he got to walk away and enjoy his life."

"Thanks, Mom, for the endorsement," Megan muttered. "No, I won't be using that money." She didn't like to think about it. "I'll pay you out of my savings." She grabbed the sheet and winced at the total. It was nearly forty-two thousand dollars. Pretty much every penny she had.

"With your father leaving me, I'm going to need someone to support me," Tina told her. "It's your fault he left, so I'm now your responsibility. The house is paid for but there's maintenance, food. Your father is keeping me on his insurance for now, but how long will that last . . ." She wiped at a tear. "I'm destitute. Dependent on the kindness of strangers. That inheritance could cover things for a long time. You could at least leave a few hundred dollars to see me through."

"I don't think so," Megan said. She waved the invoice. "I'll get a check to Dad tomorrow. See you later."

Her mother reached for her. "I still need you to get me some tea. And maybe something to eat. Nothing too heavy. I couldn't manage."

"I don't think so."

"Megan, you can't go."

Her mother collapsed, unmoving, except for the hand clutching at her chest. Megan walked away without looking back.

Fourteen

AS MEGAN WALKED TOWARD her father's office, she wondered what it would have been like to be raised by someone normal. She'd always assumed that despite her mother's insanity, she would have her dad's stabilizing influence to make everything right. Maybe at twenty-eight she shouldn't care that he was no longer a part of her life, but she couldn't seem to let it go.

She went inside and walked back to his office. His assistant was gone and his door stood open, so she let herself inside.

He sat at his computer, looking just like he always did. For a second she imagined he would glance up, see her and then smile the way he had nearly ever other time she'd come to his office. A bright, happy smile that made her believe she was the light of his life. He'd always acted like that—how could it all be different now?

She knocked on the open door and walked in. "Hi, Dad," she said, determined to sound friendly and cheerful. "How's it going?"

He barely looked up. "I'm busy, Megan. This isn't a good time."

Cold words that cut through her and made it hurt to breathe. But she wasn't going to let him win this time.

"Ask me if I care," she said, standing in front of him. When he refused to look up, she reached down and pulled the plug on his monitor.

"I was supposed to get married on Saturday," she said. "Do you remember that?"

"Of course I remember," he snapped, still not looking at her. Things had to be bad if he would rather stare at a blank screen.

"Don't you want to know why I canceled the wedding?"

"Your mother said you had a change of heart."

"Adam cheated on me, Dad. He took some nineteen-year-old bimbo to Hawaii. I was devastated."

She paused, waiting. There it was. Her final card—her last play of the game. If that didn't get a reaction, nothing would.

Please, please respond, she thought, desperate for him to turn to her, to swear at Adam, to show that he cared even a little.

"I'm sorry to hear that."

She'd heard the phrase "weight of the world" all her life, but she'd never gotten it until that moment. Until it felt like thousands of pounds sat on her shoulders, pushing her down, grinding her into the floor.

"That's it? That's all you have to say?"

He finally looked at her. "What more do you want from me?"

"Gee, I don't know. How about a little sympathy? You were my father for twenty-eight years. I would think something lingered. A hint of affection."

He turned away. "There's a lot going on."

"You're right, and not just with you. How do I get through to you? How do I make you understand what you're doing to me? Or do you know and not care? Is that it? One second I'm your kid and the next I'm just someone you used to know? That's not right. Who does that?"

"Megan, I don't know what you want from me."

"My father!" she yelled. "I want my father back. I want to talk to you about everything going on. I want it fixed."

"There's nothing to fix," he said, coming to his feet. "Nothing is the way I thought, including you. We're not going back. Don't you get that? Stop asking. You're Tina's daughter, not mine."

She refused to cry. Megan told herself a breakdown was just a short walk away, but while she was here, she would stay strong. She owed herself that.

"Thanks for making that clear," she said, pleased her voice wasn't shaking. Her throat was raw, her hands trembled, but she wouldn't cry. "Here."

She put the check on the desk.

"I know that you're going to get stuck for the wedding costs, what with me canceling so late. So I wanted to give you this." She pushed the check toward him. "I have an itemized list, so this should cover everything. If it's not enough, let me know." She could always get a cash advance on one of the credit cards.

He said nothing.

The last of her hope died.

There weren't any words. She saw that now. There was no way to convince him, no way to make him . . . what? Still love her? Had she ever been anything to him but a walking, breathing DNA sample?

"Good-bye, Gary," she said, and left.

Thirty minutes later, she was in the women's bathroom at her office, struggling for control. Coming back to work might have been a mistake. She felt frail and vulnerable, not to mention emotionally exposed. The need to bolt only increased when Felicia, her boss, walked in.

"You're looking battered," the other woman said. Despite the words, her tone was kind. "The gossip getting to you?"

Megan hadn't actually noticed it. She supposed that people stopped talking about her canceled wedding whenever she walked into the room. Right now the problem with her father seemed much more important. But as she didn't want to discuss that particular disaster with her boss, she nodded.

"It's tough to know everyone is speculating."

"There'll be something new and exciting to talk about next week," Felicia told her. "Are you sure you don't want to take a few days off?"

"Right now working really helps. If I need some time, though—"

Felicia held up her hand. Diamonds sparkled. "Just say the word. You have plenty on the books. Even if you didn't, it wouldn't be a problem. You're an asset to this company, Megan. Let us know if we can do anything to help you through this difficult time."

"I appreciate that."

Megan washed her hands, then left. No matter how awful everything else got, she had her career. At least that was one place in her life where she didn't have to worry about taking a fall.

Leanne felt like she was going to throw up. If it was the stomach flu, she wouldn't object. There was nothing like a four- or five-day run of it to take off a few pounds. But as she was seconds away from her final callback audition, she had a feeling she was suffering from a serious case of nerves.

This was it—she knew that. The make-or-break moment of her career. She'd passed round one already. Now she was on the verge. She was going to give the performance of her life and she was going to get the part based on sheer talent.

She took a deep breath and faced the five men at the other end of the room.

"I'm ready," she said.

Instantly lights snapped on. The audition would be filmed so they could see how she looked on camera. In a way, it was good news. With the lights on, she couldn't see any of them watching her. She could pretend they weren't there . . . except for Connor McKay. He stood in the corner and she could feel his gaze on her.

Let it go, she told herself as she faced the production assistant who would be reading the lines with her.

"They're coming with me," the PA said in a bored voice.

Leanne ignored the tone and concentrated on the words, on the meaning. He was threatening to take away the only family she had left. The only family she'd known since she was a child.

She tossed her hair back and stared into his disinterested eyes. "I don't think so," she said quietly. "You can try. Give it your best shot. But know this—I'll fight you. I'll fight you in ways that will leave you bleeding in the dark."

"What good will you be to them dead?" The PA practically snapped his gum as he spoke.

"I'm not the one who's going to die." She moved around him, circling him, sizing him up, like a cat stalking prey. "You think this is going to be easy. You don't know me and that was your first mistake. Your second was walking in here. This is my territory and I protect it with everything I have."

She bent down and, in a lightning-fast move, pulled a knife out of her boot. It was a prop, plastic, but the PA didn't know that. She moved behind him, wrapped her arm around his neck and put the knife against the base of his chin.

He gasped and squirmed, but in her high-heeled boots, she was about his height. She held on and didn't let him get away.

"I can't wait to feel your blood on my skin, you lying

bastard. I'm going to put your head on a stick and leave it out for the crows. You'll get in death what you gave everyone else in life."

She raised her knee and put it in the small of the PA's back, then shoved, pushing him away. The pages scattered as he stumbled. He turned on her.

"Hey, what do you think you're doing?"

Leanne smiled. "Acting."

"Gerald, back in place," a voice from beyond the lights said. "Leanne, we're going to the second scene."

Leanne nodded, then turned her back on them. The transition from anger to grief was tough, but she forced herself to concentrate.

"Any time," another voice said, sounding bored.

She ignored it and thought about how she would feel if her dreams were taken from her. If she'd made a series of lousy choices only to end up with nothing. What if it was too late? What if she couldn't do it?

She felt tears fill her eyes, then she spun toward the lights. The PA stood there, looking wary.

"It's not that I care about myself," she said, her voice thick with emotion. She felt the moisture on her cheeks. "It's that I won't see you again. I always thought we'd have more time. I wanted to get to know you enough to find you annoying."

"Val, don't talk like that," the PA said, watching her cautiously, as if expecting her to spring on him. "It's not too late."

"You were always a bad liar, Joe. It's been too late ever since we met."

"You know I love you."

"I know."

"I probably would have annoyed the hell out of you."

A few more tears fell. She managed a shaky smile. "I know that, too." She sank to the floor and closed her eyes. She'd always hated those endless death scenes, so she went for simple and to the point.

"Cut!" someone yelled and the bright lights went off.

Leanne sat up, then took her time getting to her feet. She felt good about her work—she'd done the best she could. If they didn't want her, she had nothing to be sorry for. And the rest of the pep talk could wait until she was alone in her car.

The men behind the long table huddled together in a conference. The PA had escaped to the far side of the room, eyeing her as if he expected her to attack. At least she'd scared him. That was something.

"Ms. Greene?" The director nodded. "Well done. We'll be calling your agent to discuss things. Tell her to expect to hear from us this afternoon."

There was only one reason for them to want to talk to her agent. One very good reason. She used every skill she'd ever learned to keep from shrieking with excitement. She allowed herself a small smile.

"Thank you. I hope I get a chance to work on the project."

She crossed the room to collect her purse. She knew she was walking because her boots clicked on the floor, but she felt as if she were floating.

She got it! She'd nailed it and she got it! Sure, the part

was small, but it was important and the movie would be huge and this was her shot. She knew that. Everything was going to be different now.

She stepped into the hallway.

"Leanne."

She didn't have to turn to know who was calling her name. She recognized the deep voice, the faint British accent. Bracing herself, she turned and faced Connor McKay.

"Impressive," he said, moving toward her. "The transition from anger to sadness and pain is difficult. You managed beautifully." One eyebrow rose. "Frightening the PA was a nice touch."

"I know it was probably wrong, but he couldn't have been less engaged in the audition. He gave me nothing to work with. I figured he earned a little terror."

Connor didn't say anything. Instead he stared at her, his dark blue eyes seeming to draw her to him. She felt tingles all through her body and they had nothing to do with the recent audition.

"We'll be working together," he said quietly. "I'll be doing any rewrites on location."

And his point would be?

"You're far too young," he added.

What? If she didn't know any better, she would think he was talking about getting involved. "It beats being too old."

His mouth twitched as if he were fighting a smile. "I don't date actresses. They're too emotional and interested in the limelight."

So he was talking about them. He felt it, too. The connection. "I don't date writers. They're egotistical, narcissistic and incapable of listening to a conversation without wanting to rewrite the dialogue."

"Nothing will ever come of this."

Which would be fascinating, if she knew what "this" was. She feigned boredom. "Your point is?"

"I don't have one."

That's not what the predatory gleam in his eye told her.

Three weeks ago, she would have jumped into bed with Connor in a heartbeat. Sleeping with him could be a real boost to her career. But she wasn't going to be that person anymore.

"I'm not interested in playing around," she told him. "I want to fall in love. I want magic and romance and stars in my eyes." She drew in a breath. "Which probably sounds foolish to you."

"It sounds impossible. Apparently we have nothing in common."

"Nothing at all."

"Then there isn't a problem."

"I agree."

He walked away.

She watched him go. The regret pierced her but she ignored the pain. Whatever she felt now was nothing compared with the pain she would suffer by making the wrong choice about a man.

Which only made her want to bang her head against the wall when her cell phone rang and she grabbed for it, desperately hoping it was Connor calling to agree to her terms.

"Hello?"

"Leanne, it's your father."

She walked to her car and got inside. "Hi, Dad. What's up?" It had to be her mother. There was no other reason that her father ever called.

"I was wondering what you were doing this Sunday. I thought you might like to join me for brunch."

If she'd been standing, she would have fallen. Brunch? That was his thing with Megan. Only nothing was right between him and Megan. So he was asking her instead. Why? To punish Megan? To claim the only child he had left?

She told herself she was mature enough not to want to get involved in whatever his game was. She reminded herself that her father had ignored her most of her life, that she had always desperately longed to have the attention of the only "good" parent she had. If she gave in now, wasn't she sending the wrong message?

"Leanne?"

"I'm here." She closed her eyes and grimaced. "Sure, Dad. I'd love to have brunch with you. When and where?"

After she hung up she groaned. What was wrong with her? What happened to being strong?

"I used it up on Connor," she muttered to herself, then picked up her phone again. She used speed dial.

"Megan Greene."

"Hi, it's me," Leanne said, going for a cheerful tone

that would hide the guilt. "Want some more help tonight with those wedding presents?"

Megan sighed. "Are you serious? I'd love help, but I hate to impose."

"Hey, I'm your sister. Impose away. Then we'll get drunk and pull each other's hair. I'll be there at, what? Six?"

"Make it seven. I have a couple of reports I have to finish."

"I'll bring Chinese."

Megan passed her sister the pot stickers. So far they'd talked about Leanne's great audition, how things were at Megan's work and the pleasant weather. Apparently Leanne was going to avoid mentioning anything unpleasant this evening, which Megan appreciated, but it wasn't necessary.

"Remember Travis Hunter?" she asked.

Leanne leaned back against the sofa and sighed. "In every detail. I had such a crush on him. He was so gorgeous. That long hair. The earring. I used to dream that he would dump you and take me away on the back of his bike." Leanne look a bite of dumpling. "You were such an idiot for not running off with him when you had the chance."

Megan reached for her wine. "Okay, tell me what you *really* think."

"Sorry. It's the wine. And that I'm happy about my new job. I'm going to be in a movie!" She waved her bare feet in the air, then set them on the carpet, straightened and grinned. "I'm done. As for Travis, he was totally hot."

"He still is."

Leanne stared at her. "You've seen him?"

"Last weekend. In Las Vegas. We ran into each other."

Leanne shook her head. "Do not tell me he's gained fifty pounds and lost his hair. I beg you. Some memories should stay perfect."

"He's better than he was. Just as sexy and good looking."

Leanne whimpered. "Does he still have the earring?"

"And a scar."

"Was the sex spectacular?"

Megan poked at her plate, avoiding her sister's gaze. "Why would you think we had sex?"

"You'd just broken up with Adam. You were in Las Vegas the weekend you were supposed to get married. You said he's still amazing. Why wouldn't you have sex?"

Megan wondered if she spent too much time making her life complicated. She grinned. "It was the best fifteen hours of my life."

"I'm so jealous. Are you going to see him again?"

Megan's smile faded. "I doubt it. Adam showed up in my room. Travis got dressed and left without saying anything."

"Did he know who Adam was?"

"That he was my ex-fiancé and the guy I was supposed to be marrying that day?" She sighed. "Oh, yeah. That part was very clear."

"Then you can't expect him to stick around. He was giving you a break."

"He was pissed."

"Which makes sense. But all is not lost. Do you know where he is? Can you call him? Beg? Travis looks like the type who would respond to begging."

Megan appreciated the humor even if it didn't make her feel better. She'd thought about calling Travis, but she wasn't sure what to say.

"We just ran into each other. It was one of those things. Why would I call him?"

"Because it was the best sex of your life?" Leanne dug her fork into her chow mein. "Where's the bad in pursuing that?"

"This isn't a good time for me."

"Then can I have his number?"

Megan smiled. "No."

"So you don't want him and you don't want anyone else to have him."

"Exactly."

"Just so we're clear. What's he doing these days?"

"Building custom motorcycles."

"Sounds yummy."

"But not simple." Megan put down her plate. "Everything is so confusing. Yes, it was great to see Travis and I wouldn't mind seeing him again, but there's so much to explain. Adam, for one thing. Plus, there's too much going on. The breakup. Dad." She looked at Leanne. "I went to see Mom when I got back."

"Your first mistake," her sister said. "What happened?"

"The usual. She swore she hadn't eaten in days, but there were fast food wrappers in the trash. She was bugging me about canceling the wedding, saying she'd been getting calls. Then she brought up how much the wedding had cost. I'd canceled too late for them to not have to pay. It was over forty thousand dollars."

Leanne winced. "Okay, that's unfortunate, but it's not your fault. Would they have preferred you to just marry Adam, knowing it was wrong?"

"Mom would have and I don't know what Dad's thinking right now. I . . ." She felt her throat tighten. "I wrote him a check to cover the cost of the wedding. It took every penny I had, but I did it. I took it over to him. I wanted to just talk, but he wouldn't. He barely looked at me."

She blinked rapidly, doing her best not to cry. There had been too many tears. "He took the check and when I looked online this morning, I saw he'd cashed it. He took the money. He never would have done that before. He would have starved before taking anything from me, you know?"

Leanne put her plate on the coffee table. "I know. I'm sorry."

"I'm not saying I don't have a responsibility for the wedding. Of course I do, but this isn't about the money."

Leanne cleared her throat. "I wasn't sure if I should tell you or not, but he called and asked me to brunch."

Brunch? That was Megan's private time with her father. The pain in her stomach sharpened.

Her first instinct was to tell her sister she couldn't go.

That their father wasn't allowed to replace her. Except she knew it was wrong and even if it wasn't, she didn't have the right. This was her sister's life, her sister's father. Because Gary wasn't her father anymore. Not biologically and obviously not in his heart.

"Why don't *you* go?" Leanne asked quietly. "You can just show up. It's a public place. He'll have to talk to you. Maybe you can get things straightened out."

If only it were that simple. "There's no point. I tried to force things in his office. He's done with me." She touched her sister's arm. "Go. You've always wanted a relationship with him. What happened with me has nothing to do with you."

Leanne wrinkled her nose. "I don't know if I believe that. Before, he couldn't be bothered with me. Now he's ignoring you. I would say we've both learned a lot about who he really is, and none of it is good."

"He's still your father. Go to brunch."

Leanne nodded. "I just feel bad."

"You don't have to. I'll figure it out. Maybe I should try to find out something about Elliott Scott. Maybe that would give me answers. Or at least be a distraction."

"How would you do that?"

"Talk to the lawyer who came to see me. I still have his card somewhere."

Leanne stood up and pulled Megan to her feet. "If it feels right, do it. Plus, just think how it will annoy Mom."

Megan laughed. "Good point."

Leanne headed for the stairs. "I'll go grab some boxes

so we can start on the packing. Then I'll take what we finish tonight to the post office tomorrow."

Megan glanced at her sister's barely touched plate. "That's all you're eating?"

Leanne grinned. "I'm a movie star now, remember? I have to stay skinny for my part."

Leanne disappeared onto the landing. Megan sat back down on the sofa and picked at her dinner. She wasn't hungry, either, but it had nothing to do with being famous. Her stomach hadn't felt right for weeks now. Probably not a surprise. Things would get better, she told herself. Or at least settle down.

Leanne returned with several empty boxes and a stack of drawings.

"I pried," her sister said cheerfully. "The top was off one of the bins, so I looked inside. Are you doing anything with these?"

Megan barely glanced at the papers. "Maybe. I'm going to have a lot more free time these days, what with being single. I've missed sewing."

"Make a dress for Allegra to wear to an opening. That would make a splash." Leanne dumped the boxes and held up a drawing of a cocktail dress. "Something like this. What color?"

Megan glanced at it. "Red. Blood red."

"Perfect." Leanne waved the drawing. "Say you'll do it. What have you got to lose?"

"These days? Not a whole lot."

Fifteen

TRAVIS CHECKED THE LOAD in the truck against the list on his clipboard. "That's it," he yelled. "Head out."

Shawn climbed into the truck and started the engine. The guy grumbled something Travis couldn't hear, which was probably for the best. He'd only been running his mother's business a couple of weeks now. It seemed early to start firing people, but Shawn was at the top of his list.

The place was in worse shape than he'd thought. Bids were badly done, if done at all. No one followed up on payments, and customers changed their minds and weren't charged for the extra work. The teams straggled in over a two-hour period, were slow getting out and early getting back, and somewhere in the middle of all this, someone was stealing a hell of a lot of money.

He'd been over all the invoices and payments for the past six months and nothing added up. They were hemorrhaging money for supplies without references to the different jobs. Now he was going to have to find out who was responsible for what was going on. He had a bad feeling it was an organized attempt to take as much as possible.

"We're all going to the fights tonight," Artie said, following Travis back into the small office. "You should come. You could get to know all the guys here. Be a friend rather than the boss."

"I'm not interested in being anyone's friend," Travis told him.

"Since when? Don't forget, I've known you since you were ten years old, Travis. You don't scare me."

Travis looked at the lined older man standing in front of him. "Artie, someone here is screwing with my mom's business. I'm going to find out who it is and I'm going to put their ass in jail for a long time. Nothing's right. Guys are working five-hour days and charging the company for eight. Equipment isn't being maintained. I get that taking an extra fifteen at lunch once in a while is okay, but this is a whole lot more than that."

Artie shifted uncomfortably. "Maybe a few of the boys got a little out of hand, but they're good people."

"You want to tell me what's going on? Save me the time of investigating?"

"I don't know what you're talking about."

Travis wasn't surprised. Artie either made sure he wasn't aware of what was going on, or he didn't want to rat on a friend. For all Travis knew, he was the one behind it all, although he hoped that wasn't true. Artie had stepped in to be a father to Travis when Burt Hunter had been too drunk to bother.

"No one steals from me and mine," Travis told the

other man. "Whoever did this thinks he covered his tracks, but I'll find what I need. If he comes to me with a full accounting and a way to pay it all back, I might be willing to listen. Otherwise, he's going down, as is anyone who's helping him."

"Sure thing, boss," Artie said as he backed out of the office.

Travis sank onto the wooden chair and turned his attention to the computer. His words about finding the thief were basically cheap talk. He didn't have a clue where to start.

He spent the morning doing paperwork, then got too restless to stay inside. It was raining in L.A., an event so unusual that it would be the lead story on the news that night. With the slick roads, he didn't want to go for a ride. Not when every resident was freaked about the weather. Instead he walked to the empty shed he'd taken over and started to work on one of his bikes.

Fifteen minutes later he had his blowtorch going and felt some of his tension ease away. Heat built in the small room, but he ignored it and the sweat dripping off him. Bending metal to suit his will was a hell of a good way to deal with stress.

He stopped, his arms trembling with exhaustion. After pulling off his gloves, he stripped his shirt off and draped it over a chair, then debated when he should go home and shower.

"Hello, Travis."

The familiar voice hit him below the belt, reminding him that some problems were easier to solve than others.

He glanced up and saw Megan standing at the door.
"You lost?" he asked.

She hovered in the doorway, apparently unable to look at him. If he were any kind of gentleman, he would have put on his shirt again. But he was no gentleman.

"I wanted to see you. How are you?"

One part ready to run for the hills and two parts ready to have sex with her right there on the concrete floor.

She looked good—too good. All clean and conservative, with her hair pulled back and a dark green suit covering her from neck to knees. It was the buttons on her jacket that really got to him. It made him want to pull out a knife and cut them off one by one so she couldn't do them up again. That would keep her from pretending she was so civilized. He knew better.

"What do you want?" he asked, going for rude because that was better than sounding horny. Her perfume filled the small space, imprinting itself on his brain.

"To see you," she said, her green eyes meeting his. "To apologize for what happened in Las Vegas."

"You know what they say. What happens there stays and all that."

"I'm sorry I put you in that position. I'm sorry I wasn't honest about my engagement. You didn't deserve to get dragged into that."

Good manners finally forced him to grab his shirt and slip it on, although he didn't button it.

"I'm happy to help you get back at your future husband."

She stiffened slightly. "I'm not marrying Adam. I

ended things the week before the wedding, which I also canceled before I left for Las Vegas. I don't know why I even got engaged to him in the first place. Actually, that's not true. I know why, but it was all wrong from the start. I never meant for you to get in the middle of things. I didn't mean to . . ."

"Use me?" he asked, then wanted to call back the words. They implied he'd been bothered by what she'd done and he wasn't. What did he care about Megan Greene?

She flinched. "It wasn't like that."

"It was exactly like that. Why are you here, Megan? You've said you're sorry. Great. Now go back to where you belong."

She raised her chin. "I will, but first, I want to talk to you. We used to be friends. That meant something to me. I'd like us to be friends again."

His temper burned. Once again he found comfort in the anger. "I don't think so, Megan. We were never friends. We dated and I loved you, but that's not being friends. Adam's what? A lawyer? Doctor?"

She glanced down, then back at him. "Cardiologist."

"Sure. Makes sense. I'm just some blue-collar guy who works with dirt and plants and builds motorcycles on the side. I'm not interested in driving a BMW, wearing a suit or spending two hundred dollars on a bottle of wine. My life is simple. Being in jail taught me that's the best thing for me. No complications."

She frowned. "Jail? Travis, that was years ago. You were a kid."

"The first time, babe. Not the second." He touched his scar. "That guy with the kid? They charged me with assault for attacking him. The kid was their main witness. I served sixteen months. No good deed goes unpunished, right?"

He refused to think about that time again. It had been a hard-won lesson, but he'd learned it. Keep it simple—that was how he lived his life. No roots, no ties, no complications. No beautiful redheads in suits. No women with big eyes and ways to drive him wild in bed.

"I'm not who you think," he told her. "I'm just like my old man—a waste of space. The difference is I *try* to be different. But there are days when the darkness inside wins, and trust me, Megan, you don't want me around then. I'm not anyone you want to be with. So get your good-girl ass back to the west side where it belongs."

He pushed past her, ignoring the heat of her body against his, the sound of her gasp, the way he wanted to pull her against him and kiss her until they both forgot who they were.

Instead he walked away, heading for the supply barn. As he walked, a part of him hoped. Hoped she would ignore what he'd told her and come after him. Hoped she would try to convince him they could work it out. It wouldn't take much, he admitted to himself, not that she knew that.

But she didn't. There was only silence and the reminder that he should be more careful about asking for what he wanted. Too often he got it.

*   *   *

Two days later, Megan typed in the entry and watched as the balance sheet adjusted. "It's here," she said, pointing to the third entry.

"It's the depreciation."

Payton groaned. "I should have caught that. Where is my brain?"

"Depreciation can be tricky. I only knew where to look because I had the same problem a couple of months ago. It took me hours to find and then I wanted to slap myself for missing it in the first place. It happens."

"Knock, knock." Carrie smiled as she walked into the office. "Hope I'm not interrupting the girl talk."

Megan tried to ignore the surge of irritation. "Not girl talk. We're working on a balance sheet. What can I do for you?"

Carrie waved the paper in her hands. "I have a question about a time sheet you did for Wayward Productions. There's some kind of mistake. I had to check it because of a question from billing. You've charged them for times you weren't in the office. One of the days, you show three billable hours while you and I were in a meeting for something completely different."

Carrie set the paper on Megan's desk. "I know it's important to cough up the hours for the partners, but I don't think this is a good way to do it."

Megan stared at the copy of the time sheet, unable to believe what the other woman was saying.

"I have never charged a client for hours I didn't work," she said, shocked and furious at the accusation. "I would certainly not charge them for time I spent in a meeting that was not directly about them." She rose. "I don't know what the problem is; however, I will find out and I will fix it." She narrowed her gaze. "My reputation here has never been questioned, Carrie."

Meaning, *Don't try to screw me, bitch, because I'll take you down.*

Carrie only gave her another smile. "You've been under a lot of stress lately. We all know that. Mistakes happen."

"Not like that and not to me." Megan picked up the paper and stared at it. "I'll need to compare this with my original time card. Who were you speaking with in billing?"

"Melissa." Carrie started to leave, then turned back. "Under the circumstances, I felt it necessary to bring this up with one of the partners."

"Good. Now you've saved me the effort of reporting it myself."

Carrie waved her fingers, then left. Megan waited until she left, then walked around her desk and closed the door.

"That bitch!" Payton said the second the door clicked shut. "I can't believe it. Tell me you have copies of your original time cards."

"Both here and at home." Megan stared at the paper. "I'm speechless. Who would have done this? Who would have adjusted my time card?"

"I'll give you one guess."

"She can't have done it. She's not that stupid. What if she'd been caught? But it's bold. I'll give her that. If

I didn't have the backup material to protect myself, I could be facing fraud charges. For something like that, the partners would call in the police." She went cold at the thought.

"Be careful," Payton warned her. "The partners don't seem to see her for who she really is, although most of the associates are clear. There are only going to be a couple of promotions. Obviously Carrie wants to make sure she gets one and you don't."

"I know," Megan murmured, thinking she would have to watch her back. Currently, her career was all she had.

"How did I let you talk me into this?" Megan asked as she and Leanne walked into the hotel ballroom. "What was I thinking?"

"That you look fabulous and you should share yourself with the world."

Megan thought about all the craziness in her life. She couldn't stop thinking about Travis and how he'd totally rejected her. There was the Carrie problem at work, not to mention the possibility she'd spent her whole life being wrong about the man she'd always thought of as her father. Oh, and Adam had been cheating on her. Other than that? No worries.

"I'm not feeling especially fabulous," Megan admitted.

"You will." Leanne patted her arm. "This is a local charity fund-raiser. There will be plenty of rich, single guys here. You can find one and be distracted."

"Is that why you're here?"

Leanne laughed. "I'm here because I saw this blue cocktail dress in your closet and I wanted an excuse to wear it."

Megan glanced at the dress she'd designed and made the previous year and had never worn. "It looks better on you than it would on me. I don't like that."

"Get over it and walk this way. I happen to know there's champagne around here somewhere."

The Santa Monica hotel was bathed in white twinkle lights. Well-dressed people circulated and chatted. Tables lined the room, offering items for a silent auction. Megan wasn't overly enthused about being here, but her sister was right. She needed to get out. Maybe she could bid on an afternoon at a day spa and pamper herself. She had to do something to break out of her funk.

"There," Leanne said, waving down a waiter and grabbing two glasses of champagne. "I drove so you can drink to your heart's content. Liquor always helps."

It couldn't hurt, Megan thought. She took a sip, turned and nearly choked when she saw Travis across the room.

He looked amazing. Better than that, he looked dark and sexy and five kinds of dangerous.

He wore a black suit with a white shirt, but no tie. His earring glinted, his eyes smoldered and she could feel the heat from fifty feet away.

She told herself to look away, not to risk letting him know how much she wanted to move closer, talk and touch and somehow be healed just by being around him. Where was her instinct for self-preservation?

She braced herself for a sneer and dismissal, but he kept looking. The room seemed to go silent, but that might have been just her. His gaze dropped to her mouth and she would have sworn she could actually feel the brush of his lips against her. She wished he would look other places.

"Oh, my," Leanne whispered. "I've never seen people have sex across a room before. It's very erotic."

"I have no idea what you're talking about," Megan said, never turning away from Travis.

"You're not a great liar. You know that, right?"

He moved toward her. Megan stayed where she was, mostly because she was afraid that if she tried to walk, she would stumble.

"Did you know he was going to be here?" she asked her sister.

"I saw the guest list. I thought it looked interesting. I'm going to go find a little action of my own." Leanne sighed. "If you get into trouble, or decide you don't need a ride home, just let me know."

Megan nodded, still watching Travis approach. He stopped a few feet in front of her.

"I wouldn't have thought this was your kind of thing," she said, wanting to speak first so he wouldn't guess how much he'd hurt her.

"My mother agreed to donate some landscaping. She wasn't up to coming so I'm here representing the company." He shoved his hands into his slacks pockets. "Was that your sister?"

"Uh-huh. She dragged me here."

"Last I heard, you two didn't get along."

"We don't. At least we didn't until recently. She's been very helpful the past few weeks."

"You look good," he said.

"Thank you." She didn't know what to do. While she wanted to stay and talk, she knew it would be better and safer to walk away. He'd made his position clear when she'd gone to see him. He'd more than dismissed her. Didn't she have any pride?

But she already knew the answer to that. Not where Travis was concerned.

"I was trying to scare you off," he said. "Last week. I got carried away. I didn't mean to be so much of a bastard."

"How much did you mean to be?"

"Less than I was."

Okay—that was a good start. "I wanted to apologize. I didn't plan for you to get in the middle of my messy life." She thought about Adam showing up and what Travis had heard. "Despite how things ended, I had a great time. I wanted you to know that. Nothing more. Your meltdown wasn't necessary."

He raised his eyebrows. "I'm a guy. I don't have meltdowns."

"Sure you do. You just call them something different. Which isn't the point."

"You're right. I'm sorry. I didn't ask for specifics about your personal life. I didn't much care. I had a good time, too."

She wanted to mention that he'd been wrong about

them not being friends but figured there wasn't much point. He'd apologized, she'd been strong, it was a win all around.

"I have a problem at work," he said. "Someone is stealing. I know the information is buried in the books, but I can't find it."

Was he asking for her help? "Numbers are my life," she said cautiously.

"Would you be willing to help? If I didn't scare you off."

"I don't scare that easily."

"Then I need to work on my delivery."

She smiled. "I'll help. Despite what people think, there's nearly always a trail. Once you find it, you find everything. Can you put the information on a flash drive?"

"Sure." His dark eyes stared into hers. "I'm moving on in a few months. I'm only here temporarily, working with my mom. Once that's done, I'll be gone."

Was he telling her that anything between them would be short term, or warning her off again, only more politely this time?

"Where are you going?"

"Anywhere I can build my bikes."

She thought about the hundreds of sketches in her spare bedroom, how all those years ago he'd been willing to take off and she'd been too afraid to try.

"I envy your courage," she told him. "You're not afraid of anything."

"I wish that were true."

"Okay, you're not afraid to go after what you want."

"Are you?"

"Sometimes." Most of the time.

"What do you want now?" he asked.

My life back, she thought. Well, not Adam, but her father. She wanted the innocence of belonging again. Then she looked at the man standing in front of her and knew she would add him to the want list as well.

"You sure you want to know?" she asked.

"Yeah."

She smiled. "You."

Fire brightened his eyes, even as he took a step back. "I'm not the right guy. I never have been."

"Who are you trying to save? Me or yourself?"

He looked at her a long time. "Maybe both."

Megan was shown into Mr. Johnson's office right at three.

"Thanks for seeing me on such short notice," she said, remembering the last time she'd met the attorney, when he'd told her about Elliott Scott.

He gave her a smile. "I've been expecting you. Of course you have questions."

He motioned to the sofas in the corner of the spacious office and waited until she was seated to sit down himself. Then he leaned toward her. "How can I help you?"

"I'd like to know more about my . . . about Elliott Scott."

The lawyer nodded. "Elliott anticipated this and left you several documents, along with a few letters." He nudged a large envelope toward her. "Also, his wife is willing to speak with you."

Megan stared at the envelope, not sure she wanted to pick it up. "You mean Elliott's widow? Why would she want to have anything to do with me?"

"She always knew about you. Elliott didn't keep you a secret. She was very much in favor of him getting in touch with you before he died, but he was concerned about how that would affect your life. Pam asked me to give you her phone number. It's in there. You can call any time you'd like. She also suggested you consider going to San Diego to speak with her and maybe pick out one of Elliott's paintings for yourself. Sometimes a face-to-face meeting is easier. It's whatever you'd like, Megan."

She was beyond surprised. If the situation were reversed, Tina would be in hysterics and refusing to acknowledge any child her husband had with another woman.

"I don't know that I want to go see her," Megan murmured.

"That's entirely your choice. Pam knows this is a difficult time for you and wants to do everything she can to make things easier."

A unique perspective, Megan thought, knowing neither of her parents shared the other woman's attitude. How odd that a stranger was more concerned about her than the two people who raised her.

"Tell me about Elliott," she said. "You knew him a long time, didn't you?"

"We were friends for many years." The other man

smiled. "Elliott loved life. He found humor in everything and enjoyed pointing out the ridiculous that we all took so seriously. He and Pam threw great parties several times a year. They were always for silly reasons, like a nearly full moon or cheese being on sale. You laughed when you went to their house."

Megan tried to imagine what it would have been like to grow up around parents like that. "He and Pam had children?"

"Yes. The house was always crowded with their kids' friends. And color. Always color. Elliott's studio was alive with light and half-finished canvases. One entire wall is covered with his children's artwork and a beautiful portrait of Pam he did years ago. He was a good man, someone larger than life, and we'll all miss him."

He cleared his throat and shuffled through a few papers on his desk. "I wish you could have known him."

"Me too," she said softly, feeling a sense of having missed something wonderful. *Someone* wonderful.

Her life would have been incredibly different if she'd known about Elliott, had actually met him. Ten minutes ago, she would have said that was a bad thing, but not anymore.

"Pam will really talk to me?" she asked.

"Yes. She's warm and caring. I think you'll like her very much."

"Then I should probably go see her."

"An excellent idea."

Sixteen

"DON'T EVEN THINK ABOUT losing weight," Bobby said as he pinned the jeans even tighter. "Swear to God, every time someone comes in for a fitting, they've either lost weight or gained it." He scowled at her. "You look like the type to lose weight. Skinny bitch."

Bobby's grumpy nature was legendary and Leanne was too excited to take anything he said personally. This was her first real fitting for her first big movie role. They could call her names all they wanted.

Bobby stood and stepped back. He motioned for her to turn slowly.

"Fine," he said. "Take them off. You're done, but remember what I said. Not an ounce. Do you hear me?"

"Promise," she said, shimmying out of the pinned jeans and pulling on her own. "I swear."

"They all swear, honey, and it doesn't mean a thing."

Leanne waved and left the workroom. She still had to swing by and visit her mother before heading home to pack because she was going on location.

Location! Okay, sure it was all of a hundred miles out

in the California desert, but technically it was a location shoot. She couldn't wait to get there and start filming. This was about the coolest thing ever.

She passed several people who worked at the studio and did her best to act totally casual, as if she did this sort of thing all the time. That was her—a successful, slightly jaded actress. No one had to know that inside was a screaming, jumping, happy teenager who had just—

She turned a corner and literally ran into a man. He reached out to steady her and the second his fingers touched her bare arms, she felt flames lick along her skin.

"Ms. Greene," Connor McKay said. "Leanne."

"Connor."

She expected him to release her and move on, but he didn't. He just stood there, his dark blue eyes seeming bottomless.

"I, ah, just had my fitting," she said. "Bobby's in a mood."

"He's always in a mood. Did he give the lecture about not gaining weight?"

"No, the one about not losing any."

"That's right. You're in the 'thin enough to die' demographic."

She stepped back, a bit of her happy bubble bruised. At least he wasn't touching her anymore. "Have a nice day," she said, prepared to step around him.

"Wait. You'll be getting new pages. There have been some rewrites."

Was that good or bad? "All right," she said, determined to keep her expression neutral.

"You have more lines. Everyone was impressed by your audition and the decision was made to expand your character."

She wanted to do a cartwheel, assuming she knew how, or scream or throw her arms around Connor and kiss him. Instead she squared her shoulders and as coolly as possible said, "I look forward to the challenge."

"I'm sure you do. This will mean a lot more attention. More scrutiny. Be sure you're prepared."

"Of course."

He stepped aside, as if to walk away, then he paused. "I'm not going to ask you out."

What kind of game was this? "If you did, I wouldn't say yes."

"You're far too young. Young women are inherently boring."

"Old men can't get it up."

His eyes crinkled as if he were trying not to smile. "I have no interest in talking about shoes or clothes or diets. I like my women to be intelligent and mentally challenging."

"It sounds as if you should be dating the *New York Times* crossword. I like my men to be more than elitist snobs with minimal personalities." She wished she was wearing higher heels. "I won't apologize for my age and I don't care what you think about me."

"Yes, you do."

"And you want to ask me out."

With that she walked past him, her heart pounding so loud she couldn't tell if he was following her or not.

When she reached the parking lot, she found herself alone. Which meant he wasn't. The thought made her sad.

Megan typed on her laptop, trying to ignore Travis sitting next to her on the sofa. This was business. She was helping a friend, nothing more. Except she was completely aware of him just a few inches away. Heat seemed to radiate from him, making it difficult to keep her attention on the computer program.

She could feel herself getting closer to the problem. There was a pattern in the stealing—she sensed it. The trick would be finding it.

She went over invoices, then pulled up the deposits. Everything matched all the way through, except—

"Got it," she said, and plugged in her portable printer. "It's pretty slick. Here's what's happening. Your clients agree on a total amount and then pay in installments. So much on signing, so much when the work is partially done, so much at the end."

Travis leaned closer as she pointed at the screen.

"But you don't match the bid price with the contract price," she said. "The contract price is manually entered."

"Right," he said. "A lot of times customers come back with changes to the original bid. They want more or less or different hardscape. Concrete, to you. The bid price almost never matches the contract. And contracts get adjusted all the time."

"Which someone is using to his advantage," she

told him. "Look at all these bids and the correspond-
ing contracts. The contracts have been adjusted after the
fact, by the smallest installment payment. So an eleven-
thousand-dollar contract paid out in, say, two payments
of thirty-five hundred and two of twenty-five hundred
suddenly becomes an eighty-five-hundred-dollar contract as one of the twenty-five-hundred-dollar payments
disappears. This is happening consistently. If this has
been going on for any length of time, we're talking about
significant money. Possibly hundreds of thousands of
dollars."

Travis rose and crossed to the window, then turned toward her. "Which explains why my mom is having so many
money problems. Someone is stealing all the profits."

"Who has access?" she asked. "You must have some
safety checks in place. Who can get into the contracts and
change them?"

Travis thought about their old accounting software.
"Just about everyone. There are supposed to be pass-
words in place, but they're old and I'm sure they've been
passed around."

Megan did her best not to look shocked. "You need to
change that. No one who collects money from customers
should be allowed to change a contract. You need checks
and balances. You need a money trail that is totally separate to prevent this from happening."

"What now?" he asked.

He looked good silhouetted in the light, she thought
absently. Strong and sexy. She forced her brain back to
the problem at hand.

"That depends on where you want to go with this. I don't know the law as specifically as a lawyer, but I'm guessing your thief has stolen enough to cross into felony territory. Are you interested in getting him to stop or do you want to prosecute?"

"I want him taken down and punished."

She wasn't surprised. "Then we'll need proof. A sting. There are ways to do that. First, everyone gets a new password that is unique to each employee, but you give them access to everything. You run a hidden program that records keystrokes. You monitor who is doing what. Once you have that, it's enough to go to the police, who get a warrant for bank records. I can't do the programming, but I know a guy who does this kind of thing. He's not cheap, but he's the best."

Travis grinned. "You know a guy? You don't seem like the kind of person who can say 'I know a guy.'"

"I have hidden depths. I couldn't get anyone killed, but I can get them exposed financially."

He returned to the sofa and sat next to her. "You're good at what you do."

"I've had a lot of training."

"I never would have guessed there was a numbers girl hiding behind your green eyes." He angled toward her. "You were so determined to get to New York and be a designer."

"There's still a chance. I could apply for Project Runway. It's a reality show," she added when he looked blank.

"Do you want to?"

Go into design? "That was another lifetime. I'm not sure I have the drive, let alone any talent. I was a kid and it was a childish dream. I'm an accountant now. I like what I do. It's actually pretty interesting."

He took the computer from her and set it on the coffee table, then leaned in and kissed her.

"So are you," he whispered.

His mouth was warm and firm and filled with promise. As she wrapped her arms around his neck and prepared to surrender, she closed her eyes and got lost in the sensations that being near Travis always produced.

She'd known when she invited him over that there was a better than even chance they would end up in bed. Now, as he moved his hands up and down her back, then sank back onto the sofa, taking her with him, she knew she'd made the right choice. Travis had made it clear she wasn't his type and that they had no future together. The last thing she needed was another relationship. So making love with a sexy guy she'd always liked seemed like a good way to spend a Saturday afternoon.

He slipped his hands under her T-shirt and unfastened her bra. She pulled it and her shirt off, tossing both onto the carpet. He cupped her breasts, his thumbs brushing her nipples.

Every part of her hummed in anticipation. Liquid need poured through her as each flick of his fingers caused her insides to tighten. She bent down and lightly kissed him, teasing his mouth with hers. She touched his bottom lip with her tongue but ignored it when his lips parted.

She nipped at his jaw, then licked his skin and felt the hint of stubble there.

"Kiss me," he demanded.

"Or what?"

He grinned. "You really want to play that game?"

"Maybe."

He sat up and grabbed her waist, then stood. She gasped, hanging on to him. Instinctively she wrapped her legs around his hips and he carried her upstairs to her bedroom. They tumbled onto the mattress. He loomed above her, then bent down and claimed her with an open-mouthed kiss that stole her breath.

He plunged inside of her, tasting, taking, teasing until she was wet and swollen and ready to beg. He drew back and pulled off his shirt, then reached for her jeans. Seconds later they were gone, along with her panties. He knelt between her legs.

Megan parted for him, braced for the intimate kiss he promised, then sucked in a breath when she felt the first warm brush of his tongue on her most sensitive spot.

He explored all of her. He discovered what made her gasp or squirm or moan. He gently sucked, then used his tongue to circle and arouse her.

It was pure magic, she thought, her eyes closed as she dug her heels into the bed. It was beyond amazing. How could anything feel that good? She tilted her hips to push herself closer, wanting more, wanting all that he could give her. He licked faster, more intensely, then slipped two fingers inside of her.

He pushed up from the inside, stroking to match the

movements of his tongue. She tensed as she raced toward her release. She tried to hold back, to prolong the pleasure, but it was too late. Muscles tightened, she gasped and strained, struggling to stay in control when it was impossible to do anything but let him push her over the edge.

She came almost violently, her body shaking, her muscles convulsing. He moved his fingers in and out of her, prolonging her orgasm until the last spasm had faded. And still he filled her, in and out, in and out.

She felt him shift. He kept his fingers inside of her even as he moved up on the bed and began to lick her suddenly sensitive nipples. An unexpected flash of sexual need ripped through her. Instinctively she grabbed his head, as if to hold him in place. She felt another release just a whisper away. He drew her nipple deeply into his mouth and she came again.

She rode his fingers, wishing it were his erection instead. But instead of keeping pace with her, instead of letting her find all of her release, he slowed. She opened her eyes and found him watching her.

"Undo my jeans," he told her.

She managed to undo the button and pull down the zipper, all while he kept his fingers inside of her, teasing her enough to keep her close to the edge.

"Ready?" he asked.

She nodded.

He withdrew and shoved down his jeans and briefs. She moved on top of him and settled on him.

He filled her perfectly, stretching her, going deep. She

leaned forward so she could brace herself against the bed. Her hair tumbled down, framing his face.

His dark gaze locked with hers. He pushed his hand between them so that he cupped her groin with his thumb on her center. Every time she went up and down, he went with her, rubbing in a steady rhythm that made her want to go faster.

"Sit up," he told her. "Just go for it."

She'd never been a fan of being on top. It made her feel too exposed. But in this moment, none of that seemed to matter. She straightened and began to ride him.

He moved with her, pushing up when she came down, filling her again and again. He continued to rub her center, going faster and faster, urging her on. Up and down, more and more. She could feel her breasts bouncing, but she didn't care. She closed her eyes, arched her head back and took exactly what she wanted.

She didn't care what she looked like, didn't care what he was thinking. Possibly for the first time in her life, she gave in to total abandon and when she came again she screamed with the force and pleasure of it. She kept pumping up and down until the last ounce of release had faded and she was spent.

Somewhere in the middle of this she was aware of him grabbing her hips and groaning as he found his end as well, but she wasn't sure exactly when or how that had happened.

Reality returned with an unpleasant crash. She didn't want to open her eyes, didn't want to look at Travis. But before she could figure out how to crawl away and hide, he drew her against him and breathed her name.

"You're incredible," he whispered into her hair. "You're the most incredible woman I've ever known. No one makes love like you do."

She risked opening her eyes and saw him watching her. He looked both pleased and impressed.

"I got a little carried away," she said, feeling herself blush.

"That was the sexiest thing I've ever seen in my life. Want to do it again?"

Her insides felt swollen and bruised. "Maybe later."

"Just say when."

"You wanted to see me?" Megan asked as she walked into Felicia's office, only to stop when she saw Carrie sitting with her boss at the conference table in the corner.

The two women looked at her, then at each other. Carrie smiled as she rose.

"Hello, Megan. Nice to see you."

Megan watched her leave, knowing that whatever Carrie had to say, it couldn't be good.

"Come have a seat," Felicia told her.

There were several folders spread out on the table. Megan took the chair opposite Felicia's and noticed that the records belonged to her clients. What was going on?

"I've been hearing some troubling rumors," Felicia said. "You've missed appointments with several of your clients without notifying them, Megan. I understand that canceling the wedding was an emotional upheaval and you've done very well under the circumstances, but standing up clients isn't an option."

Megan forced herself to relax. She was going to handle this meeting in a calm, professional manner. Obviously there had been a misunderstanding. She would find out what it was and get it fixed.

"I appreciate your concern and share it," she said. "While I have taken off a few hours here and there to deal with . . ." She didn't want to bring up the trouble with her parents. "To deal with cleanup, I haven't missed any client appointments. I check my schedule very carefully to make sure that doesn't happen. One of the reasons I know it hasn't been an issue is that I was supposed to be on my honeymoon for the past two weeks. I wouldn't have had anything scheduled while I was gone."

Felicia frowned. "You're right. You wouldn't. But I have an e-mail from Character Creative and Film Rats, both complaining you didn't show up for a meeting."

Megan wondered if anyone from either company had actually sent the e-mails or if they had been generated elsewhere.

"Interesting," she said, and motioned to her boss's laptop. "May I?"

"Sure." Felicia turned the computer toward her.

Megan typed in her password and accessed her calendar. She checked it, then showed it to Felicia. "My quarterly review with Film Rats is next week. Josh at Character Creative is in France. His assistant is supposed to call me and set up something when he gets back. As you can see, neither company is on my calendar."

"But I have the e-mails," Felicia murmured more to herself than Megan.

Megan didn't know what the other woman was thinking. Would she consider the possibility that Megan was being set up? Should Megan mention it?

"Who sent them?" she asked.

"One of the assistants there. I'll forward them to you. What happened with the time cards?" Felicia asked.

"I don't know," Megan admitted. "I know what I submitted. Those are not the hours that billing received. Fortunately I keep backup records of my time cards, so I was able to reconstruct them. Has anyone else had a problem?"

"No. Just you. How are you feeling, Megan? Is the stress getting to you?"

Megan sensed dangerous territory. "No. I'm feeling very good about where things are these days. I'm enjoying my work with my clients. You saw my proposal for the new company I've been speaking with. They'll bring in significant billable hours."

"I know. Honestly, I don't have any complaints about your work. Or at least I didn't until recently. Is it Adam?"

Megan wanted to scream. It wasn't Adam, it was Carrie. But would Felicia believe her enough to investigate the other manager? Or would she just think less of Megan and assume she was trying to spread the blame?

"It's not Adam," Megan said. "I'm sorry the time card

mistake has happened. I don't know what went wrong, but I'm confident it won't occur again." Now that Carrie knew she had backups, she wouldn't try a second time. But who knew what else she would pull?

"As for the e-mails, I don't know what to say. I haven't missed any client meetings."

Felicia nodded slowly. "I believe you. It's just so strange. We still think very highly of you, Megan. Stay visible. Make sure the partners see the hours you're working. Now that things have settled, I'm assuming you won't need to take off so much personal time."

A not-so-subtle hint. "Absolutely not. I'll be here, working."

"Good. All right. I don't want to keep you." Felicia smiled. "Go bill some time."

Megan nodded and left. She maintained her calm as she walked down the long hallway, but inside she was furious. What the hell was Carrie up to and how could she be stopped?

She reached her office, but before she went inside, her assistant stopped her.

"Your mother called. She says it's urgent." Lily's eyes widened. "She sounded really sick."

"She always does," Megan muttered. "Thanks. I'll call her."

She went into her office and closed the door, then dialed her mother's number.

"It's me," she said when she heard the faint "Hello?"

"Megan?" Her mother gasped. "I can't breathe." There was another gasp. "I can't get Leanne on her cell phone.

I can't—" Her breathing was raspy and desperate. "You have to come at once. I'm not . . ." More gasping. "I'm not sure I'm going to make it."

Megan gripped the phone. "Mom, if it's that bad, you need to call 911. I don't have any medical training. I can't help you if you're not breathing."

"I don't want to bother them. They're busy with important things." Another gasp. "Just come over. You can fix me lunch. That will help. Oh, and bring your checkbook. I have some bills I need you to take care of."

Great. So she was being played again. "I don't think so," she snapped. "I know you'll find this tough to believe, but I have important things to do. If you're dying, call for help. If you're not, I have to go."

She hung up and logged on to her computer. The forwarded e-mails were waiting. She read them over. The wording was different, but the message was the same. Megan had failed to show up for an appointment. She didn't recognize the name of either person sending the e-mail.

She picked up the phone to call Film Rats, only to put the receiver down again. She couldn't get her mother's phone call out of her head. Her brain told her that Tina was once again giving her professional victim performance and that it was an excellent one. But her heart wondered if maybe something was really wrong.

The battle raged for nearly a minute, then she glanced at the clock and saw it was close to noon.

"I'm going to lunch," she told Lily as she walked past her. "If you need me you can reach me on my cell."

"Sure."

Twenty minutes later, Megan pulled up in front of her mother's house. She hated that she was weak enough to have been drawn here. She was going to have to be stronger than this. Why was her mother getting to her? Because Tina was now the only parent she had left?

She thought about what she'd learned about Elliott and Pam and knew neither of them would have ever acted this way with their children. Never tormented them or dismissed them. Of course she couldn't be totally sure. Maybe every family had twisted secrets, but she hoped not. She wanted things to be better elsewhere.

Knowing she was going to hate herself for doing this, she walked into the house.

"Mom?"

There was no answer.

Megan ran to the bedroom, where she found her mother lying on the floor. She swore and grabbed the phone. But before she could dial, her mother spoke.

"No. It's fine. I'll be fine. I just fainted. Maybe you could help me back to bed. I'm just so weak these days."

Megan wasn't sure what to think, what to believe. She got her mother to her feet, then guided her back to the bed. Tina slid under the covers and sighed.

"Thank you. It's so difficult lately. I'm so alone." She sank back on the pillows. "Leanne is too busy with her career to bother about me. Not that I blame her. She's worked so hard to get where she is. But your father . . ." Tina's eyes filled with tears. "He won't speak to me. I miss him so much."

Megan stood by the bed and actually felt bad. "I know you do. Are you talking to him at all?"

Her mother shook her head. "No. I call and call and he won't talk to me. He doesn't love me anymore. It's just over. After thirty years, he's turning his back on me." She covered her face with her hands and cried.

"I'm sorry," Megan said, not knowing what to do. Her mother was normally so dramatic. It was difficult to know how to handle a genuine problem.

"He won't pay for anything," Tina continued, wiping her face. "He's leaving me to starve."

"Mom, I doubt that. You're still married."

"That doesn't matter to him. You should be helping me. You have all that inheritance money and it's only because of me. I want half of it, Megan. I think I deserve all of it, but you're too selfish to ever agree to that. So half is fine."

Megan took a step back. "Is that what this is all about? Did you plan the show to get me to give you money?"

The tears dried up. "You owe me, Megan. You know it and I know it. All of this trouble is because of you. You're the reason your father left."

"He left because you'd been lying to him for twenty-eight years. He left because you cheated on him. You pretended I was his daughter. You lied to both of us."

"It's not my fault," her mother said, the tears returning. "It was never my fault."

"You're the only one to blame."

"And you were a mistake," her mother snapped. "I should never have had you. I should have gotten an abortion. I thought about it. Then none of this would have happened. Then everything would be fine."

Megan stared at her for several seconds, turned and left.

"What about the money?" Tina yelled after her. "I want my half. I want my fair share."

Megan kept walking.

Seventeen

LEANNE LOVED EVERYTHING ABOUT being on location. It was kind of how she'd always imagined summer camp to be. She loved sharing her tiny trailer. She loved the challenge of figuring out the right focus and emotion for the scenes when they were shot out of order and in a sequence that made no sense to her. She loved the people, the food and even the desert, where it was hot and bright and keeping them all from sweating on camera was an ongoing problem.

She pulled a bottle of water from an ice chest and opened it.

"You're Leanne, right?"

Warren Hatch, a nearly A-list star who was the second male lead in the movie, grinned at her over a cola can.

"Yes. Hi."

"Hi. I think we have a scene together tomorrow."

"Uh-huh." She'd already memorized all her lines and nearly everyone else's.

"I'm looking forward to it," he said, his gaze roaming over her body. "By the way, I'm Warren."

"I know."

"Yeah?" He grinned. "Good. Want to come back to my trailer? We could hang out."

"An excellent and compelling invitation," Connor said as he approached, "but Ms. Greene has a previous commitment with me. Sorry, Warren. Maybe the two of you can hang out later."

"Oh, sure. No problem."

Warren waved, then sauntered off.

Leanne hadn't seen much of Connor, even though they'd both been at the location shoot for nearly a week. Sometimes she thought he was avoiding her. Other times she told herself that he simply wasn't paying attention to her and she should take a lesson from him.

"Your latest conquest?" Connor asked, the faint British accent adding a dash of contempt to the question.

"No, although he's much closer to my age. And that body. He works out."

"On nearly everyone. Come with me."

He walked toward the trailers. She debated ignoring the order, then gave in to curiosity and followed him.

His trailer was one of the large ones, on the end. She looked around at the open space created by the walls sliding out.

"Very nice. Jenny and I are sharing something the size of a litter box."

"Make the studio a few million and you can get one like this."

"Can I make myself the millions first?"

"Of course."

He waved toward the leather sofa. She perched on the edge, not sure why he'd brought her here. If he'd been anyone else, she would have assumed it was for sex. But Connor didn't strike her as the type to get involved without an old-fashioned seduction first.

He took the chair opposite the sofa. "How are you liking your first location shoot?"

"It's fun. The people are nice and I'm enjoying being a part of this." She rolled her eyes. "I know. I sound like I'm seventeen, but so what? I love my part. The rewrites are fabulous."

"Not missing anyone at home?" he asked, his blue eyes watching her.

"My sister," she said without thinking. "Which is weird. We've never been close. I wanted us to be, but we never were. Probably because I was totally horrible to her when we were growing up. I'm younger and I always resented how she got to do things first. I spied on her and ratted her out to our parents. But lately, we're getting along. I don't want that to change."

"Why would it? You're both adults now."

"We've been adults for a while, not that Megan's been willing to see that. I guess I feel bad because of. everything that happened to her. Our dad . . . my dad . . . isn't—"

She pressed her lips together. What was she doing, talking about all this? She knew to keep her personal life private on location. She didn't want to be gossiped about. Not that Connor was the type. Still, she barely knew him.

"Sorry," she murmured. "Family stuff must be right up there with shoes. Totally boring."

He leaned toward her. "Tell me about your sister and your father."

"Why?"

"Because I'm interested."

She narrowed her gaze. "I don't want this going into one of your screenplays. Do you have writer's block or something? Are you fishing for ideas?"

"Your faith in my talent and ability is overwhelming. I'm deeply touched."

"I didn't mean to insult you."

"I look forward to seeing what you come up with when you make an effort."

She eyed him over her water bottle. "You're a lot more sensitive than I would have thought."

"Despite what you may think, I have an artistic temperament. It's not the easiest thing in the world to live with."

"For you or those around you?"

"Both. Tell me about your sister."

Still not sure why he was interested, she explained about the lawyer visiting Megan, the discovery that her father was another man who had recently died, Gary's total rejection of her, Adam's betrayal, the canceled wedding and how all of this had, oddly enough, brought the sisters together.

"I want to be there for her," Leanne told him. "That matters to me. But I'm scared, too. That she's . . ."

"Using you in her time of need."

"Something like that."

"Would you not be there for her if you knew it was temporary?" he asked.

"No. She's my sister. I love her, even if she doesn't believe that. I do. I want her to be happy."

"You lead with your heart. That can be dangerous."

"She's family."

"The ultimate answer."

"Don't you have anyone you care about?" she asked him.

"Less and less as I grow older."

"Because they're all dead or you're getting more picky?"

He laughed. "Both."

"How old are you?"

"Forty-seven."

So there was a difference of twenty-two years. She'd never dated anyone over thirty. Of course, she'd slept with plenty of dirty old men.

"That's really old."

He raised one eyebrow. "How charming."

She stood. "Okay, Connor. Enough of the bullshit. What do you want with me?"

"I wish I knew."

"Sex?"

"In part."

She was tempted. He was funny, smart, verbal, charming, and she had an idea he would know what he was doing. But so what?

"I'm not interested in casual sex," she told him.

He stood. "I know, Leanne. I know exactly what you want. But I'm not the man to give it to you. I'm too cynical to fall in love."

"Then I guess we have a problem."

"More than you know."

He touched her face. She knew he was going to kiss her and she didn't pull away.

He leaned in, then brushed his mouth against hers. They only touched for a second, yet she felt the contact down to her toes. He drew back.

"We could have been great together," he told her.

"We still could be."

Once outside in the heat, she walked to her own tiny trailer. She could feel Connor watching her, wanting her. There was something between them. Something powerful. He was resisting, but it was just a matter of time until he realized she was exactly what he'd been looking for.

The last of the wedding gifts were gone. Megan looked at the master list she'd made and double-checked that she hadn't missed something small. Everything had been canceled, paid for or sent back. She was officially done with her engagement. Even the tan line from the diamond ring she'd given back had faded. It was as if that part of her life had never happened.

Except it had. Being with Adam had changed her. What she didn't know was if it had been for the better.

The past couple of months had been difficult and draining, but she was still far more upset about how her father was acting than finding out Adam had cheated. Was it that the events were so different in emotional size or was the reality that Adam had been more symbol than man? Why had she thought she was in love with him? Obviously she hadn't been.

She remembered the first time they'd met. It was at a party. He'd been so different from her physical type. Ever since Travis, she'd gone for dark, dangerous guys who, as a rule, made lousy boyfriends. Adam, all tall and blond and smiling, had been like a Ken doll. He'd been funny and charming and when he asked her out, she'd told herself it was time to try something different.

They'd seemed so well suited. As if they belonged together. She'd appreciated the lack of drama. Had she been so frightened by the passion she'd once felt for Travis that she'd wanted to avoid it in another man?

Her doorbell rang.

In the time it took for the sound to register in her brain, her heart rate doubled and her insides tightened. Travis? Wouldn't that be a nice surprise. Not that he came by without calling. Unless he'd been thinking about her.

She hurried to the door and pulled it open. Adam stood there looking annoyed and impatient.

"Good. You're home," he said, pushing past her. "We have to talk."

She was beyond surprised to see him. Not only because they hadn't talked but because she'd been thinking about him. It was as if she'd conjured him out of thin air.

Winning lottery ticket, winning lottery ticket, she chanted silently, then smiled.

"I'm glad you're amused by all this," Adam said as he glared at her. "Because I'm not."

He held himself stiffly as he stalked around her living room. She didn't ask him to sit. There was an air of edginess about him that made her uncomfortable.

"Why are you here?" she asked.

"Why do you think? This has gone on long enough. I've given you time, Megan. I've tried to respect your feelings on the matter, but when are you going to settle down and do the right thing? Do you know what it was like to have to call all my friends and tell them we weren't getting married? Do you know how it made me look?"

"You? You expect me to feel bad for you? You're the reason we didn't get married, Adam. You cheated on me. Not just once, but over time. You had a relationship."

"That's done. I've told you, once we're married, I'll be totally faithful. It's not as if you wasted any time finding some biker guy for your bed."

She ignored the comment about Travis. "You'll be faithful after we get married. And I should believe you why? That is not going to happen. I don't know what you want, but it isn't marriage. It isn't a partnership."

"I want you, Megan. We're good together. Come on, you have to know that. We like the same things, the same people. My partners and their wives all think you're great. Your family likes me."

"How flattering for both of us," she murmured. "Adam, no. This isn't going to happen. We don't love each other. I don't want to be with you."

"You don't know what you want," he snapped. "You never did. That's why you need someone to take charge."

"Someone like you?" Could he really be stupid enough to mean that?

"Better me than that other guy."

"You're having a hard time letting that go."

"I didn't like finding you in bed with him."

"It was one night, Adam. Imagine how I felt finding out about your affair with a nineteen-year-old." She wanted to slap him. Instead, she marshaled her self-control and went for a more reasonable line of conversation. "Aren't the other people in our lives proof that this relationship wasn't a good one for either of us? You don't want me back, you want your life settled. You don't want to have to find someone else. This is so much easier. But in the end, you won't be happy with me and I won't be happy with you. It's done. Let it go."

"I won't. This is just like you, Megan. You're not even going to try. Something gets hard and you walk away. You always have."

"What? That's not true." He was making this her fault? Talk about a weasel bastard.

"It's your pattern. You take the easy way out. This got hard, so you left."

"Relationships require honesty and fidelity, two things

you have trouble with. They require commitment, and we're equally guilty of breaking that one."

He stalked to the door. "You're going to regret this. You're not going to find anyone better than me, but once I leave, it's over. I'm not taking you back."

She sighed. "It's been over for a long time, Adam. The problem is neither of us noticed."

Eighteen

TRAVIS'S MOTHER BURST INTO his office. "The police are here. They say they have a warrant. They're looking for Artie. Do you know about this? What's going on?"

Travis glanced out the window and saw two patrol cars parked by the main gate.

He'd turned all the information he had over to them a few days before and had asked not to be told when they would show up. He didn't want to risk tipping Artie off by knowing what was coming.

He stood and faced his mother. "Artie's been stealing from you for the past ten years. Maybe longer. He adjusted contract amounts and stole installment payments. We don't have a total amount yet, but it's close to half a million dollars." He softened his tone. "That's why you haven't been making it, Mom. But with him gone, the cash flow will improve. You should be able to sell the business for a lot of money. That will fund your retirement."

"How could you? Artie is my friend. He's your friend.

You've known him all his life. He's taken care of me while your father's been gone."

He took a step back. "My father isn't 'gone.' He's in prison for a laundry list of charges, including murder. As for Artie being your friend, he's stolen from you. Don't you get that? We're talking about half a million dollars. If I hadn't come back and caught him, you would have spent your retirement eating cat food in a cold apartment because your 'friend' took advantage of you."

"You don't know what you're talking about. I want you to stop this right now. Tell the police you made a mistake."

"No. He deserves to go to jail for this."

"That's always your answer, isn't it? People make mistakes, Travis. We're not all as perfect as you."

He didn't get it. How could she take Artie's side in this? Didn't she believe what she heard? Did she think Artie was going to put the money back?

"I'm not perfect, Mom."

"You're right. You're not. You took my husband from me and then you left." Tears filled her eyes. "I haven't had anyone for years. Can't you understand what that's like? Artie was my connection to your father. You don't accept that people have problems. You don't give anyone a second chance."

He thought about all the times his father had beaten her unconscious. He remembered the long stays in the hospital when he'd been forced to lie to doctors about how she'd been hurt.

"Some people don't deserve a second chance," he said.

"I'll never forgive you for this," she told him as she walked out of his office.

He watched her go. She might never forgive him, but she also hadn't told him to leave. She was willing to have him fix her life, just so long as he played by her rules.

He watched the police talking to Shawn. A voice in his head told him nothing was worth this. He should go. Let his mother live the life she'd earned.

But he couldn't. For whatever reason, he felt he owed her. So he would stay until the business was up and running. He would find her a buyer and then he would take off. But this time, he wasn't coming back for anything.

Megan listened to the rumble of Travis's voice as she lay naked in his arms. She could feel his pain and knew that he didn't understand why his mother had reacted the way she had. Megan was on his side—the woman should have been grateful. But how often did people do what they should?

"I'm sorry," she murmured.

He tightened his arm around her. "I know. Sorry to dump all this on you."

"I don't mind. Besides, I've ranted plenty and I have a few more things, so don't think you're getting off for free."

He gave her a slight smile, then kissed the top of her head. "She blames me," he said. "That's the part I don't get. Artie was stealing and she blames me. It's just like with my dad. She doesn't care about him breaking the law and killing someone. But if he gets put away, that's the real problem."

"She loves him and that's what drives her," Megan said. "We can't understand it, but it's not going to change. You either accept it or know that it's going to make you crazy forever."

"I know." He closed his eyes. "She used to cry every night when he was in jail, but I was always happy. I liked it just being my mom and me. It was easier. Safer. I knew she was afraid of him, not that she would admit it. But when I talked back to her or did something wrong, she would say I was just like him. That I had that same blackness inside of me."

Megan sat up, pulling the sheet with her. "You're not like him. You know that, right?"

He opened his eyes and looked at her. "There's enough of him there."

"How can you say that?"

"I get angry."

"We all get angry."

"Not like this. It lives in me. I have to stay in control. It's easier to just keep my distance."

She didn't get it at first. "You mean emotionally. If you don't get too involved, then you don't have to worry?"

"Something like that."

Not exactly the words she wanted to hear. "Isn't that just an excuse not to care? To be emotionally lazy?"

His gaze sharpened. "Tell me what you really think."

"I mean it, Travis. What is this? Are you warning me off?"

"I'm telling you who I am."

Which was the same thing. "So you're the iconic American loner? Don't get too close, ma'am, I can't be trusted."

He started to climb out of bed. She grabbed his arm.

"You can't walk away from this," she told him.

"Why not? It's what you do whenever things get tough."

Ouch. "I can't tell you what I think without you getting mad at me?"

"I warned you I had a temper."

"You warned me you didn't get involved. If I'm annoying you this easily, you're already involved, so we have a problem."

"More than one."

"Meaning?"

"We're not involved. You don't get involved. You walk away."

"Are you talking about what happened ten years ago?" she demanded, unable to believe he would bring that up. "Seriously?"

"I offered you everything and you walked away."

"I was eighteen and terrified. I'd never come close to being on my own. You wanted me to run away with you and I couldn't do it. That doesn't mean I didn't love you. I was a kid. I can't control that. You have no right to judge me on that. It's not like you were willing to negotiate. It was your way or you were gone. So I'm not the only one who disappears."

"You don't know what you're talking about."

But he didn't leave.

They stared at each other for a long time. She put her hand on his chest.

"Travis, don't be like this."

"This is who I am."

"You're many things, but you're not a jerk. What are you really upset about?"

"I'm a guy. I don't get upset."

She smiled. "Sure you are. Your panties are all in a twist."

He raised his eyebrows. "Excuse me? What did you say?"

"Panties. Twisted."

"Are you calling me a girl?"

"Just about."

He reached for her, dragging her down on the bed. They were pressed together, skin on skin.

He touched her face. "I'm not the right guy. I don't know how to do this."

"You think you're so dark and dangerous, but you're wrong. You're the guy who came home to help his mom because she asked. You're the guy who worries about the darkness inside so much that you cut yourself off from the world rather than risk hurting anyone. You worry about everyone but yourself, and whatever you want to tell the world, I know the truth. You lead with your heart, Travis. You always have."

"Don't make me a hero," he said. "You'll only be disappointed."

She started to speak. He silenced her with a kiss. As his mouth claimed her, she thought that the problem wasn't that he wasn't good enough for her, but that she didn't deserve him.

He reached for her and she went to him willingly. The phone rang. She wanted to ignore it, but the shrill sound was insistent. She rolled over and grabbed it.

"Hello?"

"Thank God you're home," Leanne said, sounding breathless. "It's Mom. She's really sick this time. She's in the hospital, in a coma."

"Your mother is very lucky," the doctor said. "She's responding to the insulin extremely well. The preliminary tests show no organ damage, which is what we worry about most with people in her condition."

"How did this happen?" Gary asked, looking stunned. "She's sick all the time. It's chronic. She can't go a day without some crisis." His voice shook. "She suffered so patiently. She always looked so beautiful."

The doctor patted him on the arm. "There are patients like that. They're always unhappy so no one takes their symptoms seriously, the medical version of the boy who cried wolf. Your wife has diabetes, Mr. Greene. She has for a long time. Despite her various complaints, she hasn't had a thorough physical in years. Everything about her lifestyle is going to change. She's going to need a lot of support."

"Of course," he said. "Of course, I'll do anything."

Megan stood next to her sister, as stunned as they were at the diagnosis. But she was also aware of being in the same room as her father, of wanting to reach out to him, to have him hold her and promise everything would be all right. Instead, he didn't seem to notice she was there.

"You'll be able to see her in a few minutes," the doctor said. "Keep her calm. She's adjusting. But if all continues to go well, she should be going home in the next day or so."

"Thank you," Gary said, shaking the doctor's hand. "Thank you so much."

"You're welcome. Be sure you set up an appointment with the nutritionist. There's more involved in controlling diabetes than just not eating sugar."

"Yes. We'll do whatever we have to."

The doctor left. Gary turned to Megan and Leanne.

"We're in this together, girls," he said. "We're going to have to pull together to help your mother."

The knot in Megan's stomach relaxed a little as she waited for him to tell her he was sorry for how he'd behaved, that of course she was still his daughter and that he loved her. Instead he covered his face with his hands.

"She was really sick," he said, his voice breaking. "How could I not know? What if she dies? This is all my fault."

"It's not anyone's fault," Leanne said.

He dropped his hands. "We're all going to have to be more careful around her. Think about her instead of ourselves. She's been so giving and loving all these years and we've never appreciated her. You especially, Megan."

"What? Wait a minute. None of this is my fault. And why do you care so much? You're divorcing her."

"I'm not." He shrugged. "I might have said something before, but that was a misunderstanding. I love your mother. I'll always love her. I'm so sorry for everything." He lunged for Leanne and held her close.

Megan watched them, then turned away. She felt sick. This couldn't be happening. Watching her father with Leanne was like watching a movie. It had nothing to do with her.

No. What she meant was watching Leanne with Gary Greene had nothing to do with her. Because he wasn't her father. He might have raised her, but he wasn't interested in a relationship with her anymore. She wasn't who he'd thought, so she no longer mattered.

The truth hurt, but not as much as it would have a month ago. Maybe she'd always known that anyone who could stay with her mother for thirty years couldn't be expected to react normally to anything.

"I'm going to go see her now," he told them. "Wait a few minutes, then you can join us." He glared at Megan. "No fighting and don't be critical. She needs our love and support. We're going to take care of her the way she's always taken care of us."

"I'm sorry," Leanne murmured as he walked away. "This is too weird for me. I can't imagine what you're feeling."

"I'm finally accepting that nothing in my world is how

I thought it would be. But maybe that's just a part of life. The craziness. I felt so smug for so long because he was my dad and I knew, no matter what, he loved me. I felt sorry for you because you got stuck with Mom."

"I don't want him," Leanne said. "I've seen what he is. He could turn on me, too."

Megan hugged her. "Don't go there. He's your dad and you have to love him."

"What about you?"

"I haven't got a clue."

"I used to think my parents overreacted by putting me into therapy every time something went wrong," Allegra said as she sat next to Megan in the hospital waiting room. "But they might have been onto something. There was always someone to talk to. Someone to tell me why it wasn't my fault."

"I have you," Megan said, grateful her friend had been in L.A. for a photo shoot. "And you listen for free."

"That's true." Allegra tossed her long hair over her shoulders. "Plus, I'm much prettier to look at."

Megan grinned. "And more modest."

"I do have that humble quality."

They laughed. Megan caught herself before the humor turned to tears.

Allegra took her hand and squeezed it. "You're not having a good year, are you?"

"The last few months have really sucked."

"So it will get better."

"I hope so. I just can't figure out my—Him. Gary. He's in love with her because she's beautiful. That's pretty much the sole reason. Why is that enough?"

"He could turn around."

"Be my father again?" Megan knew better. "No. This is what it is. I'm accepting that. Wanting it to be different won't make it different. And now I don't know that I even want it back the way it was. Am I smug?"

"What?"

"Leanne said I had this perfect life and I was smug about it."

"You were happy. There's a difference."

Was there? "When I was younger, my mom told me I wouldn't ever have a good life because I wasn't pretty enough. I was so hurt and angry, I vowed to show her. I went out and made everything work—or so I thought. A great career, a handsome doctor to marry. I had my dad. But none of it turned out the way I thought. I should feel bad about that, but I keep having the feeling that there's a reason for all this. That something's coming and it's big and cool and I should make sure I'm wearing the right shoes when it gets here."

Allegra laughed. "You can borrow any of mine if you want."

"I appreciate that more than you can know."

Allegra squeezed her hand. "How's your mom?"

"Very cheerful. I think she likes being in the hospital and having all the attention. If it wasn't for the potential shutdown of all her organs, I would guess she'd want to fall into a coma every month."

"Are they getting her blood sugar under control?"

"Apparently. She's responding well to the insulin and my da—and, ah, he's monitoring every bite she takes. Keeping her food right is going to be their new hobby." Megan looked at her friend. "Am I a bitch? Should I be more worried about her? Shouldn't I take this seriously?"

"You're here. You care. But she's not going to change."

"Maybe no one changes. Maybe we are who we are and then we die."

Allegra leaned her head against Megan's shoulder. "I love it when you're perky."

Megan smiled. "Okay, yeah, that was dramatic. I need a break from my life."

"So take a vacation. Where do you want to go?"

"San Diego. I want to find out about my real dad."

Pam Scott was a pretty, plump woman with short blond hair and permanent wrinkles from constantly smiling.

"I'm so excited to finally meet you," she said as she showed Megan onto the patio behind the house.

A glass and wrought iron table stood under a patio cover. Lush plants spilled over terra-cotta containers. Elliott Scott had lived on Coronado Island, a scant couple of miles from San Diego.

Pam set the tray of lemonade and cookies next to a stack of photo albums. "I was afraid this was all too much of a shock and that you wouldn't call. I'm glad you did. Elliott wanted us to meet." Her bright eyes dimmed a little. "It's still hard for me to believe he's gone."

"I'm sorry for your loss," Megan said, feeling awkward. She didn't know this woman from a rock.

Pam sighed. "I'm handling things as best I can. The kids really help. We have three. Now sit and ask me anything you want."

Megan took a seat and a glass of lemonade. "I'm not sure what *to* ask," she admitted. "What would you like to tell me?"

Pam settled across from her. She took a cookie and broke it apart on a plate but didn't eat any. "Elliott was a good man. He was kind and sweet. Funny. He could always make me laugh." She blinked several times. "So talented. When I met him, he was a mess. Charming, but unfocused. No job, no drive. He was totally ignoring his art. I was in college, studying to be a nurse. I was very serious about everything. I've always thought we balanced each other out. I taught him to be responsible and he taught me to have fun."

She motioned to the paintings leaning against the wall. "Those are all his. I thought you might like to look them over and pick a couple you like."

Megan glanced at the paintings. They were mostly tropical landscapes with bright colors that made her think about travel and sunlight.

"They're beautiful," she said.

"I think so. He had some success with his work. Enough that he took care of us. He told me about you from the first," Pam said. "He'd met your mother one afternoon at the movies. At first he didn't know she was married. When he did find out, he assumed she was interested in escaping from her marriage. They got involved, she got pregnant, but when he asked her to run away with him, she refused."

Pam shrugged. "He wouldn't have been a very good bet back then. So I'm not completely surprised at her decision. I'm sure she loved her husband very much. People often go astray without meaning to."

Megan nodded. Pam was one of those people who erred on the side of kindness. Had Elliott liked that about her?

Pam pulled the top photo album toward them, opened it and turned it so Megan could see the pictures. The first one was a family portrait, formal, with everyone in matching chambray shirts, on the beach. They were the perfect American family—happy, healthy, laughing. Two girls and a boy, two parents and a yellow Lab.

"Your children are lovely."

"They're getting there," Pam said with a laugh. "Ryan, my youngest, has been a handful, but he's in his first year of college and doing well." She held up her right hand, fingers crossed.

She flipped through more pictures, describing when and where they were taken. Family trips to Disneyland. Camping. A weekend in Catalina. It was all so normal, so happy. The kids were her half brother and half sisters, but they were strangers to her. She could have been looking at still shots from a movie.

"I don't know what to say," she admitted. "This doesn't feel real."

"It's too much, too soon," Pam told her. "You're here.

I want you to know you'll always be welcome here. The kids want to meet you. I told them not this time. It would be too much. But maybe in a few weeks? We have a big brunch every Sunday."

Brunch, she thought, remembering happy times spent with . . . with Gary Greene. Leanne's father.

She flipped through the album. Perfect people living a perfect life. That's what pictures were about. The highlights. Her family photos would look just as ideal. But wasn't life defined by how people dealt with the weird crap?

Pam touched a picture of Elliott. "He spoke of you from time to time. Wondered about you. He wanted to get in touch, but he was afraid of how that would change everything. When he found out he was dying, he knew he had to take the chance."

She looked at Megan. "I know he took the coward's way out, dying first and telling you second. But it was his choice and I couldn't talk him out of it."

"I never thought of it that way," Megan admitted. Had he been afraid?

"He was a good man, but he wasn't perfect. Are any of us?"

"I'm not."

"Me either. But I try. I'm sure you do, too." She smiled. "He wanted you to be happy. He wanted you to live your dreams. He wanted that for all his children."

"Thank you," Megan said, not sure what to think or feel or do. She stood. "I need to get back to L.A."

"I understand. I hope you'll stay in touch and come

back. I'd like us to get to know each other." Pam rose. "Say you will."

Impulsively, Megan hugged her. Pam squeezed her back.

"I will," Megan told her, and meant it. This welcoming house with the pretty patio and the pictures from the past was a place she wanted to come again.

Nineteen

LEANNE DID HER BEST to act totally casual as she walked around the set. She'd returned to the desert after three days home while her mother was in the hospital. The director had shot around her absence, barely bothering to yell at her for leaving, which was strange. She had a feeling someone—Connor—had stepped in to smooth the way.

Which made her want to see him more. Not that he would admit anything, so it would be impossible to thank him.

She waved to a few people she knew, then moved faster as she heard a familiar laugh. She couldn't wait to see him, to have him ask how she was, to smile at him and—

Connor wasn't alone. He stood next to a stunning fortysomething woman with short black hair and an air of confidence that immediately made Leanne feel awkward and young.

They were obviously having an intimate conversation. The woman leaned toward Connor, touched his arm, then smiled in a way that let the world know she'd seen him naked.

"Leanne," Connor called, turning and seeing her. "You're back."

Trapped, she walked toward the couple. "I am," she said, smiling as if he were nothing but a little-known uncle she'd run into at a family gathering.

"How is your mother?" he asked.

"Doing well."

"Good. Dee, this is Leanne Greene, the actress I was telling you about. Leanne, Dee."

The two women shook hands. Dee wore the kind of casual clothes that cost thousands. They looked fabulous on her, emphasizing a perfect body and legs that went on forever.

Dee's smile widened. "Connor, you left off my title." She turned to Leanne. "Wife number three. Or is it four? I can never keep count."

"Three."

"But the favorite," Dee said with a throaty laugh. "You promised you would always say I was the favorite of your ex-wives."

"If you like."

Leanne knew that Connor had been married before but she'd never thought to find out the specifics. Apparently he was a man who liked a woman around but didn't generally keep her for long.

Dee excused herself. Leanne watched her go, not sure if the other woman had just been making conversation or warning her off.

"You can't take her seriously," Connor told her. "She likes to talk. Too much."

"One of the reasons you left her?"

"Maybe she left me."

"Maybe she did." Leanne suddenly felt the exhaustion of the past couple of days. "I didn't get much sleep in the hospital. I'm going to lie down so I'm rested when they call me." She started to walk away.

"Wait," Connor called.

She looked at him.

His dark blue eyes stared intently, as if he were searching for something. "I didn't ask her to come here. She's dating one of the stunt men. We ran into each other."

"You don't have to explain anything to me." She didn't want to play games anymore. She was too tired, too unsure.

He moved closer. "Why me?" he asked. "Am I some kind of father figure for you?"

Was it that? Was she trying to find the perfect dad after all this time?

"I don't know," she admitted. "I don't think so. Does it matter?"

"There are few things in life more pathetic than an old man in love with a young woman who is using him."

"Don't play me."

"I'm not playing."

Was it true? While she doubted he was actually in love with her, right now the possibility was more than enough.

She stared at him, trying to read his mind and know what he was thinking.

"You stand up to me," he told her. "You're full of passion and determination. You have faith in yourself, but you also have faith in other people. I gave that up years ago. You're achingly beautiful, with a brain and a sense of humor, which is more rare than you know."

She desperately wanted to believe him. "The problem with getting involved with a writer is you can never know when he's speaking from the heart and when he's practicing dialogue."

He touched the side of her face with his fingers. "I know what I get out of it," he said. "Anyone can see that. But what's in it for you?"

He was afraid. She saw it in a flash. He wasn't sure of himself, of her, of what she would do. He thought she might have the power to hurt him.

"You are."

"That's not enough."

She smiled. "It's everything."

Megan took her coffee out onto her little deck. She'd never bothered to sit out there, but after spending time with Pam on her patio, it felt right to relax in the sun and boot up her laptop for a quick review of her e-mail before heading into the office. Later her life would be frantic, but for now, in this moment, it was calm and happy and she was in a good place.

Two months ago, a good place would have been impossible to find. She'd felt as if everything she cared about had been ripped from her. Now she'd found her way to some kind of acceptance, if not total inner peace.

In many ways, she was lucky. She had so much to be grateful for. Her friends, her sister, a career that challenged her. Travis.

She smiled as she thought of him, then scrolled through her programs. She wanted to check on a client's tax filing date before she went into work.

She clicked on the connection to her office computer to find the file she wanted. The screen went white, with only the cursor blinking. Everything was gone.

Megan searched the other files and they were equally empty. Panic swept through her. Her heart rate cranked up and her palms got sweaty.

Every single record for Character Creative had been wiped clean. She was going to throw up.

This could destroy me, she thought, unable to believe it had happened. This wasn't an accident. Someone had deliberately destroyed all the records. Someone on a campaign to get rid of her.

OhGodohGodohGod.

What if she got fired? What if she got arrested? She would lose everything. This couldn't be happening, couldn't be real, couldn't—

Megan forced herself to breathe.

"Think this through," she said aloud. "It's not a total disaster." She wasn't an idiot. She had a backup.

She remembered the file she'd had her computer friend upload into her system. One that monitored any remote access to her client records. She had everything backed up here at home, so no client data was lost. Nothing had been compromised. All she had to do was take the information she had to Felicia. She would be vindicated. She wasn't going to jail or even losing her job. She was safe.

Which meant what?

The question surprised her. It meant everything. It was what she'd always wanted. She would make partner before turning thirty. She would move to a large corner office with a view, lease a Mercedes convertible and call herself a success.

And then what? Would she be happier? Would being a partner make her right for Travis? Would she sleep better at night, wake up more excited about her day, long for more of the same? Did she really want to spend the rest of her life where she was?

Her gaze fell on her father's painting. It showed a beach with a chair and the sun sinking low in the horizon. It was called *Sunset Bay*. The beautiful scene called to her. Not so much the location, but what it meant. Freedom.

But freedom from what? Her work? Her past? The lingering sense of emptiness she couldn't explain?

No answers came to her, so she did what she always did in a crisis. She went to work.

Travis had never much trusted men who were too well groomed. The guy standing in his office looked as if he'd been buffed and polished by an army of professionals.

He wasn't all that tall, but he was big in a way that said he worked out. He wore a black fitted T-shirt, black slacks and loafers. Travis would bet his sunglasses cost at least a grand and that the price of his leather briefcase would pay for a year of private college tuition.

"How can I help you?" he asked, because the sooner he got his mother's business profitable again, the sooner he could sell it for her and get the hell out of L.A.

"You're Travis Hunter?" the guy asked.

Travis nodded.

"Sweet. I'm Rudy James. Like Jesse James, but Rudy, you know? Leanne Greene told me about you. I'm doing some work on the movie she's in. Stunts. I specialize in motorcycle stunts." He pulled several papers out of his briefcase. "I'm producing a sci-fi motorcycle movie. It's going to be very big. Sort of like *Gone in Sixty Seconds*, but in the future and with bikes." Rudy grinned. "Here are the designs for what we have in mind. I've got a stunt guy who can make them fly if that's what we need, but he can't make them pretty. They have to be pretty." He dropped a photo of one of Travis's bikes on the desk. "I want them all to look like that."

Travis stood and stared down at the picture, the designs and the list that stated they would need fifteen working bikes and thirty others in pieces. His first thought was there was no way in hell he could pull this off. His second was that only an idiot would walk away from an opportunity like this.

"By when?" he asked.

"We start filming in eight months. You'd need to get

the first seven working bikes to my stunt guy in six. We'll pay you thirty grand a bike."

"Fifty a bike," he said absently, wondering where he could get space. Finding guys to help with the work wouldn't be hard. He knew exactly what he needed. He could go up to the San Fernando Valley. Maybe take over a lease in an industrial park.

"Forty, and that's as high as I'm going."

Forty thousand a bike? Forty thousand times fifteen and a door into the very lucrative movie business?

"I can't commit to the partial bikes until I get a complete list of what you want. A third for the fifteen up front, and the complete payment as I deliver them."

"I can get you a check as soon as we draw up a contract."

Holy shit! For real? With the money from this deal, he could start his own company. He could be doing what he always wanted to do. He could be . . .

A respectable member of society.

He had no idea where the words came from. Under any other circumstances, he would think they were bull, but not so much right now. This was his chance to be the right guy.

He stuck out his hand. "Done."

Thirty minutes later he and Rudy had worked out the rest of the details. He had an appointment with an entertainment lawyer and had been advised to bring one of his own. He would ask Megan; she would know.

Megan. What would she think of his deal? He picked up the phone to call her, then set it down when his mother walked into the office.

"You should go," she said, not looking at him. "With Artie in jail, I'll have the money I need."

Go? "You heard me with Rudy?"

"Some of it. Enough. It's a great opportunity. I won't stand in your way." She gave him a sad smile. "Not that you'd want to stay after what I said before. I understand. I don't see things the way you do. Artie's like your father. He's not a bad man. It's circumstances that he can't control."

It's always someone else's fault, Travis thought grimly. Even after Artie had nearly stolen every penny she had, his mother wouldn't see him as anything but a hero in waiting.

"I'm not going anywhere, Mom," he told her. "I'm going to get your business ready for you to sell."

"But you have this opportunity. You can't not take it."

"I'll do both. It won't be hard."

Tears filled her eyes. "Really?"

She must have been terrified he would just take off, like he had before. He wanted to remind her he'd been a kid then, and angry.

He put his arm around her. "Mom, I'm going to be around for a while."

"Thank you," she breathed, and held on tight.

She seemed smaller. He would take care of her. Ironically, he found himself thinking this wasn't her fault.

She'd always seen the best in people, especially her husband. Even when it wasn't there.

"I need your sister's phone number," Travis said.

Megan stared at her phone. "Do *not* tell me you're getting into the sister thing, because I'm so not in the mood."

Travis laughed. "No. A guy came to see me about my bikes. He's producing a movie with sci-fi motorcycles. Leanne must have told him about my custom work. He offered me a deal. A great deal."

He told her the details, then asked for the name of a good lawyer to go over the contract before he signed it.

"This changes everything," he told her. "This is my shot."

"It's wonderful. You're going to get everything you want."

"Or close." His voice dropped. "Are you free tonight? I thought we could celebrate."

She had a vision of exactly how she wanted to commemorate the moment. "I'm totally free. And yours."

Oops. Had she really meant to say that?

She braced herself for the backpedaling that was sure to follow, but Travis only said, "Great. Seven? Your place?"

"I'll be there."

She gave him Leanne's cell number, then flipped through her file of business cards until she found two different lawyers she'd worked with before.

After they hung up, she waited about twenty minutes before calling her sister.

"Hey, you," Leanne said, sounding cheerful. "I just got off the phone with your boyfriend. Rudy got in touch with him."

"So I heard. Thanks for doing that."

"I just gave a friend's name to a guy I work with. I didn't know if it was going to work out or not. I hoped it would. You know this means he's going to be hanging around L.A. for a while now."

Megan smiled. "I figured that out. Was that part of your plan?"

"Of course. You two are great together. He makes you happy. When you mentioned his bikes, it gave me the idea, but I didn't want to say anything in case it didn't happen."

"I owe you."

"Not really. We're sisters."

Something Megan had tried to avoid for years. "You were right to keep pushing me."

"I always wanted us to be close. Now we have that chance."

Megan picked up her pen and traced a line on her desk blotter. "I shouldn't have been so distant and judgmental," she said. "I'm sorry for that. And for the lost time."

"It's not lost anymore."

"You're being really nice to me and I don't deserve it. How's being on location?"

"Great. I love it. This is going to be an amazing movie. I can't wait for you to see it. You'll come to a screening, won't you? I want you there."

"Of course. Is this a red carpet event?"

Leanne laughed. "No. Sorry. Just a showing at a multiplex. But it's catered."

"I guess I can take food instead of paparazzi. You sound happy."

"I'm delirious. I've kind of met someone. He's a writer and totally cynical, but sweet, which seems weird. We're going really, really slow, getting to know each other. I like him a lot. Actually I think I'm falling for him."

"Okay, now I need details."

While Leanne talked about Connor, Megan thought about how Travis was following his dreams and Leanne was following hers. They'd both overcome a lot to get where they were. She looked around her office and thought about the possibility of making partner. Not exactly a dream that kept little kids up at night. There'd been a time when she'd wanted more. She'd wanted to create something beautiful, special. She'd wanted to design clothes that make women feel sexy and touchable and capable of taking on the world.

She thought about Elliott's painting and the two hunded and fifty thousand dollars sitting in an account, collecting interest.

"What the hell am I waiting for?" she asked aloud, before standing up and grabbing her purse. She'd put her dreams on hold long enough. It was time to take action . . . starting today.

The best garment workers in the city could be found in East L.A. Most people drove by the large factories near the freeways and never thought about what went on inside, but Megan had always known. Now she stood in a cramped office surrounded by fabric samples, facing a bored-looking man with a measuring tape around his neck and a pincushion where a watch would normally be.

"You want the good material, you pay the higher price. Making only two or three of each size is very expensive. I don't make these things up. It's how business is done."

Arturo was one of the best around. She'd come to him because she wanted everything to be perfect. Sewing the garments herself would have taken months. Paying him meant everything would be perfect. It would also use up a big chunk of her inheritance from Elliott Scott.

"Do it," she said. "I have more designs I'll bring after these are made."

"You have patterns?" he asked.

"For some."

"Get the patterns. That will save you money." He fingered the sketches. "These are good. Yours?"

She nodded.

"Are you starting a line?"

"I don't know," she said honestly. "I might just sell them to a few stores."

He looked annoyed. "If that's all you're going to do, why waste my time?"

She pulled out her checkbook. "Do you want the deposit or not?"

He named an amount that nearly made her faint, but she wrote out the check and handed it to him.

"Give me two weeks," he told her. "Maybe less."

Once in her car, she did her best to steady her breathing. Arturo was right. Putting a few items in stores around town wouldn't do anything for her. She would never get noticed, never take off. The way to be successful was to make a splash. Go out big.

"Fly high, crash hard," she said out loud as she backed out of the parking space.

This was her dream. Did she take it all the way or did she play it safe?

She drove back to the office via Santa Monica, which wasn't on her way, but there was a storefront she wanted to check out.

It was next to a couple of upscale stores and across the courtyard from the Cheesecake Factory. There would be built-in foot traffic. And she would never go hungry. At least not while the money lasted. Not sure if she would ever call it, she wrote down the phone number for the leasing agent. Fifteen minutes later, she was back at her desk.

Felicia hurried in seconds later.

"You're back," her boss said in a tone that implied she'd been waiting. "What do you have against your cell phone?"

"Nothing. Oh, sorry. Is it off?" Her mother had been calling and Megan had been avoiding her. "Is there a problem with a client?" Had Carrie struck again? If she had, Megan was going to take the information she had to Felicia. She was tired of being the good girl in all this.

"There's a problem, but it's not with a client and it's not with you." Felicia sank into the chair on the other side of the desk. "You never said anything about what Carrie was doing. Changing time cards, erasing files, lying about appointments. She was out to destroy you."

Megan breathed a sigh of relief. "I knew she'd done some of that," she said carefully. "I wasn't sure about all of it."

"She had obviously decided she wanted to get the promotion and make sure you were fired along the way. I caught her going through some files she shouldn't have been in and started investigating. There had been rumblings, but I thought that was just jealousy about the new girl." Felicia stared at her. "You never complained."

"I didn't know how it was going to play out. I was collecting information, and if necessary, I was prepared to use it. But as long as our clients were getting a hundred percent from me, I . . ."

Megan paused. The truth was she hadn't known what to do or how to complain. Politics were a necessary part of doing business, but not one she liked.

"I understand," Felicia told her. "The partners and I have been talking about this situation. Obviously Carrie has been fired. Of everyone attacked by her, you have impressed us the most." Felicia smiled. "Congratulations, Megan. The partnership is yours, along with a raise and, of course, a much bigger office."

She kept talking about the benefits and responsibilities that came with the new position. How everything would be different. She was one of them now.

Megan moved her leg slightly and felt her briefcase. The leather bulged from all the designs she'd crammed inside. She and Arturo had picked a dozen of the best, but while talking to him she'd thought of ways to improve some of the others. She also had ideas for a spring collection. Soft fabrics in perfect colors. Clothes that would make women feel good about themselves while making them look beautiful.

"There's a comfortable security in making partner," Felicia was saying. "As a single woman, I'm sure you appreciate that as much as I do. I was married when I got promoted, but since then . . ." She grinned. "Let's just say men come and go but a great job is forever."

Forever. That was a long time.

Megan thought about months and years in this highrise, dealing with clients and the tax code and all the details that made her a great accountant. She thought about the rooms of beautiful fabric at Arturo's factory and how inspiring that had been. She thought of her father's paintings. Had she inherited her creative ability from him?

She saw her life clearly then, at a perfect crossroads. One direction led to safety and security. She could see exactly what she would be doing every day until she retired.

The other direction was in shadows. It could end in disaster. Fifty percent of all new businesses failed in the first year. Eighty percent in the first three years. The statistics were worse for retail. Did she really want to risk all that? Take the only money she had and potentially throw it down a rat hole? What would her father think?

Her father. Not Gary Greene, who had turned his back on her, but Elliott Scott. A man who laughed in every picture she'd seen of him. A man who painted with passion and light and color. A man who loved his children and his wife, who had reached out to a daughter he'd never known to leave her a legacy that could change her life.

"Megan? Are you all right?"

She stood and looked at her boss. "It's a great offer."

"I know. Congratulations. Welcome to the team."

"I'm going to turn it down."

"What?"

"I quit."

Twenty

"I MAY NEED TO breathe into a paper bag," Megan said, looking wild-eyed. "What was I thinking? Ohmigod! I wasn't thinking. I reacted. I was insane. They'll take me back, right? I can call Felicia and get my job back. That's what I should do. This is Elliott's fault. His life of painting and colors. Or it's sex with you. I'm under the influence." She pressed a hand to her stomach. "I think I'm going to throw up."

Travis hid his smile as he put his arm around her. "You're not going to throw up."

"You don't actually know that. And won't you feel stupid when I do."

He moved in front of her, cupped her face in his hands and stared into her green eyes. "Are you excited about the future?"

"Excited and scared and worried and terrified and hopeful and, you know, queasy."

"Then you're doing the right thing."

She pulled free and slapped his shoulder. "That's easy for you to say. I gave up a very impressive 401(k) program, benefits and a corner office. I was going to lease a new Mercedes. I had security and paid vacation."

He enjoyed the sound of panic in her voice, the way she pushed back and how stressed she looked. There was a fire inside her again—one that he'd first fallen for ten years ago. This was the Megan he knew . . . this was the Megan he'd missed.

"Now you have a future," he said.

"I had a better future before."

"You had a more secure future before. This one's going to be more fun."

"Sure. Until I lose everything. You know this condo isn't paid for, right? I have a very crabby bank that's expecting regular checks. Telling them I'm off following my dream isn't going to change that fact. I used my entire savings to pay back Gary for the wedding. It took nearly half my inheritance from my dad to get my clothes made and it'll take the other half to buy inventory, lease the place and get it ready. Then I'll have about eight dollars to my name. I can't live on eight dollars."

"You'll be fine."

"You don't know that." Her voice rose shrilly. "You're just saying the kind of stuff you say to a crazy person right before they threaten to jump off a building. You think I'm a jumper. I can't breathe." She clutched her chest. "And now I'm turning into my mother."

He grabbed her arm, pulled her close and kissed her. When she started to draw back, he deepened the kiss, claiming her with his tongue until she melted against him and her breathing deepened.

"Better?" he asked.

Her eyes were closed. "It could be if you did that again."

He grinned, then kissed her until they were both straining toward each other.

"Now?"

She opened her eyes and smiled at him. "Much better."

"Good. Now sit."

She collapsed on the sofa. He sat on the coffee table.

"You're going to be fine," he said. "You're smart and determined, you're not afraid of hard work and you know a hell of a lot about business. Plus this is your passion and going for your passion gives you an edge."

"Says who?"

"Everyone who matters. Come on, Megan. I know you're scared, but if you could go back to this morning, wouldn't you still quit your job?"

She nodded slowly. "I have to do this. It's where I need to be. But it's scary." She smiled. "Okay, and it's fun." She grabbed his hands. "Don't you get scared? Or are you too macho to feel fear?"

"I started my business out of the back of a garage, building one bike at a time. There wasn't anything to be scared about." He thought about the deal he was going to sign and how it would change everything. "Until now."

"Soon you'll go Hollywood and start wearing chains."

He stood and drew her to her feet. "I'm not a chains kind of guy."

"You will be. You'll be getting facials and manicures

before you know it. Sleeping with starlets and partying on private jets."

He kissed her. "I doubt that," he murmured against her mouth.

She parted for him instantly. As their tongues danced together he thought about how it had always been right with her. When he was around Megan, his world got brighter, better. She made him laugh, chased away the darkness. There was a part of him only she touched.

Ten years ago he'd vowed he would never care about anyone ever again. It had been the promise of an angry kid, born out of hurt, but it had been easy to keep. Not loving anyone else was easy. Not loving Megan?

Her doorbell rang.

She put her hands on his chest. "Did you order take-out?"

"No."

"Me either. I guess I'll see who it is."

He watched her walk across the room. His gaze dropped to the sway of her hips and he imagined what would happen later, when the two of them were naked, in bed.

The door opened. He recognized the guy on the porch—Travis had first seen him in Las Vegas. The cardiologist.

"Adam." Megan sounded surprised. "What are you doing here?"

"I want to talk to you." Adam glanced past her and saw Travis. He stiffened. "I called you at the office and they said you didn't work there anymore, so I came by." He lowered his voice. "You're seeing him? I thought it was a one-time thing."

"It's not," she said. "I don't understand. We don't have anything to talk about."

"We were engaged," Adam said, keeping his gaze on Travis. "We have some unfinished business. We have a joint account to deal with—that time-share we bought. You owe me a conversation, Megan."

Travis stayed where he was, hoping he looked intimidating to a soft-handed doctor. Adam might know how to put people back together but Travis was really good at taking them apart.

Megan sighed. "Okay, fine. We have to talk, but not tonight."

She'd bought a time-share? With the doctor? Travis couldn't explain the anger inside, except that he knew she would never buy a time-share with him. He wasn't the type. But was she? Had he been fooling himself all this time? Did he really think he got to keep someone like her?

Without wanting to, he remembered everything she'd said about her parents. How their twisted relationship worked because there was one who worshipped and one who was adored. Was he that guy?

And then he got it. He would be that guy. He would be anything to keep Megan. Because she was the best thing that ever happened to him. Only he didn't belong here, in her world. She *should* marry a doctor, a lawyer. Somebody who owned a lot of suits and cared about time-shares.

He grabbed his leather jacket.

She left Adam at the door and moved toward Travis. "What are you doing? You don't need to leave. I'll talk to him later. All of this can wait."

"Why? Deal with it now. He wants you back. You know that, right?"

"Travis, no. Why are you leaving? What's going on?"

"He's who you belong with. Remember that when you're talking to him."

Words he didn't mean and didn't want to say. What was wrong with him? He should fight for her. She was the one he'd always wanted.

Except she was light and promise and everything else he didn't have. She should be with a guy who wore sweaters and drove cars with good safety ratings. Adam was a much better bet than he would ever be.

"Good-bye, Megan," he said.

She glared at him. "Don't do this. Don't make him showing up here more than it is. Dammit, Travis, this is crazy. What are you doing?"

"Bowing to the inevitable."

"That's crap and you know it. You're looking for a reason to run. Stay and talk to me."

"See ya, babe."

He walked to the door and pushed past Adam. Then he was out on the street. It was still sunny, which was odd. It should have been cold and raining. Only this was L.A.—a place where you could count on sunshine and the blond-haired guy always getting the girl.

*   *   *

Megan watched Travis leave. She wanted to go after him, to at least punch him hard enough to hurt. Not that she could, but a fantasy life was important. Why did he have to go and be a butthead just because Adam showed up?

She looked at her ex-fiancé and knew the answer to the question. Travis and Adam couldn't have been more different. If she'd wanted one, why would she want the other?

She stepped aside and motioned for Adam to come in. He looked a little uncomfortable.

"I wasn't trying to make trouble," he said, sounding almost genuinely sorry.

"It's a timing thing," she said. She would deal with Adam, then figure out what to do with Travis. "Why did you come by? Why now?"

He handed her an envelope. She opened it and saw a check for twenty-one thousand dollars.

"My half of the wedding expenses," he said.

She stared at him. "You're kidding."

"I don't like what happened to us. I think you're wrong to end things, but I can't force you to marry me and I acknowledge that telling you about my affair was where it all started to go wrong."

If she hadn't been so surprised, she would have smiled. It wasn't his telling her that was the problem. It was that he'd done it in the first place. But Adam wouldn't get that and she didn't care enough to fight with him.

She waved the check. "We're still not getting back together."

"The money isn't conditional."

No, but it *was* a surprise. She would put it in a savings account and pretend it didn't exist. It could be her emergency stash in case her business totally failed.

"Thank you," she said, leading the way into the living room. "You're being very fair and I appreciate that."

He shoved his hands into his slacks. "I never wanted to lose you. I'm sorry about that."

She nodded because she couldn't bring herself to say she was sorry, too.

He glanced around at the designs and fabric covering nearly every surface. "What is all this?"

"My life," she said, knowing it was true. "I'm going to open a boutique in Santa Monica. I rented the space this morning."

He frowned. "Retail? You quit your job to work in a store selling clothes?"

"I quit my job to open a boutique that sells unique designs, some of which are mine. I'm having a couple of dozen things made for the store. Tomorrow I'm going to the fashion school where I took classes years ago. I want to see about putting some of their students' designs in the store, too."

"Who wants to buy clothes from a kid in school? Megan, why are you doing this?"

"Because it's what I've always wanted to do."

"You're an accountant."

"Not anymore."

"Is this about your dad?"

"In part. I've had a chance to look at my life, to figure out what it is I want. I've taken the safe road for a long time now. I've made easy choices. Ten years ago, Gary told me I couldn't go to design school. That I had to study business. And I agreed." He'd also told her to get rid of Travis and she'd done that, too.

"I've been so afraid of losing that I haven't bothered to try too hard. But I'm starting to figure out that life is a game of risks. We have to lose some things we think we need to find what we really want."

"Is he what you really want?"

"I don't know," she admitted. Travis had always had a direct line to her heart. But she needed more than passion and a guy who looked great in black leather. She needed someone willing to be with her through the tough times. Someone who loved her fearlessly. Was that him?

"Either way, you don't want me," Adam said.

She shook her head.

"At least I know." He hesitated, as if he was going to say something, then smiled. "Take care of yourself, Megan."

"You too."

And then he was gone.

Megan carried a couple of large boxes down the hall.

"I would have done it myself," her mother said, following her. "Only I don't know what you want to keep. Plus, I have to be so careful with my energy. The diabetes can be so draining. Once we move, it will be better. I'm taking a water aerobics class. Did I tell you that? Your father spoke with the instructor himself. He wants to make sure she understands that I'm dealing with a serious illness. She has to take special care of me."

Tina sounded thrilled with all the attention. Megan walked into the bedroom that had been hers for eighteen years and told herself not to be cynical, that she should just take the events as they came and not read too much into them.

"When are you listing the house?" she asked.

"Friday. We want to buy a smaller condo here and then a place in Hawaii. Your father is cutting back to part-time work. We've been talking about it and we want to take advantage of the few years we have left together." Tina sniffed. "With my health being so precarious and all."

Megan did her best not to roll her eyes. Her mother's diabetes was under control. With the right diet and exercise, she could easily live to be a hundred.

"I'm back," Leanne yelled. "I got the fresh vegetables from the farmer's market, like you asked. Is Megan here? I saw her car."

"She's cleaning out her room." Tina fanned herself. "I need to make sure she's putting everything in the right place, then go lie down. My energy just isn't what it should be."

"Sure. I'll be fine, Mom. You go rest."

She didn't bother pointing out that since the diagnosis, Tina was more mobile than she'd been in years. She also didn't tell her to stop referring to Gary as her father. Tina being in the hospital might have caused him to start speaking to Megan, but nothing about their relationship was as it had been.

She didn't like it, but she'd accepted that she couldn't change it. He saw things differently from her; he always would. The loss was there, the hurt, but it got smaller every day. Eventually it would only be a scar that ached when it rained.

She set to work going through her room. She'd cleared out most of it when she'd gotten her first apartment, after college, so it didn't take long to sort through the few items left. There were some old books that she put in the give-away box; pictures and clothes she dropped in the box to take with her for further sorting at home. A few minutes later Leanne joined her.

"Need some help?" her sister asked.

"No, I'm good. Did you do your room already?"

"Yesterday. It didn't take long. I can't believe they're selling the house."

"All the better to enjoy the few years they have left."

Leanne grinned. "She is enjoying the drama of having a real disease. When she says diabetes, I swear the word is in italics. Dad is constantly fussing, which she loves. I always thought he resented her craziness, but now it seems as if he likes it."

"Maybe it gives him purpose," Megan said.

Leanne settled on the bed. "Are you dealing with him at all? Has he called?"

"No, and he's not going to. I'm not his daughter and I'm in the process of accepting that."

"Megan, he could come around."

"I don't think he will—and even if he did, I'd never trust him again."

"I know. It's just that I hate to see you sad."

Megan sat across from her on the bed. "I'm not sad. I'm happy. And scared." She'd already told Leanne about quitting her job and opening the boutique.

"No being scared," Leanne said. "This is an amazing opportunity. We're still on for our painting party, right?"

"Yes. Thursday. Dress grubby. I have a cleaning service coming in tomorrow to take care of the worst of the dirt, but the whole place needs painting and I can't afford a professional."

"Do you have a date and time for the opening?"

"I don't know. As soon as possible. The clothes I designed are nearly ready, but I have to find other stock, pull a guest list together, send out invitations."

"What about doing a fashion show?" Leanne asked. "I know a lot of skinny out-of-work actresses you could use as models. That might draw some press."

"I hadn't thought of that."

"I finally have Hollywood connections. Let's use them. Oh, and I found out there's going to be an actual premiere for the movie, so I'll need a dress, which you can design. I'll talk you up and you'll be famous."

"I'd like that." Megan smiled. Whatever else she'd had to go through, at least she'd found her sister. "Speaking of sharing the love, thanks again for putting that guy in touch with Travis about the motorcycles. It's a big deal and Travis is excited."

Leanne grinned. "I know. He sent me the biggest bouquet of flowers I've ever seen. Connor was very jealous, even after I explained why I got them. I would be a little upset, but he's not one to admit to jealousy, so that was kind of cool. He's—" She frowned.

"What's wrong?"

"You look funny."

Probably because she hadn't heard from Travis in three days or because he'd never sent her flowers. "He left."

"What do you mean?"

"Travis is gone. He was at my place and Adam came over and said we had to talk. I told Adam another time would work better, but Travis got upset anyway. I don't get it. He said Adam was a better choice, then he left."

She'd managed not to fall apart, but the more time that went by, the more she wondered if he was gone for good.

"Did you explain that you weren't interested in getting back with Adam? Did you tell him you were just cleaning up old business?"

"Yes, and he knows that's all it is. He completely over-reacted."

"Did he?" Leanne asked. "You're a successful professional who was engaged to a pinheaded cardiologist. Only Travis doesn't know Adam's a pinhead. He sees this outwardly powerful guy who wants to marry you. A couple of months ago you and Travis hook up in Vegas where he finds out he was your distraction on the day you were supposed to be getting married."

Megan winced. "It wasn't like that. I'd broken up with Adam. I wouldn't have married him even if I'd never run into Travis."

"Do you think Travis believes that? He's not a professional. He's some guy who builds custom bikes. You're like the princess he can never have, except he almost did once. Then you walked away. Now he's afraid of it happening again."

"That's not fair. Not any of it. I'm not a princess. As for having me before, he didn't give me any time or even a choice. I had to go with him that second or it was over. I was a kid."

"And this time?"

Megan drew in a breath. "I want to make it work with him. I . . . I love him. I think I always have. He's the one who makes my heart beat faster. But he's so damn quick to walk away."

"You hurt his pride," Leanne said softly.

"What?"

"Travis is a very proud man. He doesn't ask for anything from anyone. He never has. He makes his own way. No one gets close, except for you. He offered you all he had, all he was, once. And you're right—you were too young and he was too impatient. But he thinks he knows how this story ends and he's terrified of it playing out the same way again."

Megan didn't know what to think. Her sister's words made sense, even if they were impossible to believe.

"How do you know all this?" she asked.

"I'm very smart."

That made her laugh. "Since when?"

"It's a recent thing." Leanne shrugged. "I've made a lot of mistakes in my life. I've done a lot of stupid things and I've gone places I never thought I would go. I want to change that. I want to be a better person. So I'm trying to be different. Some days it's harder than others."

Megan hugged her. "Thank you for being my sister."

"You're welcome. Thanks for being mine."

Twenty-one

TRAVIS HAD SET UP shop in north Van Nuys, in a small industrial park that housed a couple dozen businesses. There were a few car repair places, a printer, a machine shop. Megan parked next to a truck that advertised window and gutter cleaning.

She crossed the narrow parking lot, checking numbers until she found the one she was looking for. The big bay door stood open.

He was there by himself, bent over a partially built bike. He wore jeans and a T-shirt; his hair was too long. His leather jacket lay across the bike he'd ridden that morning.

Her own personal bad boy, she thought, her whole body quivering at the sight of him. Years ago she'd been too young to take what he offered. She'd been too afraid. Now . . . Now everything was different.

She spoke his name.

He paused, then straightened and looked at her.

She'd come here looking for something she couldn't define. As he stared into her eyes and did his damnedest to keep her from knowing what he was thinking, everything became clear.

Knowledge gave her strength. She walked up to him and smiled.

"I love you," she said clearly, so he couldn't later say he didn't understand. "I love you. All of you—even the bad stuff. You're not perfect. So what? I'm not either. We can screw up together. Because that's what I want. You and me together."

He stared at her without speaking. Was he testing her? Regardless, she was going to go for it, without worrying about the consequences.

"Ten years ago I wasn't close to ready. You pushed and I totally freaked out. We were too young. We would have crashed and burned. We may still. The difference is this time I know it's worth trying for. I'm willing to give my whole heart, Travis. It's yours. Forever. I'm serious about this, about us. I want it all, if you're interested. But I don't think you are."

Emotion flickered his eyes, but she couldn't read it.

She touched the scar, then dropped her hand. "It's too easy for you to be a loner. You never have to worry about anyone but yourself. You never have to put anything on the line. You don't have to take a step of courage or believe in anything. I believe—in myself, in you and in us. I'm stepping up. What are you doing?"

He turned away and picked up a wrench. "This isn't a good time for me."

Disappointment weighed on her. "That's just what Gary said when I wanted to talk about why he wasn't being my father anymore. There's never a good time, there's only the right time." She pulled a business card out of her pocket. She'd picked them up that morning. She set one on the small workbench by the bike.

"So you can find me when you're ready."

She walked out into the sunlight. It was a perfect Hollywood ending. All she needed was a slight breeze, the swell of music and the credits to roll. Everything would look great on film. But in life, her heart was breaking.

"Oh, please!" Payton turned in front of the mirror and looked at herself from the back. "You have to let me have this. I'll pay retail. Come on. Or at least hold it until the opening. Megan, we've been friends a long time. I need this dress."

Megan looked up from the artfully arranged flowers she'd been moving from place to place in an attempt to display them in the best possible light. After paying a hundred and twenty dollars for them, she wanted to get her money's worth at the launch party.

Payton twirled in a pale green halter dress that was part of Megan's spring collection. The empire style fell softly to just above her knee, making her waist look impossibly small and her legs look longer than usual.

"If she gets that, I get these," Allegra said, pushing Payton out of the way so she could see herself in the three-way mirror. "If you had told me that you could make me look good in high-waisted pants I would have laughed in your face. But I like these. Jeez, next you'll have me eating spinach."

Megan managed a smile, but that was the best she could do. She was so tired her bones ached. In the past month, she'd been getting by on maybe three hours of sleep a night. She'd pushed hard to get the boutique ready to open and now she was less than twenty-four hours from D-day.

As her friends argued about who looked better, she straightened and looked around at the bright, open space that was her store.

Large windows let in plenty of natural light during the day, while recessed lighting added ambience. A dozen or so outfits had been put up on walls. Most were her own designs, but a few had been created by students at the design school. The shoes and bags were on consignment from an accessory store in the Third Street Promenade a few blocks away. Her father's artwork—some hers, some on loan from Pam—hung on the walls.

The carpenter had finished with the dressing rooms less than a week ago, which had meant a rush of more painting before the carpeting arrived. She'd spent the last forty-eight hours arranging stock, decorating and being grateful for Leanne, who was handling most of the details for the opening party.

"I can't wait to wear this to some fabulous party in New York," Allegra said with a sigh. "I'll be sure I'm photographed."

Payton rolled her eyes. "At some point you're going to have to enter the real world."

"My life is the real world."

"On what planet?"

Megan sank into a chair. "We're done," she said, so tired it was hard to talk.

They both looked at her. "What do you mean, you're done?" Payton looked around the store, then grinned. "You're right. Everything looks incredible. You should be proud of yourself."

She would be, after she'd had a chance to sleep.

Allegra bent down and kissed her cheek. "We'll get out of here so you can go home. What time do you want us back tomorrow?"

"The party starts at seven. So five?"

"Sure. Do you need help with anything?"

"Leanne's handling the details, so you should ask her. She's back from her location shooting." She had a couple of weeks off until she was needed back in the studio for the interior shots. At least Megan thought that was what she'd said. She couldn't remember right now.

Her friends changed back into their own clothes and promised to collect their new outfits tomorrow. Megan waved as they left, then forced herself to stand. The quicker she closed up, the quicker she could get home and collapse.

She walked to the front door to make sure it was locked and nearly jumped out of her skin when she saw a man standing in front of the store. Gary.

They stood there, just staring at each other. For a second it was like nothing had changed. He was her dad and he'd come to check on her. But even as the thought formed, she knew it wasn't true. He couldn't have changed that much—he wasn't capable.

It had taken her a long time to figure that out.

He'd raised and maybe even loved her—at least while it was easy. But when times got tough, he got gone. She supposed she could have fought harder, demanded he see her as his child, but to what end? She couldn't force him to love her, just like she couldn't force Travis to want to be with her. People made their own choices.

She'd lost her father but found her sister. She was pretty sure she'd ended up with the better bargain.

She opened the front door. "Hi," she said.

"Megan. Your mother wants me to remind you to stop by with the dress you're giving her. She wants to be at her best for the opening."

Tina had called and demanded Megan create something just for her. Megan had agreed because it was easier and because her mother would certainly talk about the creation.

"It's on my calendar for tomorrow," she said. "Anything else?"

He looked past her to the shop. For a second, she thought he might say something. Maybe he felt the pull of the past, but it wasn't strong enough. He shook his head and turned away.

"Good-bye, Dad," she said, and meant it.

Megan closed the door and locked it, then turned out the lights and walked to the rear of the store.

When she reached the stock room, she turned for one more glimpse of her dream. She'd managed to pull it together in an impossibly short amount of time. Of course she'd had help, but knowing all the people who cared about her were a part of this only made it better. Well, nearly all the people. She hadn't seen Travis in weeks.

She missed him constantly. It was like a part of her was gone. She didn't regret anything she'd said or done. She'd told the truth, and if that was too much for him, the problem was his, not hers. Which sounded very mature but didn't make it easier to forget.

She looked at her store and felt both anticipation and pride. She'd done it. Despite everything that had happened to her in the past six months, or maybe because of it, she was here. Ready for whatever the future might bring.

She stepped out the back door and carefully locked it behind her. As she moved to her car, she heard the sound of an engine. It was deep and powerful and familiar. A man on a motorcycle pulled up next to her.

Her exhaustion fled, pushed aside by a surge of hope. Travis pulled off his helmet and looked at her. Her insides quivered just like they had the first time she'd seen him. His earring glinted in the fading light.

He stared at her as if searching for something. She wanted to tell him that she would love him forever but forced herself to keep quiet. She'd done the talking last time. Now it was his turn.

"You scare the crap out of me," he said. "You make me want things I know I can't have. To lose again . . ." He shook his head. "Just when I think I know how it's going to end, you show up and tell me you love me.

That you believe in me. No one's ever believed in me before."

"Okay," she said cautiously. "And?"

He grinned. "Damn, you're never easy, you know that?"

"It's part of my charm."

His smile faded. "I believe in you, too. I believe in us. Jesus, Megan, I nearly blew it. We could have lost everything, only you wouldn't let that happen. I don't know how I got so damned lucky. I found you twice and this time, I'm never letting go. I love you. I always have. I've been a jerk about it, but the love never died. I tried to forget you, but I can't. I want you too much. You're the one for me. I want to be the one for you."

There was so much they needed to say to each other. So many lovers' questions, like when had he first realized he loved her and who loved the other more. Silly questions and questions that would make her cry.

But that was for later. For tonight, there was just the man and where he was going to take her.

She picked up the extra helmet from the seat behind him and slid it on. After fastening the strap, she climbed on behind him, wrapped her arms around his waist and said, "Let's go."

LOS ANGELES TIMES
STYLE SECTION

There are Hollywood parties where one goes to be seen and Hollywood parties that are just plain fun. The opening of Santa Monica's latest trendsetting boutique—Sunset Bay—was the place for the latter. It wasn't just somewhere to be seen, it was a great time for everyone lucky enough to get an invitation.

New designer Megan Greene dazzled with a fashion show of wearable, beautiful, stylish designs from her new collection, as stars and other A-listers circulated.

Following in the footsteps of actor/designer siblings such as David Spade and his sister Kate Spade, Megan Greene's sister, Leanne Greene, is an up-and-coming actress already getting award buzz for her latest role. Leanne, on the arm of handsome writer and director Connor McKay, glittered in an elegant gown by Megan. Supermodel Allegra also wore the designer's clothes and raved about the new fashions.

Megan is modest about her overnight success. "I want to make clothes women love," she said, her handsome fiancé at her side.

The party lasted until well past midnight as the crowd devoured snacks and bought out nearly the entire inventory. The only bump in an otherwise perfect evening was when the designer's mother seemed to faint, but she quickly recovered.

Next time you're in Santa Monica, check out Sunset Bay. It's going to be a hit.

Turn the page for a preview of Susan Mallery's
next heartwarming novel

The Best of Friends

Coming in February 2009
from Pocket Star Books

> *"No gold-digging for me . . . I'll take diamonds. We may be off the gold standard someday."*
> —Mae West

THERE WERE TWO TYPES of people, Jayne Scott told herself as she hurried from the waiting car toward the international terminal at the Los Angeles airport. Those who skated through life, never spilling coffee on themselves or tripping or showing up at the wrong time for the wrong event. Then there was the rest of the world. As she dabbed at the growing damp spot left by her grande nonfat latte, Jayne knew exactly which camp she fell into.

She scanned the crowded "arrivals" area, ignoring the dozens of different languages, the happy families reuniting, the couples in love. Instead she looked for a tall, beautiful blonde with an excessive amount of luggage and a half-dozen or so minions. Seconds later she spotted two porters with overflowing luggage carts, a burly guy with a briefcase strapped to his wrist, and a head-turning woman wearing leather pants and a leopard duster. Leave it to Rebecca to make an entrance.

Jayne waited until her friend spotted her, then waved.

"I'm late," Rebecca called, then hurried forward and hugged her. "I got stuck in customs. They thought I was a jewel thief. Don't you love that?"

"Anyone offer to do a strip search?" Jayne asked, hugging her back and inhaling a floral perfume that was probably custom blended.

Rebecca straightened and wrinkled her nose. "No, and I didn't want anyone to."

"No one cute enough?"

"Pretty much. Jayne, this is Hans, my bodyguard."

The burly guy barely made eye contact before returning to scanning the crowd.

Jayne glanced at the briefcase in his hand. "You couldn't use a courier service like everyone else?" she asked, leading the way to the waiting limo. "You had to bring them yourself?"

"That's what the customs people said. They lack imagination."

"Or maybe they were overwhelmed by seeing a couple million in loose gemstones."

"I'm a jewelry designer. It's what I do."

"If you were a ship builder would you travel with a three-ton hull?"

"Thanks for coming to meet me," Rebecca said, linking arms with her. "I've missed you."

"I've missed you, too."

They walked out to the waiting limo that Jayne had arranged. She'd known better than to bring her own car. Not only did Rebecca prefer to travel in style, there was no way all the luggage would fit in Jayne's Jetta.

Rebecca stared at the vehicle with approval. "It's a stretch limo."

"I know you love them."

"I do. Wait until you see the place I rented in Santa Monica. It has a view of the ocean and everything. I'll have to get a car, of course. Everyone needs a car in L.A."

"You could just hire the limo permanently. It could go with you everywhere."

Rebecca slid into the backseat, then looked up at her. "Now you're mocking me."

"I can't help myself." Jayne settled in next to her. "Do you want to talk about your mother now or later?"

"How about never."

"She's the reason you're back."

"I've returned to announce myself," Rebecca said, leaning back in the leather seat. "To reintroduce myself to society."

"You're here to be a pain in her ass."

"That, too."

"Rearranging your life to annoy your mother is expected at thirteen. At twenty-nine, it's just kind of sad."

Rebecca turned to her. "Tragedy keeps my art fresh."

"I see you're still dramatic."

"I see you're still dressing badly."

Jayne glanced down at the faded magenta scrub shirt she was wearing, now decorated by the latte stain. "I came straight from work."

"Maybe something more tailored."

"I'm a nurse, Rebecca. This is what I wear."

Rebecca gave a little sniff, then pulled a bottle of water out of her carry-on.

She was the only person Jayne knew who could fly from Italy to L.A. and look ready to step into a photo shoot. Carefully highlighted blond hair hung past her shoulders in layered curls. Her skin was flawless, her lips full and lush. Gold and diamond earrings, her own design, glittered as she moved.

Hans finished supervising the luggage being loaded into the trunk, then walked to the front passenger seat and slid in next to the driver.

"What about a work space?" Jayne asked. "You're not going to be making jewelry at the condo you rented, are you?"

Rebecca laughed. "I think the landlord would object to me melting gold in my living room. I've got a place in an industrial park."

"You're not the industrial park type."

"People grow and change, Jayne. I have."

Jayne ignored the smug smile. "Is this where I remind you that you're back in L.A. to piss off your mother?"

"Not if you love me. Speaking of the socially correct Mrs. Worden, how is Elizabeth?"

"Stuck in France."

Rebecca raised her eyebrows. "Seriously? Did the private jet develop mechanical trouble? Are my parents being forced to fly commercial?"

"Nothing that dramatic. There's fog. She and Blaine are delayed a few hours." Jayne glanced at her watch. "Which means I'll be leaving you shortly and heading to the house."

"Why?"

"I have to open it up for David."

Jayne was careful to keep eye contact with Rebecca. Her friend might be self-absorbed, but she wasn't stupid. But after nearly twelve years of keeping her secret, she was an expert at making sure nothing ever showed.

It was foolish, really. One of those freak things that happen every now and then—like plane-grounding fog in France. Fourteen years ago, at the age of sixteen, Jayne had gone on vacation with the Worden family. They'd spent the holidays at an exclusive resort in the Bahamas. The hotel had been fabulous, the weather perfect, but what Jayne remembered most was how she'd taken one look at David, Rebecca's older brother, and had fallen madly and completely in love.

Well, as completely as a sixteen-year-old could.

Since then, she'd seen him every couple of years. The conversations had been casual and he'd barely noticed she was alive. Better for both of them, she thought wryly. It was one thing for her to be friends with Rebecca and an unpaid part-time assistant to Elizabeth. It was quite another to get involved with the heir . . . or as Rebecca loved to call him, the young prince.

Over time Jayne had accepted that her feelings were little more than an intense crush. But knowing they were irrational didn't make her knees tremble any less when he was around.

"Carmine can do it," Rebecca said. Carmine was the Worden's housekeeper.

"Carmine is visiting her daughter in Chicago."

"Let me guess . . . Mother called and asked for your help."

"A few hours ago. She had planned to be back this morning, but fate intervened."

"You're choosing her over me?"

"On nearly a daily basis."

Rebecca pouted. "You're my best friend. You can't do what she says. You have to take my side."

"It's an hour," Jayne said calmly, used to the tantrums and mostly immune to the guilt. "I'll be by later. Besides, if I don't do what Elizabeth asks, she'll want to know why. If she starts asking questions, she might find out you're back before you want her to."

"I hate it when you use logic on me."

"Yes, I know."

"Fine. Go be dutiful. One of us should be. It's a family thing."

Jayne didn't bother pointing out she wasn't family. At least, not from their perspective. From hers, the Wordens were the closest thing she had to relatives, which made her relationship with all of them complicated.

The driver pulled off the freeway. Rebecca looked out the window. "You still live in your condo?"

"We can't all have a villa in Milan."

"It wasn't a villa, exactly."

Jayne had seen Rebecca's Italian house a few times. It was pretty damned fabulous, with seventeenth-century tile and the original stained glass windows. "It was amazing."

Rebecca shrugged. "I never did learn enough Italian to fit in with the locals. Your place is nice. Homey."

"I like it." The condo was close to work, affordable, and a safe haven from the craziness of the Worden world. Rebecca didn't need to know it was for sale.

The limo pulled up in front. Before opening the door, Jayne hugged her friend. "I'll be by later."

Rebecca nodded. "You have the address?"

"You e-mailed it to me about forty times."

"We'll have dinner?"

"Yes, and drink wine and tell lies about boys. Here." Jayne pulled the current issue of *OK!* magazine out of her handbag. "I bought this for you."

Rebecca took it and hugged her. "You're so sweet! All I brought you is a pair of earrings I made."

Which was why, after all this time, they were still friends. Jayne knew that in Rebecca's mind, the cheap magazine and the no-doubt fabulously expensive earrings were on par—because, she and Rebecca were freakishly addicted to celebrity gossip, and the magazine showed Jayne cared.

"You make me insane," she said, hugging Rebecca tightly. "I'll see you later. Welcome home."

"Rearrange the pictures on the mantel," Rebecca called after her. "It will make my mother crazy."

"If I have time."

Jayne waved, then hurried to her condo at the back of the building. She had less than an hour to shower, change, and get over to the Worden house in Beverly Hills. While she'd been willing to pick up Rebecca in her scrubs, her crush was powerful enough that she wasn't willing to face David in shapeless hospital wear and no makeup.

She raced to unlock the front door and stepped inside. Bright light flooded the spacious room where her comfy Ikea sofa divided the living room and eating area. There was a kitchen around the corner to the left and a hallway to the right, leading to the bedroom and bath.

What she liked best about the condo was the patio out back. It was nearly as big as the whole unit, with Mexican pavers and potted plants. She could sit out there in the morning and have her coffee. She often ate dinner at the glass-top table. There was a small barbecue and a little fountain in the corner. It was her haven.

But there was no time to enjoy it now, she thought as she flew into the bedroom, tearing off her clothes as she went. She brushed out her long, brown hair and quickly rolled it in electric curlers. She replaced her plain, white bra with a lace one that pushed her breasts together and up in a way that made the most of what little she had, then washed her face and applied a tinted moisturizer. She smoothed on eye shadow, mascara, and blush.

She'd spent more time than she wanted to admit planning what she was going to wear. A dress seemed too fancy and obviously jeans were just . . . jeans. It was spring in L.A. , which meant high seventies and clear skies. She pulled on a pair of tailored white pants and a fitted cotton shirt with a scoop neck. After taking out the curlers, she finger-combed her hair, sprayed the life out of it with hairspray, prayed the curls would last more than six minutes, then ran back toward the front door. She had less than thirty minutes to make it to Beverly Hills.

Blaine Worden's great-great-great grandfather had established Worden's Jewels in New York back in the 1800s. Blaine's grandfather, excited by the fledgling movie business, had moved the family and the company headquarters to Los Angeles in the 1920s. He'd bought in Beverly Hills when land was cheap and houses were the size of airplane hangars. Over the years the mansion had been remodeled and some of the land had been sold off, but the estate was still one of the largest and most elegant in town.

Jayne hit the remote control on her passenger visor, then waited for the big wrought-iron gates to swing open. She sped up to the main house, jumped out, and ran to the front door.

Her concern was silly—she knew that. Carmine would have taken care of everything before she left. It wasn't as if David was expecting a marching band and floats to announce his return. But Elizabeth had asked and Jayne . . . well, Jayne didn't mind welcoming David home.

She'd seen him only a couple of times in the past few years. Before each meeting she'd desperately hoped that he'd gotten old-looking or fat or had grown an unattractive hump on his back. She was twenty-eight—a crush on her best friend's brother was no longer cute.

But every time she saw him her heart pounded, her knees went weak, and she found herself torn between wanting to bolt for cover and beg him to take her, just one time, up against the wall. Okay, she thought as she hurried up the steps and opened the front door, against the wall would be tacky and was probably one of those positions that only looked sexy in movies. But she wouldn't turn down a nice, slow, private seduction.

She punched in the alarm code, then checked her watch. David was due any minute. She scanned the foyer, with its marble floors, two-story ceiling, crystal chandelier, and custom furniture, then frowned when she saw that the large, round table in the middle of the department store–sized space was empty. Elizabeth always put flowers there. Well, technically Elizabeth told Carmine, who always put flowers there, but still. Hadn't the flowers been delivered?

"No one was here," she said aloud. She dropped her purse onto the chair by the wall, then raced down the hallway, through the kitchen, past the utility room—which was the same size as her entire condo—to the back door.

Sure enough, a gorgeous spray of flowers sat on the wide, rear step. It was done in Elizabeth's signature white—a combination of Casablanca lilies, calla lilies, Dendrobium orchids, and roses.

Jayne bent down to grab it and nearly lost her balance. Not only was the glass vase wet, five or six hundred dollars' worth of flowers was damn heavy. She tried again and got the arrangement off the pavers, then stood. Her hands slipped a little. She swore. Dropping the vase wasn't an option.

She made her way through the house to the foyer, where a series of events conspired to ruin her day.

First, she heard someone put a key in the front door. Trying to get rid of the armful of flowers before David walked in, she started to run . . . only to catch the side of her right foot on the leg of a small, curved sofa. She was moving too fast to stop her forward momentum. Scrambling only caused her to skid like a cartoon character. Then her fingers slipped on the wet glass of the vase. She threw herself forward in an effort to keep it from falling.

The vase went up, the flowers rained down, and Jayne was caught in the middle. She stared helplessly at the soaring glass vase. Even as cold water and flowers

drenched her, her only thought was to keep it from hit
ting the marble floor and shattering. She reached up and
grabbed it. The unexpected weight caused her to stag
ger back, where her heel came down on a lily stem. Her
foot shot out from under her and she fell, just as David
walked into the house. She landed on her hip and her left
wrist. The unfortunate cracking sound didn't come from
the glass—it came from her.

David Worden—tall, handsome, blond, and blue
eyed—immediately rushed to her side. "Jayne? Is that
you? Are you all right?"

She sat in a puddle of water, wet flowers, and greenery
hanging off her—the picture of humiliation. If only she
could believe the pounding in her chest was a result of
her fall and not him crouching next to her, looking all
concerned and drool-worthy. Even the sharp pain from
her wrist wasn't enough to jolt her out of her longing for
that private seduction.

So much for being over her crush, she thought sadly,
as he took the vase from her arms. So much for the so
phisticated first impression she'd planned. She probably
looked like a drowned rat.

"Where does it hurt?" he asked.

"My wrist. I think it's broken."

"Then we'd better get you to the hospital," he said,
helping her to her feet. "Can you walk?"

"It's my arm, not my leg."

"You have wet flowers in your hair. Do you really think
attitude plays well with that look?"

Despite her humiliation and the pain and the fact that she would never be able to look David in the eye again, she smiled. "Attitude is all I have going for me right now."

"Rebecca would tell you to work your strengths." He pulled a couple of flowers out of her hair then put his arm around her. "Let's go get you X-rayed."

Get intimate
WITH A BESTSELLING ROMANCE
from Pocket Books!

Janet Chapman
THE MAN MUST MARRY
She has the money. He has the desire.
Only love can bring them together.

Starr Ambrose
LIE TO ME
One flirtatious fib leads to the sexiest
adventure of her life....

Karen Hawkins
TALK OF THE TOWN
Do blondes have more fun? He'd love to know—
but it takes two to tango.

Hester Browne
THE LITTLE LADY AGENCY
IN THE BIG APPLE
She's a manners coach for men, and
she's working her magic on Manhattan!

Available wherever books are sold or at www.simonsayslove.com

POCKET BOOKS
A Division of Simon & Schuster
A CBS COMPANY

19584

Fall in love

with a bestseller from Pocket Books!

FERN MICHAELS
The Delta Ladies
When one man confronts two women from his past, there's
bound to be a little trouble … and a lot of passion.

JULIE GARWOOD
Heartbreaker
A thrilling excursion into the soaring heights—
and darkest impulses—of the human heart.

LINDA HOWARD, MARIAH STEWART,
JILLIAN HUNTER, GERALYN DAWSON,
AND MIRANDA JARRETT
Under the Boardwalk
Experience the cool breezes and hot passion of
summer loving in this unforgettable new collection!

And look for the thrilling
new Bullet Catchers Trilogy
by Roxanne St. Claire!

First You Run
Then You Hide
Now You Die

**Available wherever books are sold
or at www.simonsayslove.com.**

POCKET BOOKS
A Division of Simon & Schuster
A CBS COMPANY

**POCKET
STAR BOOKS**
A Division of Simon & Schuster
A CBS COMPANY

19098